THE FORGE

Alexander James MacDonald

ISBN: 9798386038083

Publisher: Alex J MacDonald
www.alexjmacdonald.co.uk

PART 1
THE FIRE

CHAPTER ONE

Iolair surveyed his kingdom from his lofty throne on the Corrag Bhuidhe pinnacles. The morning sun of a late summer's day glowed on the red Torridonian sandstone of the sheer cliff faces of An Teallach and on Iolair's golden neck. Iolair's chosen vantage point was called by mountaineers 'Lord Berkeley's Seat', but Iolair cared nothing for lords or mountaineers. He was lord of the sky.

He launched himself from the pinnacle and with a couple of strong wing-beats he caught the thermals spiralling up from the corrie below and rose swiftly into the airy pathways of the heavens. His keen golden-brown eyes scanned the cliffs and screes, the loch in its dark corrie, the tumbled rocks and the long slopes to the strath below. Nothing moved—not even a vole—in the shimmering heat.

It was one of those rare August days in the North-west Highlands—from early morning the sun blazed in a cloudless cobalt blue sky. It was too hot even for the midges. Only the occasional cleg bothered the few people who were out in this largely empty wilderness area.

As he glided north across the sea loch to the moorland and lower rocky hills on the other side, Iolair spied some movement. Two men, one old and one young, were gathering sheep. Iolair surveyed them casually for a moment. The old man he knew—tall and lean with shaggy grey hair, wearing green trousers and a checked shirt. At lambing time he was always out early, no chance of stealing a lamb from his flock! The young man was not so familiar—not as

1

tall, but wiry with long dark hair, in blue jeans and a grey T-shirt—but he'd seen him from time to time. And there was that big dog with them—long-limbed and grey, like no sheepdog he'd ever seen anywhere else. Losing interest, he wheeled away, hoping to spot some grouse breaking cover.

Just then the younger man caught sight of the soaring eagle. His hazel eyes lit up and his sharp features broke into a smile.

'Look, Grandad! It's the eagle. He'll have just come down from An Teallach.'

The old man craned his neck, and as his dark green eyes glimpsed the great bird, his weather-beaten, craggy face put on a look of mock horror.

'Mr Hetherington will no' be pleased, Rory. He'll scare the grouse!'

They both laughed and moved on over the hill looking for stray sheep in hidden corries or behind rocky outcrops. It was a fine day to be out on the hill, although hot work. The honey fragrance of the flowering purple heather and the distinctive fresh tang of bog myrtle filled the air.

Every so often they'd spot a sheep and her lamb and the older man would call to the sheepdog, "Come by, Fleet!" And Fleet would set off across the rough hillside, his long loping stride eating up the ground. Fleet was no ordinary sheepdog; he was a cross between a Border Collie and an Alsatian, with perhaps a little bit of Scottish Deerhound somewhere in his ancestry as well. There was nothing he resembled more than a wolf, and he could cover the hill tirelessly.

Dan Mackay was delighted to have his grandson out on the hill with him gathering the sheep for the lamb sales. Rory would soon be off back to university in Edinburgh, and Dan would miss having him about the place. When home from Uni, Rory stayed with his mother around twenty-five miles away in Ullapool on the neighbouring sea-loch of Loch Broom, but whenever he wasn't working at his part-time job in a hotel he was over at the croft with his Grandad having hitched a lift or borrowed his Mum's car. Sometimes he stayed the night, and Dan appreciated that. He still found it difficult to get used to the empty house. His wife had died ten years before, but she had left an emptiness that nothing on this earth could fill.

Later in the day, Iolair from a great height spotted more movement at the end of the single track road that runs from Dundonnain to Badrallaich and, sensing danger from the long implements the figures were holding, he drifted away. A group of people had just returned to their vehicles after a day's grouse shooting. Two Range Rovers and a Land Rover were parked at the side of the road. The shooters, gamekeepers and ghillies were dressed in a variety of tweeds, waxed jackets and expensive outdoor gear. They were putting away their guns, and the ghillies were getting the dogs into the Land Rover.

The party consisted of Anthony Hetherington, the local landowner, and his guests, along with his son, Jonathan Kenneth (aka JK or Jake) and some of his younger crowd, together with head gamekeeper, Lachie Maclean, a short burly man in his late fifties, and a couple of local ghillies. Hetherington and his son were big, heavy men. The father was in his fifties, balding and corpulent, his round red face betraying his overindulgence in rich food and drink. The son was in his early twenties, with short dirty blonde hair and watery grey eyes. Jake's two friends were also big young men, looking every bit the rugby players they were.

'Bloody poor shooting today, MacLean', snapped Hetherington. Lachie shook his head and rather nervously adjusted his tweed bonnet.

'Aye, it wasn't good, Mr Hetherington'.

'It's all these bloody eagles and birds of prey, and these bloody crofters and their bloody sheep.'

'Oh aye, you'll be right there, sir. And we can't do anything about any of them!'

Hetherington made sure that his guests were out of earshot before replying in a lowered voice, 'Something will have to be done about it, or by the time Jonathan Kenneth inherits the estate, it will be worth nothing, in fact less than nothing—just debts—and you'll all be out of a job!'

'What's that, Father?' said Jake, as he and his friends came up, 'Thinking of passing on the estate to me?'

'All in good time JK. All in good time. I'm not ready to pop my clogs yet!'

'I should think not, Mr Hetherington', interjected Ben, one of Jake's friends. 'The thought of Jake being in charge of anything doesn't bear thinking about!'

'Ha! Ha! Very funny, Ben.' The sarcasm in Jake's voice didn't quite manage to conceal his annoyance with his friend.

The truth was that the Hetherington family fortunes were at a low ebb in 2008. Although they regarded themselves as very much part of the upper crust, Hetherington's father having become a multimillionaire as a merchant banker, the reality was that Hetherington himself was inclined more to the ostentatious spending of wealth (and his wife even more so), than to the hard work of earning it. The combination of poor investments, the purchase and running of the Dundonnain estate and their properties south of the Border, their children's private education, together with their expensive lifestyles, meant financial resources were running desperately low. Added to that was the general financial downturn since the sub-prime mortgage scandal in America the previous year and the more recent collapse of various financial institutions. And to Mrs Hetherington's chagrin, none of their wealth had brought her husband the honours she thought he was due, nor the family the status to which she thought they were entitled. How she envied the titled nobility! And she never ceased letting her husband and family know it.

They all got into the vehicles and drove off, Hetherington driving the first Range Rover with Jake in the front passenger seat and Jake's friends in the back. Just out of Badrallaich, they rounded a bend and discovered their way blocked by a large flock of around 200 yowes and their lambs being driven by Dan Mackay. The road had a fence on the right hand side and rough rocky hillside on the left, so Fleet was up on the left and Rory had gone ahead to open the gate on the road that led down to Dan's croft.

For the exasperated Hetherington, this was the last straw. He swore. "Wouldn't you just know it? The end to a perfect day! And if it isn't bloody Dan Mackay! When he's not poaching my deer, he's blocking the Queen's highway with his bloody sheep!'

He blasted the horn. Dan half turned and raised his hand in acknowledgement, but kept on driving the sheep along the road.

Hetherington revved the engine impatiently and started moving forward. Dan turned and stood facing the oncoming vehicle impassively. The engine revved louder and the Range Rover lurched forward, but Dan didn't move. Hetherington was forced to stop. He stuck his head out the window scowling.

'Get your bloody sheep off the road, Mackay.'

'Oh, it's yourself, Mr Hetherington', said Dan in mock surprise, 'I thought it was one of those tourists who didn't know any better.'

Dan's jibe hit Hetherington on the raw and he spluttered, 'You don't own the road, you know.'

Dan tilted his head and his eyes crinkled into a smile. 'No, you're right there—none of us do—not even you, Mr

Hetherington. But just a bit of patience. We'll have the sheep off the road and down to the croft in a couple of minutes.' With that he turned back to driving the sheep.

'Well, of all the bloody cheek!' Hetherington exploded.

Jake saw his chance to prove himself. 'We'll move him. Come on Ben!'

He jumped out followed by Ben. Dan never heard their approach, what with the bleating of the sheep and the revving of the Range Rover's engine. They came up behind Dan taking him completely by surprise. They grabbed an arm each and threw him in the deep ditch at the side of the road, then jumped back in the Range Rover. As Dan climbed out of the ditch, the vehicles passed, with smug, laughing faces in the windows, and drove on, scattering the sheep in all directions.

Dan got back onto the road and whistled Fleet to stop the sheep from breaking back the way they'd come. Meanwhile the vehicles ploughed through the flock of sheep, Hetherington blasting his horn, and Rory had to jump out of the way to avoid being run down. He saw Jake sneering at him.

Once Dan and Rory had managed to gather the sheep together again and had got them down the road, past the house, across the burn and into the field, Rory finally got a chance to ask his Grandad what had happened.

'Jake Hetherington and one of his pals. They put me in the ditch.' Dan smiled ruefully.

'What?' Rory couldn't believe what he was hearing. 'You should get the police to them!'

Dan shook his head. 'No. No use. No witnesses. You didn't see what happened, so it would be my word against theirs. And you know who they'd believe.'

'But that's not right.'

'No, it's not, but there's a lot of things that'll not get put right in this world, Rory. And it'll not be us that'll put them right, you know that.'

'It's still not right.'

They stood for a time, leaning on the gate, looking at the sheep spreading out in the field that sloped down to the north shore of An Loch Beag, the bleating lambs finding their mothers again after the confusion.

Dan's flock were North Country Cheviots, sheep that had been specially bred for the challenging conditions of the Northern Highlands. They were introduced in the early nineteenth century after the indigenous people had been evicted by the landowners.

After a time the bleating of lambs and their mothers quietened and a great silence again descended on the wide landscape of hills and loch, made all the more still somehow by the constant wash of the sea on the sandy beach.

Looking across the great gulf of air to the foothills of An Tealach, Rory asked, 'Are you coming to the Ceilidh tonight?'

'Oh, I don't know, Rory. I haven't been to a ceilidh since your Granny died.'

'Mum says you should get out more!'

Dan raised a quizzical eyebrow in Rory's direction, 'Is that right?'

'And not just to Church!'

Dan turned his head and looked at his grandson. 'It would do you both good if you were there more often yourselves!' he teased.

'Touché', smiled Rory in return, and added, 'The new Minister will be there—at the Ceilidh.'

'Aye?' said Dan, in seeming surprise.

'I saw him in Ullapool, and he asked me how my music was going, and I said Jamie Macleod had asked me to play guitar tonight, and he said he'd come along to hear me.'

'That'll raise a few eyebrows!' Dan laughed, and after a pause added, 'Well, if the Minister is to be there, I'd better go along to keep an eye on him!'

He laughed again, and Rory joined in. He loved these kinds of moments with his grandfather.

'A bit of a change for you, Rory, isn't it—ceilidh music instead of metal? I hope I'll not be deafened!'

'You mean deafer than you are already?'

'Less o' your cheek!' Dan gave Rory a playful shove and they headed off back towards the house.

Dan's croft house at Cill Donnain was situated on the west side of the burn, the Allt Mor Chill Donnain, in an isolated spot with a dramatic view across Little Loch Broom to the massive bulk of the foothills of An Teallach. This Cill Donnain in Wester Ross is one of several of the same name in the Highlands and Islands of Scotland, all named after the sixth century Celtic Saint Donnain, who must have been a great itinerant missionary, as the churches named after him are widely spread from Argyll to Sutherland in the northwest Highlands. There are still the remains of a small church on the west bank of the burn, and higher up an old burial ground. On the other side of the burn, the east side, are some more fields, with sheep pens and barns near the shore of the loch, and up above them the remains of the original crofting community of Cill Donnain.

Dan's house dated back to the mid nineteenth century when a sheep farm was established by the landowner, Mackenzie of Cromartie, after he had evicted the original crofters of Cill Donnain. It was a traditional Highland house, slated, stone-built, harled and whitewashed. At the front of the house there were two downstairs windows, one on each side of the front door, and upstairs, unusually for a Highland house of that type, three dormer windows, the middle of which was larger than the others.

Dan and Rory parted at the side of the house where Rory's Mum's car was parked. Rory got into the driver's seat. 'Right. See you tonight then, Grandad.'

'Aye, right. See you then.'

Rory spun the wheels as he did a sharp turn and roared off.

Dan shook his head and smiled. 'Mad driver! I wonder who he took that from?'

CHAPTER TWO

Dundonnain Lodge stands near the banks of the Dundonnain River in Strath Beag. It is a solid, stone-built, complex house, in the Scottish Baronial style, with crow-step gables and various wings added to the original structure. It had been owned by various clan chiefs in times past, but around the beginning of the twentieth century, like so many other similar properties, it had been sold to the highest bidder to pay off the chief's debts. Towards the end of the twentieth century it had been acquired by Anthony Hetherington Esq.

That late summer evening, after a somewhat frustrating day grouse shooting, the guests were assembling for drinks before dinner. In addition to Mr and Mrs Hetherington, Jake and his younger sister, Charlotte (on holiday from her private school in England) and Jake's friends, Ben and Will, there were three couples: Sir Percival Maberley and his wife Caroline; Colonel Richard Brandon and his wife Rowena; and Mr and Mrs Sheringham. The Maberleys had an estate near the Hetheringtons in Buckinghamshire, Colonel Brandon was a friend of Hetherington's from his London club, and Sheringham was an investment banker. Some of the ladies had been playing golf in Ullapool, but Lady Maberley had been out with the grouse shooters (she was a notable shot).

The décor of the drawing room was traditional for the lodge of a Highland estate: light wood panelling on the walls with an ornately corniced cream ceiling. The walls were adorned with various expensive paintings and prints of the Highlands, the carpet was a green tartan and the furniture was modern but in a traditional style. To the side opposite the marble fireplace and in the corner near one of the high windows was a table laden with bottles and decanters. Everything from malt whiskies and brandies to gins and martinis and much more besides was available, all being dispensed by a local girl in traditional maid's uniform. The air was replete with the enticing mixture of the aroma of alcohol and the perfume of the ladies, and the atmosphere was full of bonhomie. There was much amused laughter over Hetherington's recounting of how Jake and Ben had put Mackay in the ditch. Mrs Hetherington, however, was not amused. Not that she had any liking for Dan Mackay's sort, but she felt such ploys were beneath the dignity of her family, and she feared that under their polite laughter, Sir Percival and the Colonel would not really approve.

The conversation turned to the awful economic situation, and all felt that the Labour Government should be doing much more to stabilise the situation and reimburse those who had lost small fortunes. 'After all', remarked Sheringham, 'it's people like us who have invested our assets in this country, and it's not our fault that the American banks got things so badly wrong.' To that the Hetheringtons heartily agreed, just as the gong rang for dinner.

After dinner, the ladies were about to withdraw to the drawing room, while the men had brandies and cigars. Jake said he and his friends were going to take a run down to the village hall, as there was a Ceilidh on. 'It should be rather amusing', he said. Charlotte wanted to go too, and was most put out when her mother forbade it. 'Young ladies like you should not be mixing with the kind of people who frequent these places. From what I hear, there's a lot of drunkenness and even fighting.' It did no good for

Charlotte to point out that Jake and his friends were going. 'They're rugby players,' said her mother, 'No one is going to bother them.'

Before Jake and his friends left, his mother had a quiet word with him. 'Now, look here, Jonathan (only his mother called him that), I'm not particularly happy with you going to this dance, but I didn't want to make more of a fuss in front of our guests. But I want you to be very careful tonight. After that incident with Mackay, there may be some who might take some sort of revenge. So be on your guard and stay out of trouble. We don't want anything unsavoury happening while our guests are here.' Seeing the bored look on her son's face, she added, 'Do you hear me?'

'Yes, mother', and he gave her a kiss on the cheek, before following the others.

She looked after him with a troubled expression on her face.

*

Dan was standing by the window of his bedroom in his old croft house. Outside the rays of the sinking sun were highlighting the ripples on the sea loch and, here and there, clumps of grass and bushes stood out against a darker background. Inside, the electric light showed the furniture and décor were rather tired looking. Since his wife Mary had died, he hadn't the heart to change things. He was wearing a green and black checked shirt, black jeans and black boots and he was looking at a framed photograph in his hand with a tender smile on his face. It was of his late wife, Mary. She had been around forty when the photo was taken, but she had still been a strikingly beautiful woman with dark blue eyes and glossy dark hair. Memories came flooding back.

'"Comb your hair Dan!" That's what you always used to say when we were going out.'

12

He put the photo down and looked in the mirror of the old dressing table. He ran his hand through his unruly grey hair and then opened the top drawer.

'There's a comb here somewhere.'

Fumbling in the drawer, he touched something that caused him to stop his search for the comb. He pulled it out. It was a large, slim, dark red box. He clicked the catch and opened it. A large, ornate piece of jewellery lay on the black silk lining. It looked oriental. It was an intricate gold necklace with various sizes of glittering diamonds and a very large red jewel in the middle. This central stone was an Alexandrite which has the very rare property of appearing green in daylight and deep red in incandescent light. Dan picked up the necklace and handled it carefully in his rough brown hands.

'It was in her family for five generations,' he said softly to himself. 'But she never wore it—said it was too costly. The price of blood... redemption. But it was not with silver and gold and precious stones that she was redeemed.'

He put the piece back in its box and placed it thoughtfully in the drawer and forgot all about the comb. He pulled on a black leather jacket, but then stood for some time gazing out the window at the long grass at the edge of the field swaying slightly in the light breath of wind before the dying of the day. The words sung at Mary's funeral came back to him, and he sang them softly to himself to the old tune Kilmarnock.

For he remembers we are dust,
and he our frame well knows.
Frail man, his days are like the grass,
as flower in field he grows:

For over it the wind doth pass,
and it away is gone;

*And of the place where once it was
it shall no more be known.*

*But unto them that do him fear
GOD's mercy never ends;
And to their children's children still
his righteousness extends.*

He sighed, then turning quickly he strode across the room and down the stairs, the sudden lithe movement of his tall, lean frame belying his sixty-four years.

Outside, his old Transit van was parked in front of the house. It looked as though it had seen better days. It was a muddy green colour, but most of it was real mud – underneath it was an iridescent, metallic green. It had low suspension and wide tyres. The lights went off in the house. Dan and Fleet came out. 'Come on, boy. If I've to go to this ceilidh, then you've got to come and sit in the van to make sure I get home safe!'

Fleet raised his nose to Dan's hand and laughed at him, his tongue lolling from the side of his mouth. As well as being a working sheepdog, he was Dan's constant companion. Dan paused to look up at the sky flecked with light grey clouds in the west which were rapidly turning rose pink and amber in the setting sun. He took a deep breath, walked to the van and opened the driver's door. Fleet jumped up and sat in the passenger seat. Dan climbed in and fired up the engine. It coughed a couple of times and then roared into life. In a few minutes he was approaching the local village hall.

The hall was like many other such halls all over the Highlands, with timber walls and a corrugated iron roof, although it had recently been renovated with the help of local donations and a grant from the government. It had a large car park at the rear that was surrounded by Scots

Pine trees.

At the back of the Hall, three elderly local people, Norman 'the Elder' Ferguson, John 'Speedy' Campbell and Maggie 'Achbeg' MacKinnon, were heading home early from the ceilidh and they got into John's car. They were just about to drive off when Dan's van roared into the car park.

'The same old Dan Mackay', laughed Maggie. 'What a noise!'

Norman, who didn't exactly approve of Dan, said, 'It's a wonder he still keeps that old wreck.'

'Well, you know you wouldn't believe the speed of that thing', said John. 'I was coming home from Ullapool the other day and he passed me as if I was hardly moving!'

Maggie retorted, 'That's probably because you were hardly moving!' She and Norman laughed as John moved off at a very sedate pace.

Dan got out and gave them a wave. He told Fleet to lie down in the van and, leaving the window open, he paused and listened to the faint strains of ceilidh dance music emanating from the back of the hall. Those rhythms and melodies were in his blood — the achingly lovely cadences of the slow dances and the stirring rhythms of the marches and reels.

As he approached the door, he greeted a group of young men who were standing outside passing round a half bottle of whisky.

'You know, you'd make more of an impression on the lassies if you were in there dancing, instead of out here drinking. But maybe you need the Dutch courage.'

They laughed. They all liked Dan, but were a little bit in awe of him, having heard of some of his exploits. One of them held out the half bottle, 'Do you want a shot yourself, Dan? It's a while since you've been at a ceilidh.'

'Aye, it is that. Maybe I need some Dutch courage myself.' He laughed and took a slug from the bottle. He grimaced, 'Man, that's rough! I hope Hector has a good malt inside to put away the taste of that!' They all laughed as he went in the door.

The five piece ceilidh band was belting it out—accordion, drums, bass, electric guitar and fiddle—Rory on electric guitar and Jamie Macleod on fiddle. A wild "Strip the Willow" was in full swing. Dan stood for a moment taking in the scene—the honey-coloured wooden interior of the old hall; the three mounted stag's heads on the wall behind the stage; the polished wooden floor; the laughing faces of all ages; the hooching and the squealing of the dancers.

Men were lined up on one side, facing the women on the other, and every fourth couple were engaged in a complex, interweaving dance down the middle of the lines, swinging each of the other dancers in turn, but always coming back to swing their own partner. Dan made his way round the edge of the birling, sweating lines to the bar, asked Hector for a Talisker malt whisky, added a drop of water and stood listening to the music and looking at Rory playing guitar.

Rory was left-handed, and Dan smiled as he remembered having to help him move the strings around when he got his first guitar. He hadn't needed to do that with this electric guitar—it was a left-handed black Fender Stratocaster. Rory was right into it and wasn't paying attention to anything around him. He was playing complicated rhythms and chord patterns, blending with the traditional music but adding something wild and ethereal to it. 'He knows it and he feels it,' thought Dan. "It's in his blood too."

The dance finished and a few people came up and spoke to Dan—Muhammad Hussain, a local shopkeeper and a good friend of Dan's, with his wife Jasmine, quickly followed by the new minister, Neil Cameron and his wife,

Eilidh. Muhammad was middle-aged, short and fat, with twinkling eyes in a merry face. He wore a light blue shirt outside a pair of dark blue trousers and was sweating rather profusely after the energetic dance. His wife was slim, dark-haired, dark-eyed and strikingly beautiful in a fuchsia pink trouser suit. Neil Cameron was about forty, medium height, strongly built and, with a flattened nose, looking like he had been a boxer in his younger days. He was in an open neck shirt and jeans, while his blonde wife wore a smart green dress.

Dan shook his head and looked at them with exaggerated disapproval. 'Well, I can just see the headlines tomorrow: "Muslim shopkeeper and Free Church minister dance at Ceilidh!"'

Eilidh was not quite sure how to take Dan, but was relieved when the others all laughed and Dan joined in.

'Aye,' said her husband, 'but we weren't actually dancing together!'

'Now that would have caused a real scandal!' laughed Jasmine.

Just then Dan's daughter Fiona Williams came up. Fiona was almost forty, dark-haired like her mother but a little bit overweight. She wore a blue patterned dress. Her pleasant face would have been very attractive were it not for her almost perpetual frown and the downward curve of her mouth.

Fiona had been a bright young girl and had had a special relationship with her mother. They shared a lot of interests in literature and history and art. Because of Dan's army career, especially in Northern Ireland, she didn't see a lot of him as she was growing up. She loved him, but was slightly in awe of him when he came home on leave. He was always full of fun, but she was quite a sensitive child and didn't enjoy the rough and tumble and outdoor pursuits Dan loved.

She now taught history in Ullapool High School, since she'd came back home with little Rory from Newcastle in 1995 after her husband had left her for another woman. She didn't always get on with her father, whom she considered rather old-fashioned in his ideas, especially what she regarded as his very inflexible Christian faith. Fiona had been devastated by her mother's death in 1998. She'd been full of anger and resentment against God, and felt that her father couldn't answer her questions.

But now as she saw her Dad, her face lit up as she smiled, and she gave him a hug.

'Hi Dad, Rory said you might come.'

'Aye, Fiona, I thought I'd better come to keep an eye on our new minister—to keep Muhammad here from leading him astray!'

They all laughed again and Dan introduced Fiona.

'Fiona, you know my good friends, Muhammad and Jasmine, and this is our new minister, Neil Cameron and his wife, Eilidh. My daughter Fiona.'

'You're the minister!' Fiona looked surprised. 'I didn't know Free Church ministers went to ceilidhs!'

'There's a lot you don't know about Neil Cameron!' said Dan, tilting his head and winking in a way that was all his own.

'Well, I came to hear Rory play—at least that's my excuse!' smiled Neil. 'He's very good isn't he?'

Fiona smiled and nodded, pleased. She turned to her Dad and said, 'Well, since you're here, you'll have to give your daughter a dance!'

Dan looked reluctant. 'Och, I only came to hear the music. And anyway it's so long since I danced.'

But Fiona would have none of it, and soon had her father up on the floor. Thankfully for Dan, it was a slow waltz, and soon the rhythm and the steps came back to him. Rory was now playing lead, high soaring notes pouring down in longing and heartache. Somehow in Dan's mind was con-jured up the long, slow music of the hills, the sea and the river, and the memory of love won and love lost.

'You know I haven't done this since your mother died.'

'I know, Dad." Fiona's eyes were moist, feeling some-thing of her father's emotion. But she soon became her sen-sible self again. 'But you know you should really try to get back to normal again. Get out more.'

Dan laughed. 'Rory said you would say that!'

'Oh, he did, did he? Well, it's true, you know.'

'He's a good lad, Rory,' smiled Dan, changing the direc-tion of the conversation which he sensed was heading into choppy waters. 'But he'll soon be off back to Edinburgh. I'll miss having him about the place.'

'I know, but he has to go away to make something of himself. They all have to—all the young ones.'

'You mean those of us who stayed, or came back, haven't made something of ourselves?' said Dan narrowing his eyes and smiling.

'Let's not go there, Dad!'

There was silence between them for a little, and Dan no-ticed Jake Hetherington and his friends in a corner drink-ing heavily, and noisily trying to chat up some local girls. 'Now what are they doing here?' Dan asked himself.

Just as the dance finished, Jim Matheson came up. Jim was a burly man in his late fifties, with a round smiling face and thinning grey hair, a police superintendent in In-verness and an old friend of Dan's. He'd come home to see his aged mother and popped into the ceilidh on his way home. Dan introduced him to the others and asked them all what they wanted to drink.

When Neil asked for a whisky and Jim and Muhammad asked for soft drinks— Jim because he was driving back to Inverness and Muhammad because of his religion—Dan joked, 'Well, it's a sorry do when it's just the Free Church men out of the four of us who can have a dram!'

After a few more dances which Dan managed to body-swerve, the ceilidh was over. Most people had drifted off. Jim had already left. At the front of the hall, Rory helped the rest of the band load the van and then waved good-bye as they drove off. As he passed the darkened side of the building on his way round to the car park, carrying his guitar case, three figures lurched out in front of him—Jake and his friends, who clearly had had too much to drink and hadn't had any success with the local girls.

'If it isn't little Rory', sneered Jake. 'How's your old man? No worse for a dip in a ditch? Oh sorry, he's not your old man—no one knows where he is.' He turned to his friends. 'Little Rory's a bastard, you know. Or is it Rory's a little bastard? It's one or the other...' His friends laughed.

'Shut your mouth!' retorted Rory. 'You're nothing but cowards—attacking my Grandad like that.'

Jake leaned menacingly over Rory. 'Who are you call-ing cowards? Come on boys, I think little bastard ought to learn a lesson.'

They all piled into Rory who tried to use his guitar case as a shield, but they wrenched it from his grip and tossed it aside. Rory fell to the ground with Ben and Jake on top of him.

'Put his hand on the floor!' rasped Jake.

'Why? What for?' asked Ben, but doing it at the same time.

'He's not going to play that god-awful guitar for a while!' Jake sneered, viciously stamping on Rory's hand, but the force was partly deflected by his foot hitting Ben's arm on the way down. Ben let out a yell, 'You've kicked my arm, you idiot!'

Just at that moment a van came roaring round from the car park at the back of the Hall, headlights blazing, and screeched to a halt. Dan leapt out, and made straight for

Jake and his friends.

Ben jumped in Dan's way, but Dan feinted with his left and his long right arm curved upwards and his fist hit Ben right on the point of the jaw. Ben's head snapped back and he went down like a sack of potatoes. Jake swung at Dan and, as Dan stepped back, Will tripped him and he fell backwards on the ground.

As Ben was struggling to his feet shaking his head, Jake took a step towards Dan and tried to stick the boot in, but Dan twisted to the side like a cat. Things were looking bad for Dan, surrounded by three drunken young men closing in on him, when suddenly Fleet sprang clean through the open window of the van landing square on Jake's back sending him sprawling. And at the same moment Muhammad and Neil Cameron ran up and, with Fleet, got between Dan and Jake's friends. Fiona came screaming round from the front and went to Rory who was struggling to his feet clutching his hand.

Jake quickly got to his feet and aimed another kick at Dan, but this time Dan, half on his feet, caught Jake's foot and, springing up, whirled Jake round making him hop on one leg. Will lurched forward to come to Jake's assistance, but Neil Cameron stepped to meet him, light on the balls of his feet, looking every inch the boxer he once was, 'Uh uh. Not a good idea.' The young man took one look at the minister's face and decided discretion was the better part of valour.

Dan slammed Jake into the side of the van and punched him in the midriff just above his belt. Jake doubled up gasping for breath. Dan grabbed him by the collar.

'Didn't they teach you in that private school of yours never to use your feet in a fight?'

Dan turned to Fiona, who'd come up with Jasmine and Eilidh, 'Is Rory all right?'

Rory groaned, 'I'm OK.' But he felt his bruised hand

gingerly.

Dan grinned to Neil and Muhammad, 'Thanks, but nothing I couldn't handle. Me and Jake here are going to have a little talk.' And with that he dragged Jake off into the darkness under the trees at the end of the car park with Fleet in attendance. Ben and Will retreated to their car.

Neil turned to Muhammad, 'Well, that was a bit of a revelation!'

'Beware the wrath of a patient man!' replied Muhammad. 'There is more to my friend Dan than meets the eye. People underestimate him at their peril.'

Still holding Jake by the collar, Dan put him up against a tree. Jake was beginning to get his breath back. He rasped, 'You've had it. Just wait till my father hears about this.'

'Oh aye, I'm sure he'll be delighted—and all his posh guests as well—to hear his son was involved in a drunken brawl at the local dance. And we have the local shopkeeper and minister as witnesses.'

'You bas…'

'Shut your mouth! And listen to me! Along the road there, up the hill from Corrie Hallie, there's a bog—the Dubh Lochan bog. No one knows how deep it is. It's said that a man once tried to ride a horse through there. Horse and rider were never seen again.' Dan paused to let his words sink in. 'If you ever do anything to harm Rory again, I'll put you in the Dubh Lochan bog myself.'

Jakes eyes widened. There was no mistaking the cold threat in Dan's eyes. Dan shoved him, 'Now get back to your friends!' Jake staggered off back towards the hall lights. Dan watched him go and clapped Fleet on the back. 'Well, boy, you did for him there all right!' And Fleet nosed Dan's hand and laughed.

Slowly they walked back, as Jake and his friends drove off noisily. Neil and Muhammad came towards Dan.

'What was all that about?' asked Neil, curious about this

unexpected side to one of his new parishioners.

'Oh, nothing much. I had to tell him something he needed to hear.'

'I think you did more than tell him!' chuckled Muhammad.

'Aye, maybe I did,' smiled Dan a little ruefully.

'But you'll have stirred up a hornets' nest there, Dan,' said Neil, 'His father won't let this drop.'

'He's not going to tell his father—let's say for reasons of his own self-preservation—and I don't suppose either of you will feel the need to tell Mr Hetherington what a fool his son is! But thanks,' he added. 'I didn't want to admit it earlier, but you came in the nick of time—you and Fleet here.'

They came up to the women and Rory standing beside the van. Rory was holding his hand.

'Are you all right boy?' asked Dan concerned.

'Aye, it's just my hand. He stamped on it.'

'Let me see. Can you move your fingers?'

'Aye, it's sore, but.'

Fiona was angry. 'That was an evil thing to do. There's a nasty streak in that Jake Hetherington.' She turned to her father. 'You should have got the police to him, instead of fighting. Now you're as bad as them. What happened to all the turn-the-other-cheek stuff?'

Dan looked a bit sheepish. 'Aye, well...'

Aid came from an unexpected quarter. 'Well, even Jesus threw the money changers out of the Temple.' It was Neil Cameron. 'Sometimes you've just got to stand up to evil—to oppressors or bullies—to stop something worse happening to others.'

Fiona looked in surprise at the minister and opened her mouth to respond, but not knowing where to begin, she instead ushered Rory towards her car, saying goodnight.

Dan called after them, 'Are we still on for An Teallach

before you go back, Rory?'

'Aye, I'm fine.'

'You're surely not thinking of going up there at your age?' asked Fiona, exasperated.

'Age! I'm fitter than Rory there!'

'That wouldn't be hard. Look at the state of him!' The others all laughed. And then Fiona joined in. They both got into the car and Fiona drove off.

Fiona loved her son. Rory was the apple of her eye. She was so proud of him—especially his getting to university. She hoped he would become an English teacher, because he was so good with language and loved poetry and reading in general. But truth be told, she was a little bit jealous of Rory's relationship with his grandfather and the time they spent together. They seemed so free and easy in their relationship, whereas, try as she might, she never seemed to be relaxed enough, but always seemed to be uptight about what Rory was doing or not doing.

Rory loved his Mum too, but sometimes he found her mothering a bit suffocating. She was always worried about the impression he would make on others and what people would think; whereas his Grandad didn't care two hoots what people thought—he was only concerned with what he thought was right and wrong in itself.

Rory could understand how his mother felt so protective of him, as she'd had to bring him up on her own and had a special bond with him, but sometimes it was good to escape out onto the hills with his Grandad.

CHAPTER THREE

It had the promise of being a glorious early autumn day, but there was mist lying in the corrie of Toll an Lochain below the jagged teeth of the Corrag Bhuidhe pinnacles. Dan and Rory along with Fleet set out up the hillwalkers' path that started at Corrie Hallie on the A832 and went up through the birch woods. But then they turned right off the path, went down through the bracken and crossed the burn. They climbed up the other side and started walking up the rocky escarpment on the edge of Coir a' Ghiubhsachain, much of it like a stone pavement. Rory was carrying their rucksack. They paused about halfway up the escarpment and looked up at the mountain. The full panorama of the awesome red sandstone towers of An Teallach had opened out, from the near ridge of Sail Liath at the southern end, round by the jagged edges of Cadha Gobhlach and the red cockscomb of the Pinnacles to the shapely cone of Sgurr Fiona and the massive bulk of Bidein a Ghlas Thuill, the highest summit. The corrie of Toll an Lochain was now full of mist.

Rory smiled, 'It's a great day for it!'

'It is that', agreed Dan, 'But never forget the conditions up there can change in a moment. That mist should clear, but you never know. It's not called An Teallach, The Forge, for nothing. Sometimes the mist just boils up like the steam in a blacksmith's smiddy when he puts the red hot iron in the water.'

An Teallach is one of Scotland's greatest mountains, a

25

long, complex, sinuous ridge with ten tops over 3000 feet, but only two classed as Munros. A summit is only classed as a Munro if it is over 3000 feet and is considered a separate mountain—the latter qualification being much open to debate! A traverse of all An Teallach's tops and pinnacles is one of the best mountain expeditions in the Highlands, requiring some competent rock scrambling skills to climb the Corrag Bhuidhe Pinnacles.

Dan was having a last outing with his grandson before Rory headed back to University in Edinburgh. It had been a busy few weeks since the ceilidh, including the Lairg lamb sales. This sale in the small Highland village of Lairg in Sutherland was generally recognised as the biggest one day sale of hill sheep in Europe, when farmers and crofters from all over the Highlands gathered to sell that season's lambs. Up to 30,000 lambs could be sold to buyers from as far south as Yorkshire and Cumbria.

But now it was a quieter time for farm work and Dan was glad to have the chance to spend some time with Rory climbing An Teallach.

As they climbed onto the shoulder of Sail Liath, the mist was swirling out of the corrie to their right, and suddenly Dan caught Rory's arm and pointed. There, right on the edge of the mist was an amazing sight that sent a shiver down Rory's spine. A huge black horned shape loomed out of the mist. It took a moment for Rory to remember there were wild goats on An Teallach.

'Some people refer to them as a non-native species', said Dan, 'but they've probably been in the Highlands since after the last Ice Age when Stone Age farmers brought them with them from Europe. So I reckon they're more native than a lot of the people! It's even said that Robert the Bruce passed a law to protect the goats after a herd of them saved his life by distracting soldiers searching for him as he hid in a cave by Loch Lomond!'

'They certainly look primitive, as if from another world,' said Rory, gazing at the shaggy black creature with long, swept-back, curved horns, who had now been joined by two of his curious fellows.

'Aye, that's probably why some folk think they have something to do with the devil. Maybe it's the horns that do it—like the Beast in the Book of Revelation. But he had seven horns and ten heads!'

'I wouldn't like to meet him on An Teallach!' said Rory.

'No indeed!' laughed Dan. 'But he probably represented the persecuting Roman Empire. No, these fellows are harmless, and they probably do some good in an area like this, grazing on the cliffs that not even blackface sheep can reach. And the eagles will no doubt control their numbers by taking some of the kids every year.'

They reached Cadha Gobhlach, the Forked Pass, about the middle of the day, and although the sun was shining from behind them, the abyss below to the right was still full of swirling mist. Fleet, who arrived first, started barking like mad at the mist. Rory, who came next, suddenly saw an amazing sight—two enormous ghostly figures of a man and a hound looming out of the mist, surrounded by a bright circular rainbow.

Rory, awestruck, turned to Dan, 'Grandad! Look!'

'Aye. I thought we might see it today,' smiled Dan. 'Fleet! Be quiet!'

'What's that called again?'

'It's a Brocken Spectre. The sun behind us casts our shadows on the mist and it also makes a complete rainbow round them.'

'You'd told me about it before, but this is the first time I've seen it. It gave me quite a scare, with Fleet barking like that!'

'Aye. It would. But you know,' Dan said, 'Any time I've seen it, it's reminded me I'm safe. It's like Noah's rainbow—the sign of God's covenant promise—only it's all round you. You know, I once saw it from the air. We were on an op in Northern Ireland—during the Troubles—it was a bad time.' Dan paused as the memories came flooding back of another lifetime.

Rory loved when his Grandad would tell him stories of when he was in the Army, although there were some things he'd seldom talk about—mostly about his time in Northern Ireland.

'Anyway,' Dan went on, 'We were in this helicopter and it was in Bandit Country in South Armagh. We'd lost a few good men there. I was praying that the Lord would protect me and my men that day, when I looked out the window and I saw it. We were flying over low-lying cloud. I think they call it an inversion, when the cloud is on the low country and the tops are in the sunshine. I've seen it here too. But there it was—the shadow of the chopper surrounded by this complete circle of the most brilliant rainbow I'd ever seen! Then I knew we'd be all right.' He looked over the mist to the far horizon and some of the most spectacular mountains in the land.

Rory felt the hairs on the back of his neck stand on end as he gave Dan a sidelong look, half envying his grandfather's faith.

A few minutes later Dan and Rory were standing looking up at a huge forty foot high, slightly overhanging rock, blocking their way.

'This is the big one,' said Dan, 'the Corrag Bhuidhe Buttress. The bad step they call it—the *mauvais pas.*

'Some step!'

'Will we try it? Or do you want to take the path round?'

'No, let's do it. Remember the first time you took me up?

'Aye. You were only a wee fellow then. Your Mum was mad at me for taking you up here. Do you remember?'

They both laughed.

'On you go, Rory, you know the way.'

Dan turned to Fleet, 'But you can't go up here boy. Round you go on the path.' He gestured with his hand to the left, and Fleet ran off along the path. Dan climbed after Rory traversing to the left and then up towards the top. The weathered red sandstone felt warm in the sun as Rory gripped various handholds. He felt completely engrossed and focused. All other thoughts, whether bright or dark, were banished in the extreme concentration required for the climb.

At the top of the ridge they were joined again by Fleet, and they sat between two of the pinnacles on the edge of the abyss eating their sandwiches, drinking tea from a flask, and gazing out at the huge vista of the unique hills of Assynt and Coigach which rose up as distinct mountains out of the surrounding moorland. The mist had cleared below them and they could look down well over a thousand feet to Loch Toll an Lochain below their feet.

'So you're off back to the university next week,' said Dan, feeding part of his sandwich to Fleet who gratefully accepted it.

'Yeah, I've got to go. There's nothing else for it.'

'Are you happy there, Rory?'

Rory paused. 'I don't know… it's not like… it's not like climbing An Teallach. You know, here you've got a clear goal in front of you—to get to the top. You know where you're going.'

'And you don't know where you're going…'

'No, not really. I'm not like you. You know what you believe and you know where you're going. And I'm different from Mum too. She knows what she doesn't believe and she thinks she knows where she's going, but I don't know if she does…'

'Your mother's had a hard time—bringing you up on

her own—when your father left, and she had to come back here with you as just a little fellow. She blames herself—and I think she blames God too.'

'Yes, it's funny that—blaming someone you don't believe exists.'

'Oh, He exists all right. You can't sit here and look at all this with the feelings it rouses in your heart and think it all came about by chance'.

'No, you're right,' said Rory slowly, 'When you're in a place like this... but it's different in the city...'

'Aye, you're surrounded by the works of man's hand, and it's difficult to see the work of God's hand. You can't see the stars. The little lights of the city are too bright.'

'It seems brighter, but somehow it's darker,' Rory reflected, 'And more dangerous. This is a dangerous place, but here you can see the danger. In the city it's not so obvious.'

'And you know, that's what women like your mother can't see. They see the danger of a place like this, but they don't see the dangers—the spiritual dangers as well as the physical dangers—of the city, the place they're driving their sons and daughters to.'

'No, Mum wasn't keen on our coming up here!" smiled Rory, and after a pause, 'What about Granny? Was she like that? Did she want Mum to leave home?'

'Well, yes and no. She knew she had to leave to become a teacher, but she always hoped she'd come back, and she was so glad when you both came back from Newcastle—even in the circumstances—because she had a love of the land and the people's relationship with the land.

'I remember the old minister spoke of that at her funeral. I've got a copy of what he said back in the house, but I actually know most of it by heart. It goes something like this,' and Dan tilted his head back and closed his eyes.

'*Mary was born Mary Munro in Strathnaver, in Sutherland,*

and she was very proud of the fact. She knew intimately the history of the Clearances and how Patrick Sellar, the Countess of Sutherland's factor, evicted her forebears from their own land. She felt keenly the injustices of those days. But she was very proud of the achievements of the crofters in establishing their rights in the late nineteenth century...

'But her sympathies were not limited to past ages. There are many here today who can testify to her kindness and the hospitality of her home...

'But she knew that none of these things earned her God's grace. She knew herself as a sinner who needed a Redeemer. She trusted in Jesus as her only hope and knew redemption by his blood...

'Though she loved this country and these hills, she was looking for a better country—a heavenly one—where she is now at home with the Lord...

'For her, all weakness is now over. "They shall mount up with wings as eagles, they shall run and not be weary, they shall walk and not faint."'

'I like that,' said Rory, '"They shall mount up with wings as eagles".' He was deeply moved by his Grandad's words, but he wanted to lighten the mood. 'I think the eagle should appear right now, soaring up above us!' He laughed.

They sat for a while in silence.

'Grandad, why did Granny have to die?'

Dan looked at the side of his grandson's face as he gazed out over the wide, wild country. It was a lean face, without being hard; his eyes were keen and searching.

'Well, she had cancer. You know that.'

'I know, but that's not what I meant. It's just that... Granny believed in God, and God wasn't able to save her. We all prayed that God would save her, but he didn't. It just doesn't seem fair. She didn't deserve that.'

Dan was thoughtful, 'Deserve? No, we all deserve a lot worse. We've turned our backs on God. What we deserve is hell. But He offers us heaven. That's grace—the gift your

Granny accepted long ago.' He paused. 'Heaven or hell, judgement or grace—in the end it's one or the other.'

A strange feeling crept over Rory. He was suddenly aware of the thousand foot cliffs below him and his own smallness. It was as if he had an out of body experience and he saw himself from above like a little child sitting on the edge of an unfathomable abyss. The child Rory and the huge cliffs receded, as if in vision he was a huge eagle soaring away from the earth, until they were just specks in a huge and wild landscape. He suddenly felt dizzy, and he got up quickly and stood back from the edge.

Dan looked quizzically at him, 'Are you all right, *a bhalaich*? Are you dizzy?'

'Aye... a little. It was just... well, it was a funny feeling. I felt very small sitting on the edge and the world was very big...' Rory's voice trailed off.

'The world is big, right enough,' said Dan, 'but remember there's Someone bigger still.'

Rory sat down again away from the edge with his back to a rock. 'Grandad... did you always have faith?'

Dan gave a little chuckle, 'No! When I was young I was a bit of a rebel—even worse than you—if you can believe that! You see my parents—you didn't know them—but they were very strict, especially about Sabbath observance and various rules, like no dancing or drinking or even playing football. But I feel it was all more to do with what other people thought of you, rather than what God thought of you—all external, rather than the heart. You know what God told the prophet Samuel when he was looking for a new king: "Man looks on the outward appearance, but God looks on the heart."

'Anyway, I rebelled against all that. I suppose I was a bit of a tearaway, out drinking and chasing girls, and of course playing football!' He laughed.

'But it was your grandmother who started to change

me. We started going out at the beginning of our last year at Dingwall Academy... 1960 that would have been. Of course I was in digs but she was from Dingwall, so I was always round at her house. Now, her parents were believers, real Christians, but they were really kind with it, especially to me, because they could have wanted their lovely daughter to have nothing to do with someone like me!

'You said Granny started to change you.'

'Yes, well I suppose at first it was like she and her parents had a good influence on me. I would go to church with them, but it didn't really have much effect on me, although I know that Mr Leitch, the minister then, was a good preacher.

'But then we left school in 1961, and she went off to Edinburgh to do teacher training in Moray House. I didn't get enough Highers to go to College. My mother said that I had a good brain, but I'd never taken it out of the polythene bag! And that was true enough! Anyway I got a job in a bank in Inverness (which I hated), but every weekend I could I would cadge a lift or hitchhike down to Edinburgh to see Mary... your Granny, that is.' He smiled.

'But then we had a falling out. You see she was going to a church in Edinburgh with a lot of other students and young people, and she was converted. She became a committed Christian, and I didn't understand it. All she wanted to do was go to church things and Christian Union meetings, and I thought she was turning into someone like my parents, so we fell out.

'I was fed up with the bank of course as well, so on the spur of the moment I joined the army—the Queen's Own Highlanders. Now it turned out they were based at Milton Bridge camp outside Edinburgh, and it wasn't long before I met up with Mary again. And she would drag me along to St Columba's Free Church, up near the Castle where George Collins was the renowned minister. She wouldn't allow me to take things any further, because I wasn't a believer. But I was just happy to be sitting beside her and didn't pay much attention to the sermons.' Dan smiled ruefully to himself.

'Well, a year later—that would be 1964—the regiment was moved to Osnabrück in West Germany as part of the British Army of the Rhine, and your Granny started teaching. We would write and I'd see her when I was home on leave, but we didn't seem to be going anywhere. She was a teacher and I was a bit of a hell-raiser, getting drunk, fighting with local lads over girls and so on. I was constantly in trouble with the Regimental Provost, especially when we moved to Berlin in '66. I was really getting near to being kicked out of the Army, and I don't know what would have happened to me then. I felt lost.

'That was when I was befriended by Major Calum Macleod who was the regimental chaplain and a fellow Highlander. Although I wouldn't admit it at first, I was feeling angry and resentful and ashamed and guilty all at the same time. Major Macleod impressed me because he didn't talk down to me or judge me. Instead he was sympathetic, but he stressed what I knew myself deep down—that the root cause of my trouble was sin—running away from God. He read from Genesis 4, God's words to Cain when he was angry and resentful against his brother: 'If you do well, will you not be accepted? And if you do not do well, sin is couching at the door; its desire is for you, but you must master it'. Of course Cain didn't listen and he didn't master his sin and he ended up as a restless wanderer, East of Eden. You know John Steinbeck wrote a whole book on that theme and he called it East of Eden. Have you read it?'

'No, I haven't, but it sounds interesting.'

'It is. I've read it and, while I couldn't go along with all of it, I think he understood something about the grip of evil on the human heart.

'But then Calum Macleod did something I will never forget. We were sitting having tea and biscuits, and he took a biscuit in his big left hand (he was a big burly man), and he said, "That's your sin. It's weighing you down. It'll weigh you down to hell in the end. But the Good News is that Jesus took your sin on himself on the cross". And here he tipped the biscuit from his left hand onto his right and he said, "That sin weighed him down to the hell you deserve." In that moment I understood what Mary and ministers back home had always been trying to tell me. I finally understood it wasn't about my efforts to appear good to other people. It was about what Jesus had done for me. It was a revelation – that simple action.'

'And then you were a changed man?'

Dan smiled, 'Well it wasn't exactly a Damascus Road experience, but it was the beginning of a change. I wanted to find out everything Major Macleod could teach me, and after a few weeks, I could write to Mary and tell her I'd accepted Christ as my Saviour. And the rest is history. We were married in '68 when the regiment returned to Edinburgh.'

'But you stayed in the Army and went on to join the SAS. Didn't you find that difficult as a Christian—I mean fighting and even killing?

'It was difficult being a Christian, but in some ways no more than in any other walk of life. I got a lot of stick from some of the other squaddies. I thought I should just turn the other cheek, as Jesus said. But in fact the bullying got so bad I had to ask Major Macleod what I should do about it. He said when Jesus told us to turn the other cheek, he was talking about personal insults; he wasn't talking about allowing people to bully you or beat you up—that would only allow the evil to grow and flourish and get other people hurt. And he gave me the best piece of advice I ever got.

So the next time someone started to lay into me, I hit him right in the midriff and then a left hook to his chin, and he went down like a sack of coal. I never had any trouble after that!'

Rory laughed, 'Just like you did to Jake!'

'Aye, and I hope we'll have no more trouble from that quarter either!'

'But what about being in the SAS? You must have felt conflicts of interest then?

'No, not really. Of course there were times things went wrong and innocent people got killed, but on the whole we were fighting a war with ruthless men who wouldn't bat an eyelid over deliberately bombing and killing innocent people.

'But for a lot of the time I was in Northern Ireland I was in "The Det", 14th Intelligence Detachment, to give it its proper name. I was involved in covert intelligence and surveillance operations. That's how we managed to discover so many arms caches and either arrest or kill so many IRA gunmen. I suppose one reason I was recruited was because I spoke Gaelic and could understand Irish Gaelic, and they thought that my accent wasn't unlike the Southern Irish accent. It isn't really. It sounded like that to English officers, but wouldn't really fool an Irishman!'

'I suppose knowing how to stalk deer would have helped too!'

Dan laughed, 'Aye that helped as well!'

'But did you actually kill anyone?

'Aye, I did. I don't take any pleasure in it, but I don't feel guilty about it either. Sometimes it was kill or be killed. Like one time we got a tip off that they were going to kill a retired policeman who worked as a security guard at a construction yard on the edge of town. Well we got there first and lay in wait behind hedges and walls and in unmarked cars—Q cars, they were called. This van appeared—we'd been tipped off it had been stolen earlier in the day—and three gunmen jumped out and opened up on the security post with AK-47s. They'd seen what they took to be two security guards at the window. In fact they were cardboard cut-outs. They were then challenged to drop their weapons, but they started firing in all directions. The van tried to turn, but was rammed by a Q car and the driver got out and surrendered, but the gunmen scattered over walls and under hedges, and one came over the wall where I was hiding and came face to face with me. I told him to drop his weapon, but he raised his AK-47 to shoot, and I shot him in the chest. If I hadn't downed him, he'd have killed me and gone on to kill who knows how many others.'

'But what about the commandment, 'Thou shalt not kill?' Rory persisted.

'That clearly means you shall not commit murder—that's unjustified killing. In the Bible it is recognised there is justified killing, like in killing a murderer or in war. The problem with killing the murderer is that that could descend into a blood feud. And even with a legal system, there can be miscarriages of justice, so I'm not really in favour of the death penalty today. But in war it's a different situation. It's kill or be killed. The only question is if the cause is just.'

Dan stood up. 'Well, we'd better get going if we're to reach the top today!'

Rory packed up the rucksack and they set off on the last leg of the climb, past Lord Berkeley's Seat, over Sgurr Fiona and up the last steep haul to the top.

As they walked, Rory remarked, 'You said "if the cause is just", but that's the really difficult thing isn't it? I mean, a lot of people think that Britain should have got out of Ireland a long time ago. And there's a whole history of oppression behind that.'

'You know, I had a lot of sympathy with some of the

nationalist community in Ulster. In some ways I felt closer to them than my fellow Protestants. We shared a common heritage in language and culture, although not many people there actually spoke Irish Gaelic. But there are tremendous similarities and cross-fertilisation in the music and the songs especially. Of course, the links go way back, right back to Columba.

'Anyway, it's good that the Troubles are over now since the Good Friday Agreement, but I feel myself there won't be real peace until all sides agree to a united Ireland.'

'I'm surprised. I thought you were fighting to keep North and South separate!'

'No. We were fighting to stop both sides killing each other. The Border is a totally unnatural one, and really impossible to defend. It's not like the Border between Scotland and England which is pretty well clearly defined geographically by the Solway, the Cheviots and the Tweed.'

'But there was plenty fighting over that border in the past!'

'Aye, too true! But I hope "Those days are past now" as it says in the song "Flower of Scotland"!'

'But can we "still rise now and be the nation again that stood against him"?'

'Not as long as we define our nationhood by standing against others. We need to rediscover what we stand for. And I don't think we'll do that by jettisoning fifteen centuries of Christian influence on this nation, which is what I think many of our present movers and shakers are all about.'

They fell silent as they climbed the last steep slope to the summit. Rory had a lot to think about. He loved it when he could be alone with his Grandad like this and when he opened up about what he really thought. But what his Grandad thought and believed was in direct contradiction to so much of what Rory had been taught in school and now university, and what was flowing around him in the general zeitgeist. He wasn't sure what he believed, but he felt that the various ideas flowing around him were like the shifting wind, whereas what his Grandad believed seemed somehow solid, like the rock of An Teallach beneath his feet.

CHAPTER FOUR

The afternoon autumn sun was shining red on Edinburgh Castle Rock, making the usually grim, grey, volcanic rock glow as if it was about to melt back again to molten lava.

Edinburgh Castle is one of the oldest fortified places in Europe. The huge volcanic plug of dolerite rock formed the perfect defensible site. There was certainly an Iron Age fort here in the second century AD. It became a royal residence from the time of David I, and changed hands between Scotland and England several times in the fourteenth century Wars of Independence. There too, Mary Queen of Scots gave birth to her son James who later became the first king of the United Kingdom. Subsequent to that union, the Castle became a purely military garrison (which it continues to be to this day), until in the nineteenth century it was opened up to the public. This was largely due to Sir Walter Scott discovering the crown jewels of Scotland hidden in the castle. The Honours of Scotland (as the jewels are called) are the oldest Crown jewels in Britain. They were created in Scotland and Italy during the reigns of James IV and James V in the 15th and 16th centuries. The crown, sceptre and sword of state were used together for the first time for the coronation of Mary Queen of Scots in 1543. The ancient Stone of Destiny, used for many centuries in the coronation of monarchs, was returned to Scotland from London in 1996 and is also on display in the Castle (although there is some doubt that the stone Edward I stole was in fact the real stone). But in spite of all these romantic historic associations, Edinburgh Castle has never lost its rather grim military outline as it towers over the city.

Down below on Castle Terrace, a man got out of a large white BMW—a 740i with the personal registration number B16 TAM. He was a big heavy man in his fifties with a round shaved head that seemed to dwarf his small features especially his eyes. He was well dressed in a bespoke grey suit, polished black shoes and dark grey Crombie coat and, as he locked the car, he displayed an expensive watch and signet ring. He looked up at the Castle and smiled. He seemed well satisfied with life. He appeared to think his life as secure and immovable as the Castle Rock. He walked up to an impressive door which had a polished brass plate beside it saying 'MONCRIEFF PROPERTY SERVICES'. He unlocked the door and strode in.

His secretary rose from her desk, where she'd been typing, and took his coat. She was a petite, pretty blonde in her twenties. Her hair was expensively coiffured, her make up expertly applied, and her nail polish exactly the same shade of bright pink as her lipstick. She wore a light grey pencil skirt and pink blouse.

'Good afternoon, Mr Moncrieff. A late night last night?'

'Less of your cheek, Gina!' He slapped her rear playfully as she turned to hang up his coat. 'I've been busy elsewhere, smarty-pants. It's not all office work, you know. Time for a coffee and some paper work before five. And maybe a little fun!'

He tried to grab her, but she evaded him round the other side of the desk, squealing rather excitedly, "Now that's quite enough of that, Mr Moncrieff!" But the little game of chase was interrupted by the door bell ringing long and loud.

'Who's that?' he snapped in exasperation at his fun being interrupted.

Gina disappeared gratefully to answer the door.

'Tell them I'm busy!' he shouted after her.

He heard voices and then two people entered. One was a wee hard man, not tall but powerfully built, in his 30s, with short reddish hair and a scar down the side of his cheek. If it wasn't for the scar, his features would have seemed pleasant. As it was he looked rather menacing, particularly as he was scowling. He wore a blue suit and open-neck white shirt. His name was Billy King. He was Tam Moncrieff's right hand man.

The Scottish surname 'King' belongs to a sept of the Clan MacGregor—probably originating from the time when the MacGregors were outlawed and the very name proscribed, together with the fact that the motto of the clan is the Gaelic 's rìoghail mo dhream—'Royal is my Race'—preserving the legend that the MacGregors were descended from an early king of the Picts. The most famous bearer of the name was the red-haired outlaw Rob Roy MacGregor of the late seventeenth and early eighteenth century from the southern Highlands, and Billy King, whose people had originated in the County of Stirling, prided himself as a latter day Rob Roy. The red hair helped, but Billy was far from Rob Roy's stature. Billy had first got to know Tam at the gym they both attended, and when he'd been laid off from his work in the construction industry, Tam had offered him a job as an enforcer.

The other person entering Moncrieff's office—actually being propelled by Billy—was a weedy youth with spiky orange hair and wearing ripped jeans and a hoodie. He looked nervous.

His annoyance evaporating, Moncrieff greeted the hard man, 'Billy, my man! How's it going?'

'Aye fine, Big Tam... But we need to talk.' Billy twisted his head and glanced towards Gina, who had just entered.

'Oh aye. Gina, you can call it a day, doll.'

'But I thought we were working...' she responded with

a sarcastic smile.

'Beat it!'

Gina made a face and, grabbing her coat and handbag, she headed out the door.

When she'd gone, Big Tam turned to Billy. 'What's the problem?

Billy shoved the youth forward. 'This wee shite's the problem.'

Tam frowned, 'How come?'

'He's been screwing us around. Been working for the dark side.'

'What, the polis?'

'Naw. Genghis Khan's lot.'

'The Pakistanis?'

'Aye. They have some direct supply route—getting their smack straight frae Pakistan or Afghanistan or some place.'

Tam turned to the young man, who was visibly shaking. Tam spoke very reasonably to him, but Tam's sheer bulk so close to him was immensely threatening.

'You're Carol Fulton's boy—Mark, isn't it? From Niddrie?'

'Aye—I'm sorry Mr Moncrieff... I didnae mean no harm... It's shan, but it's just that my Mam's no' well... and I needed the money, like... and our normal supplies weren't coming through, and I've got a lot of punters... and they were going radge.'

'I can understand that, Mark. But you know I have a business to run. And I can't have people working for the opposition. You know that could put me out of business? Aye?'

Mark nodded uncertainly.

'And you know you have to think about your Mam,' Tam continued. 'There are some nasty people about—even some who work for me—and they might no' be as understanding as me, Mark. You know what I'm saying?'

Mark was clearly terrified. 'Aw, Mr Moncrieff, you wid-nae let anything happen tae ma Mam...'

'Of course not, Mark, but you know you've got to be loyal. OK? Now, there's something you can do for me.'

'Yeah, anything, Mr Moncrieff, anything...'

'I want you to go on working for the Pakistanis.'

'Wha...?' Mark looked shocked and uncomprehending.

'I want you to find out all you can about their operation. And I want you to come and tell me everything. Right?'

'Aw, Mr Moncrieff, I don't know—I mean—they'd kill me if they found out!'

'Kill you? Don't worry about the people who can just kill you, Mark. It's what they do to you before they kill you, you need to worry about. Is that no' right, King Billy?'

'Aye, that's right, Tam,' said Billy with a mirthless grin on his face.

'So it's a deal, Mark, eh?'

'Aw, sure, Mr Moncrieff, that's barry... thanks, Mr Moncrieff.' Mark was relieved he was getting out of there alive, but he didn't know what he was letting himself in for.

Billy ushered him out, and returned.

'They say God works in mysterious ways,' said Tam pondering this unexpected development. 'This is maybe just the breakthrough we need.'

'It's an ill wind...'

'It'll be a whirlwind by the time I'm finished,' Tam slammed his fist hard on the desk.

Mr Thomas Moncrieff gave every appearance of being a respectable businessman, but the truth was that he was the biggest gangland boss in the city. His nefarious activities included supply of illegal drugs, organised crime, money-laundering, prostitution and people trafficking. He had long been a target of the drug squad and serious crime squad, but all operations came to nothing. It was suspected that his elusiveness was due to the fact that he was being tipped off by some unknown member or members of the Lothian and Borders police. There was a lot of money sloshing around the kind of activities Moncrieff was involved in. Plus, when bribery didn't work, he was not averse to resorting to blackmail, and his prostitution racket gave ample scope for that.

Big Tam Moncrieff had been born and bred in Gracemount, a council scheme on the southern edge of the city. The name Gracemount can be traced to a post-Reformation change of name from Priesthill, reflecting the Reformers rejection of the necessity of the mediation of a priest, and their emphasis instead on one of the mottos of the Reformation—*sola gratia*, by grace alone. Unfortunately by the time Tam was growing up there in the Sixties and Seventies few people knew anything about either priests or grace and cared even less. Gracemount was well on its way to becoming one of the most deprived areas in Scotland.

The surname Moncrieff (there are various spellings, including Moncrief and Moncrieffe) has a noble history in Scotland. The Clan Moncrieffe originated in the area of Moncrieffe Hill, which lies on a peninsula between the Rivers Tay and Earn, 3 miles southeast of Perth. The name derives from the Gaelic name of the hill—Monadh Croibhe—meaning 'the hill of the (sacred) tree', and the first historical record of the name is in a charter of King Alexander II in 1248 gifting land in Perthshire to a Matthew Muncrephe. Over the centuries, many influential people in church and state have born the name Moncrieff, but as in the case of all such noble names, it also belongs to family lines that have long fallen on hard times.

No one knows when or how the Moncrieffs came to Gracemount, but their history is an all too common one of a fall from privilege, through clerical work and manual labour to unemployment, poverty and alcoholism. Young

Tam grew to despise his parents and spent as much of his time as possible out of the house. He was always big for his age and very quickly became the leader of the pack. He didn't get his kicks from alcohol or drugs, but from dominating others and putting the fear of death into them. He was smart, but school bored him and he left with minimum qualifications. He worked for a building firm renovating old buildings, and realised how much money could be made from property. However, you need money to make money, and he had none—not, that is, until he and his gang took over the local drug dealing network. Some people disappeared; some were permanently disfigured and disabled. Soon the name 'Big Tam' was feared right across south Edinburgh. The rest, as they say, is history.

*

Back out on the street, Mark was walking away when a guy passed him coming towards the office—a young guy about his own age, but much bigger. Mark vaguely recognised him. He'd seen him somewhere before, but he couldn't remember. Was he a cop or was he a past customer? Didn't really look like a cop, and he seemed too healthy to be one of his clients. In his line of business you couldn't be too careful. He stared blankly at the pavement. He had other things on his mind anyway. If he had turned and looked he'd have seen the young man stop at the very door he'd just left and press the intercom button.

'It's Jake.'

After a minute, the door clicked and Jake Hetherington entered.

*

Night had descended on the city. A chill wind was blowing along the Grassmarket, causing litter and a few early autumn leaves to swirl in eddies. The Grassmarket is a large open street which is dominated by the Castle that towers over it to the northwest. It was originally, as the name suggests, an open air market, but is now surrounded by hotels and hostelries and is the site of open air performances during the Edinburgh Festivals. But this autumn night there were no Festivals or performances of any kind, and the snell wind had driven most people indoors.

A strikingly beautiful young woman was walking towards the West Port. Her long dark red hair was getting blown around in the swirling wind. Her classically neat features and complexion were flawless, although there was a certain weariness about her dark eyes, and a sad resigned look to her full lips. Her short green coat flapped in the gusty wind and her high heeled black boots beat a staccato rhythm on the pavement. A little further on, she stopped at a doorway. The sign said 'PARADISE—SAUNA AND MASSAGE'. She spoke into the intercom.

'Hi, Sharon, it's me—Claire.'

A woman's voice answered, 'Come on in, doll.'

Claire entered and was nearly knocked over by a middle-aged couple who seemed rather irate.

The man spoke over his shoulder in a strong Swedish accent, 'We thought this was a respectable sauna!'

Claire was greeted at reception by a plumpish woman in her forties—Sharon Henderson. She was almost the caricature of a madam—heavily made up, with curly bleached blonde hair, and was dressed in a pink satin blouse, tight black skirt, dark nylons and stiletto heels.

'Hi Claire', she greeted the girl. 'Another hard day at the Uni?' Her sky blue eyes seemed to twinkle with mischief.

'Yeah, Sharon, that'll be right. What was that all about?'

'A couple from Sweden who thought this was "a respectable sauna"', she giggled, attempting to mimic a Swedish accent. Her plump face creased in a wide smile as she giggled. She liked Claire.

'But you'd better get your ass into gear. Mr King and Mr Moncrieff are bringing some important guests. You know

Big Tam'll want you as usual—so you'd better be quick.'

Claire rolled her eyes, blue eyes so dark they looked violet in some lights. 'Yeah, yeah,' and exited though another door. Sharon took a vanity mirror out of her handbag and checked her makeup and hair. Her glance was drawn to the lines and dark circles around her eyes that the makeup couldn't quite conceal. She sighed, snapped the mirror shut and slipped it back in her handbag. She had been too long in this game, although now she was mainly at reception—the punters wanted younger flesh. But sometimes she wished she was a million miles from it all. She hated seeing a beautiful (and smart) young girl like Claire get dragged down. She often wanted out of it, but she knew that wasn't going to happen. Big Tam wouldn't let it.

Her mind went back to when she'd first got involved with Big Tam in Gracemount. She'd only been in her early teens when her Dad was killed. He was with the Army in Northern Ireland. That was the beginning of a downward spiral in her life. Her Dad had been a rock for her. Then she'd married young to someone she thought was the strong silent type like her father. The truth was he was just silent. When he left her for a younger model when she was pregnant with her second child, she was in dire straits financially, trying to hold down a dead-end, part-time job in a supermarket and bringing up her two small children, with no help from her ex who'd left her with nothing but debts. She couldn't pay her bills or her credit card. That's when she made her first mistake. A friend told her about a local guy who would lend money. She'd heard the term 'loan-shark', and she only focused on the 'loan' part, but she quickly experienced the 'shark' part. When she couldn't pay back, her children were threatened. That's when Big Tam came to the rescue like her knight in shining armour and put the frighteners on the loan shark. She didn't know then that Tam ran the loan shark. But he told her she could make a lot of money and pay off her debts by taking a job in one of his 'establishments'. That's when she made her second mistake. She just thanked God that her children were now grown up and married and well out of the area.

She was shaken out of her painful memories by the buzzer going again, and she admitted Billy King and Tam Moncrieff with two friends. One looked in his forties. He was tall and fit with cropped dark hair, a long face and eyes that seemed to narrow as he looked at anyone as if he was assessing them sceptically. He wore a black suit and shirt and tie. The other was in his thirties, medium height and build with longish fair hair. His face was fleshy and flushed, and his eyes glanced here and there, never seeming to stay focused on one spot. He wore designer jeans, open neck shirt and a brown leather jacket. They were all laughing.

Billy was in full flight, '… and he says "What are you looking at?" And I goes…' He head butts an imaginary opponent. "I'm looking at a guy wi' a broken nose!"

'Language, gentlemen!' Sharon remonstrated, 'We don't want to scare the clientele!'

'Sorry, Sharon, but you know what Red Billy's like — you can't take him anywhere. And how are you tonight, doll?' asked Tam, putting his arm round her and kissing her gallantly on the cheek.

Sharon extricated herself. 'Fine, Mr Moncrieff. And aren't you going to introduce me to your guests?'

'Sure. This is DI Matt Lawson,' Tam pointed to the taller of the two, 'and this is DS Jack Reid. They're both undercover — or they soon will be!'

'Ha! Ha! Very droll, Tam,' said Matt, poker-faced. 'You're some wit.'

Sharon went behind the bar. 'What would you gentlemen like to drink?'

'Make that four large whiskies, and four G&T's' said

Tam, 'And take them through to the private lounge.' He leant over Sharon and said quietly, 'And you never saw them here, Sharon. You know what I mean?'

'Aye, sure, Tam.'

They made their way through to the private lounge with its plush furnishing and décor. By the time Sharon brought in the drinks, they had been joined by three seductively dressed young women and they were soon laughing and drinking. Just then Claire entered. She looked stunning in a short purple dress and very high heeled black stilettos, her make-up and hair immaculate. Tam turned and gave a wolf whistle.

'Wow! Hullo, gorgeous! How's my pretty baby to-night?'

He enveloped her in a bear hug, lifting her off her feet. She laughed and squealed, pretending to love it, but Sharon thought that for a moment Claire's face over Tam's shoulder looked sad like the face of a little lost girl.

*

In Scotland in 2008, prostitution was covered by various pieces of legislation including the *Civic Government (Scotland) Act 1982*, the *Criminal Law (Consolidation) (Scotland) Act 1995*, and the *Prostitution (Public Places) (Scotland) Act 2007*. This effectively meant that prostitution itself was not illegal, but soliciting in a public place was, as was pimping and brothel-keeping. However, the 1982 Act gave local councils the power to license places of entertainment. Edinburgh Council issued licenses to massage parlours and saunas, effectively allowing brothels. The reality was that in Edinburgh, both Edinburgh Council and Lothian and Borders Police turned a blind eye to saunas and massage parlours that were really fronts for illegal prostitution.

Tam Moncrieff had very early on realised the benefits of owning 'saunas'—not only an outlet for his own sexual interests, as well as good financial returns, but also the possibility of blackmail of prominent politicians, councillors and members of the legal establishment and police force. That's how Lawson had been reeled in by Tam. He had, let's say, some unusual sexual proclivities, and he didn't want the videos that had been taken at one of Moncrieff's other establishments to be seen by his wife and family, far less by his police bosses. In Reid's case it was his gambling addiction that led to his falling under Tam's control. Lawson let him know there was money to be made by turning a blind eye or by passing on information about police activity.

*

Next day Claire was back at university, in a lecture theatre off George Square. The lecturer was droning on about some obscure points of T S Eliot's play *Murder in the Cathedral*. She couldn't concentrate. She was restless. But certain words and phrases kept piercing her boredom—*behind the face of Death the Judgement…Emptiness… separation from God… the soul is no longer deceived… what beyond death is not death, we fear.*

She shuddered and started looking around to check for someone she wanted to see. That's when she spotted a guy across the aisle a little further back. She'd never really taken any notice of him last session. Maybe he hadn't been in any of her lectures then. Long dark brown hair, and tanned as if he'd been working outside all summer—dressed completely in black—black leather jacket, black T-shirt, black jeans, black Cons. Then she spotted the person she was after, and lost interest in Black Leather Jacket Man.

The lecture came to an anticlimactic end and, with a clattering of seats and a general hubbub of conversation, all the students began to make their way out. Claire stuffed her half-written notes in her bag and struggled through the crowd to catch the person she wanted. They were out in Buccleuch Place before she caught up with him.

'Hey, Jake, wait up.'

Jake Hetherington turned with a sardonic expression on his face and was just about to greet her, when Black Leather Jacket passed them.

'Well, if it isn't little Rory Williams, the Man in Black!' The sarcasm was heavy in Jake's voice.

Rory just looked through Jake as he walked past, and Claire noticed that Jake looked away.

'Who was that?' asked Claire, intrigued by Jake's reaction to her Black Leather Jacket Man.

'Just some hick from the sticks. A nobody. Why? You fancy him, Claire?'

'I think he's kinda cute. Why don't you like him?'

Jake was impatient. 'A long story, babe. Another time maybe. Anyway, what do you want? I gotta split.'

Claire lowered her voice to almost a whisper. 'It's just I need some stuff—for tonight.'

'Got some clients tonight, have we?' Jake sneered, starting to walk away.

Claire tried to ignore his tone of voice and said, 'Same time, same place?'

As Jake walked off, he called over his shoulder, 'Yeah. OK. But don't be late. I'm busy.'

'Bastard!' Claire cursed to herself.

Jake crossed Buccleuch Street and headed through the pend in the building opposite into St Patrick Square. Suddenly a delicious idea occurred to him—a way he could hit back at Rory and, indirectly, at his grandfather. It would be so satisfying to see Rory dragged down into a destructive and corrupting relationship with Claire. And best of all, none of it could be traced back to him. He just needed to think of a way to persuade Claire.

Rory had just came out of Scayles music shop on the corner of St Patrick Square (where he had a part time job and was checking when his next shift was) when he noticed

Jake crossing St Patrick Square and heading south towards South Clerk Street. Rory had heard some unsavoury rumours about Jake and, on the spur of the moment, he followed him.

Jake turned left into Montague Street. He was amused that the locals pronounced it 'Montaygie' Street with the emphasis on the middle syllable. If he had turned to look, he'd have seen Rory some distance back. But he didn't look and he entered an antique shop. Intrigued, Rory dodged into a nearby close entrance. A minute later, a big white BMW pulled up outside the shop. The number plate was B16 TAM. He saw a big man in a Crombie coat get out and go into the shop.

'Big Tam. Where have I heard that name before?' Rory asked himself. Then he remembered. Some guys he knew from the music scene had stayed in a flat owned by Moncrieff Properties. There were some dodgy dealings involving drugs. Rory walked past the antique shop, which said 'King's Antiques' on the sign, and turned north onto St Leonard's and on towards his flat down the Cowgate. As he walked he mulled over what he'd just witnessed. So Jake had something to do with Tam Moncrieff. And Tam Moncrieff, as well as owning a lot of property in Edinburgh, was somehow involved in the drug scene. Was that what Jake was into?

What Rory didn't know then was that Jake also had been staying in one of the Moncrieff Properties flats, and discovered that one of the other students always seemed to have plenty of money, whereas Jake himself, with his expensive tastes, was struggling on the allowance his father gave him. Very soon he had found out the secret was drugs, and he lost no time in offering his services and had quickly risen up within the ranks to become one of Tam's trusted henchmen because of his wide range of friends and acquaintances among the wealthier students.

THE FORGE

*

That evening Claire was walking north-east through the Meadows along Jawbone walk. The Meadows is a large public park in Edinburgh consisting largely of grassland and tree lined paths, created when the Burgh Loch was drained in the eighteenth century. It is bordered on the north by the University of Edinburgh's George Square campus, and the Quartermile development on the site of the historic Royal Infirmary, and on the south by the sandstone tenements of Sciennes, Marchmont and Bruntsfield. Jawbone walk, which leads north-east from Marchmont to join Middle Meadow walk just before it passes between the University and the Old Royal Infirmary, is named after the jawbones of whales erected at the south end of the walk. These jawbones were originally part of a display from Zetland and Fair Isle at the International Exhibition of 1886.

It was a cold and rainy night. Claire was wearing a black jacket, skinny blue jeans and purple Cons, with a black bag over her shoulder, and she was struggling to keep dry with a small umbrella that kept getting blown inside out by the gusty wind. She left the Meadows and walked along the south side of George Square, once an elegant Georgian square, but vandalised by the University in the 1960s by the erection of the modernist concrete and glass buildings of the Library, the George Square Theatre and the David Hume and Appleton Towers on the south and east sides of the Square. The Towers are by far the tallest buildings in the area apart from the graceful steeple of Buccleuch Free Church on the junction of Chapel Street, Buccleuch Street and West Crosscauseway, which matches them in height, but far outclasses them in its neo-gothic elegance.

Claire threaded her way between some of the older sandstone buildings and the David Hume Tower, onto Windmill Street, across Chapel Street and into the Orchard pub on West Nicolson Street.

As she made her way to the bar, she looked around for Jake, and eventually spotted him drinking with some friends and watching the football. She bought a G&T, made eye contact with Jake and moved to a quiet corner. She sat sipping her drink, looking agitated, and glancing across at Jake who took his time to come over. He sat down beside her, and put his arm round her, too close for Claire's liking, but she didn't show it. She smiled like he was an old friend.

'Have you got my stuff?'

'Nice to see you too, Claire!'

'Very funny. Have you got it?'

'All in good time. There's a little deal I want to propose.'

Claire looked suspiciously at him. 'A deal?'

Jake leaned back, taking a slug of his lager, clearly enjoying himself. 'Mmm. You know that bloke you fancied earlier today?'

Claire looked blank.

'You know—the Man in Black…'

'Oh him. I don't fancy him.'

'OK, fine. It doesn't matter. In fact for what I have in mind, it's even better.'

'And what have you got in mind?'

'Something rather amusing. I want you to pretend to become his girlfriend.'

'What? Why on earth would I want to do that? What are you up to?'

'You don't need to bother your pretty little head about what I'm up to. But I can make it worth your while…'

'How?'

'I can give you a BOGOF every week.'

'BOGOF?'

'You know, Buy One Get One Free.'

'Are you serious?'

'Interested?'

Claire stared across the crowded room. Black Leather Jacket Man slowly walked across her mind and how he'd made Jake look away. 'All right then,' she said suddenly, 'Starting tonight?'

'Why not? But remember I'll be watching you.'

'Nothing new there then,' said Claire smiling sarcastically. 'OK, where's my stuff?'

'It's in your bag.' Jake looked down mockingly at her. 'Now where's my money?'

Claire felt in her handbag and looked relieved. She took out some folded bank notes and handed them to Jake, asking him to get her another drink. Jake went to the bar, bought her a G&T and stuffed the rest of the money in his pocket. Anyone observing them would have just seen a young man buying a drink for his girlfriend.

As Jake moved back to his friends, Claire sipped on her drink, looking wistfully out the window through her own reflection. How had she got herself into all this? She'd always wanted to go to Uni and study English. It was her favourite subject. She was a voracious reader—everything from the classics to modern crime and fantasy. She was thrilled when she got into Edinburgh University—a chance to move away from home in London and come to Scotland's capital city. She'd fallen in love with J K Rowling's Harry Potter series and knew that the author had started writing in Edinburgh. She also loved the Inspector Rebus crime novels of Ian Rankin which were mainly set in Edinburgh.

Then everything had turned sour. Her father's business went bust. Her parents had already divorced, but her father had continued to pay for her school fees and would have gone on supporting her through Uni, until just in the previous year, her first year at Uni, his business enterprises had gone belly up. She was still determined to go on with her course and said she would find work. She started working in pubs, but the hours were long to try to make enough money to make ends meet. Edinburgh was far more expensive than she'd imagined. She was constantly tired and found it difficult to concentrate on her studies. That's when she bumped into Jake in a pub (they had been to the same school) and he introduced her to Bennies. He said they'd help her to stay awake. And they did. But then when she needed more he told her what they cost. It was a vicious circle. The more she needed Bennies to keep her high, the more she had to pay, and the more she had to pay, the more she had to work in the pub. That's when Jake said he knew about some work that would pay a lot better than pub work. He could introduce her to someone—who turned out to be Tam Moncrieff. He could give her accommodation at half the price she was paying. Then Tam needed a favour. One of his girls at the Paradise Sauna had fallen sick. The money was good. She kicked herself for being so naïve. Now she was trapped, and she was really scared of Tam Moncrieff.

She finished her drink, got up and went out into the night, heading to The Paradise.

CHAPTER FIVE

It was late September and Dan was out on the hill. It was getting late in the day, nearing dusk, and rather damp. Heavy grey cloud was down on the mountains and there was a light drizzle, as if the very air itself was weeping. Dan was stalking some stags behind Beinn nam Ban which lay to the east of his croft on that peninsula of rough hilly land that lies between Loch Broom to the north and An Loch Beag to the south. The red deer's sense of smell is very acute so, although there was very little wind, he had circled round so he was well downwind of the deer. Their eyesight and hearing are also excellent, so he took care not to be seen or heard as he slithered on his belly through the wet grass and heather until he got into position. He was wearing an old brown tweed suit of his father's, consisting of jacket and plus-fours, which was perfect for two reasons: compared to modern fabrics the tweed made no sound as he crawled, and it provided great camouflage against the dying heather and grass.

He took his rifle out of its cover, fitted a silencer and looked through the telescopic sights. He focused on one stag—an older beast.

He murmured to himself, 'You've seen better days, *a bhalaich*… a bit like myself.' His mouth twisted lopsidedly in a rueful smile. 'I think it's time.'

He squeezed the trigger. There was a muffled shot and the stag leapt, staggered a few steps and went down. The other stags moved off at speed.

Dan slipped his rifle back in the cover and started running to the fallen beast. He knelt at its head and paused a moment, his face filled with a look of tender regret. 'Not for you now a slow death this winter. At least I saved you from that. And maybe the sacrifice of your life may help others too.'

He took out his knife and gralloched the lifeless stag, carefully burying the entrails in a nearby peat bog. That done, he dragged the carcase down to the top of a large rock, lifted it across his shoulders and carried it for a few hundred yards. The weight of over 150 kg would have brought many strong young men to their knees, if they had even managed to lift it in the first place, but Dan kept up a steady pace. After he was well away from where he had shot the stag, he started dragging the carcase down the hill.

Half an hour later he reached a disused quarry by the side of the road where his old van was parked out of sight. Using a large sheet of plywood as a ramp, he dragged the dead stag into the rear of the van and closed the doors. As he opened the driver's door, he noticed the glow of car lights approaching from the direction of Dundonnain in the gathering gloom, the vehicle out of sight over the brow of the hill. It was still some distance away. He jumped into the driver's seat. The engine coughed and then spluttered into life. Dan's hand rested gently on the six-speed gear shift as he caressed it into first.

The van eased out of the quarry slowly, but when it hit the road, Dan opened it out and took off at high speed. Only when he was well out of sight of the following car, round a sharp hairpin bend and down the hill, did he switch on the headlights in the rapidly falling darkness.

When he reached the road down to his croft, he killed the lights again, and drove slowly past the house and over the ford across the burn to his barn. He opened the door and drove in. As he closed the door he saw the car lights pass on the road.

*

Maggie Achbeg sat dozing by the peat fire which was burning low. She was wearing a comfortable green tweed skirt and twin set, and her pleasant round face was perfectly relaxed. She had been knitting, and the wool and needles and unfinished jumper lay on her lap. A fat tabby cat was curled up comfortably on a rug in front of the glowing peat fire which was burning low. The furnishing and decoration were basic and old-fashioned. Apart from the glow of the fire, a standard lamp which illuminated the old woman and her knitting was the only light. An old carriage clock ticked loudly in the peaceful silence.

There came a knock at the outside door. Maggie stirred but did not wake. There was a click and a squeak of the outside door opening and a muffled voice, 'Hello, Maggie.'

Maggie sighed and smiled in her sleep, dreaming of summer days in the hayfields of her youth. The door into the room opened, and Dan stood in the doorway, a large carrier bag in his hand. He stood for a few moments gazing at Maggie with a tender smile on his face.

'You're having a bit of a snooze, Maggie!'

Maggie woke up with a start, but as her bright eyes focused, she exclaimed, 'Oh, it's yourself, Dan.' Her face broke into a smile, and she struggled to her feet. 'Come away in. You'll have a cup of tea.'

'I will that. But you'd better put this in the freezer first,' said Dan, handing her the bag.

'What have you got there?' Maggie took the bag and looked inside.

'Just a little something. You have the family coming at the weekend.'

'Oh Dan! Dan, you shouldn't have! They'll catch you

one of these days.'

'Aye. That'll be the day, Maggie!

Maggie reached into the bag and lifted out a large cut of dark red venison.

*

In a dark Edinburgh close off the High Street, a bloodied face was caught in the shaft of light falling from a distant street light. It was the face of a young Asian man who was sprawled against a wall. Two darkly clad figures stood over him, balaclavas concealing their identities.

'Tell your boss to stay off our patch,' hissed the shorter of the two, 'Or there may be one or two more 'accidents'!'

'And this is just a wee reminder!' said the taller one, sticking the boot in.

The man groaned and retched, as the two made off. Just before they exited the dark close, they pulled off their balaclavas. It was Red Billy and Jake. They had followed their target up from a club in the Cowgate where he'd been touting his wares. Some of Mark Fulton's information was beginning to pay off. It was the beginning of a turf war for domination of the drugs scene in Edinburgh.

*

It was Tuesday 14th October when Rory's life took a surprising new turn. In the late afternoon he, Jake and Claire were all in a philosophy lecture in the David Hume Lecture Theatre. The lecturer, Dr Lowther, a late middle-aged man looking rather dishevelled and wearing a crumpled cord jacket, was trying to introduce the class to existentialism. Rory, dressed in his habitual black, was bored, twirling his pen and looking absent-mindedly at it. Claire was sitting slightly behind and to the side of Rory. She kept glancing over at him. She was in her normal student uniform of skinny jeans and blue jumper.

The lecturer's voice droned on in the background of Rory's thought, occasional soundbites penetrating his daydream as he doodled on his notebook. 'The major French existentialists were Jean Paul Sartre and Albert Camus....

'But the origin of all existentialism lies in the statement by Dimitri Karamazov, one of the characters in Fyodor Dostoyevsky's novel *The Brothers Karamazov*: "Without God... everything is allowed. You can do anything you like", often expressed "If God does not exist, everything is permitted... "

At this Rory's head came up suddenly, he stopped doodling and gazed intently at the lecturer. Seeing Rory's interest, Claire also became interested.

Lowther droned on, 'Of course Dostoyevsky, who was a Christian, believed everything is not permitted, but he believed the consequence of atheism is that there is no moral absolute. This is the starting point of the existentialists...

'Sartre wrestled with the problem of ethics without God... You have to authenticate yourself by an act of the will...

'If you see an old lady trying to cross the street, you can authenticate yourself by helping her. But can you also authenticate yourself by pushing her in front of a bus? And if not, why not?...'

The lecture ended and the students were making their way out. Claire grabbed her bag and papers, and as she stepped into the aisle trying to put on her coat at the same time, she contrived to bump into Rory, so that she dropped her bag, and her papers were scattered. Rory blushed, all flustered from still feeling the warmth of this girl's very shapely body as she'd bumped into him. He bent down to pick up her things at the same time as Claire, and they bumped heads. This made Rory even more embarrassed, but Claire was laughing and their eyes met. For a moment Rory gazed into her deep violet-blue eyes and for the first time really saw what a beautiful girl she was. Of course he'd seen her in some of his lectures, but had always felt she wouldn't be interested in someone like him. He sensed they were from totally different worlds.

'Uh, I'm sorry,' he muttered self-consciously. 'Are you OK?'

'Yeah, I'm fine. No damage done!'

Rory helped her to gather up some of her fallen things and ventured, 'Can I buy you a coffee—as a sort of an apology?'

'A sort of an apology?' Claire tilted her head and raised her eyebrows.

Rory blushed again, 'I'm sorry... I mean a real apology, but...'

Claire laughed, 'Of course you do—and a coffee would be lovely. But something stronger would be even better.'

Rory brightened, 'Oh, OK. Yeah, right, there's a wee pub I go to sometimes. It's not far...'

'Great. I'm Claire, by the way.' She held out her hand and after a moment Rory took it, feeling it warm and slightly trembling in his hand.

'Oh right. I'm Rory'.

They walked down the stairs together and out of the lecture theatre. Jake saw it all from a distance and smirked.

As Claire and Rory headed out of George Square, the sky was clear, although the sun was sinking in the west in a bank of cloud. It was reasonably mild for the time of year with a light westerly wind. They crossed Bristo Square in front of the University's imposing, Italian Renaissance style McEwan Hall and turned west along Teviot Place. After they'd talked a little about what courses they were doing, they fell into an awkward silence, which Rory felt obliged to break, and he started telling about how the pub they were going to was renowned for its live traditional folk music, and how he was getting interested in all that. He felt he was talking too much and that Claire wasn't really interested, although she asked the occasional question.

They turned into Forrest Road and were going to cross the street. Claire stepped out, just as a car came round the corner fast. Rory grabbed her arm and pulled her back.

'Hey! Watch out! You'll get yourself killed like that.'

Claire clutched his arm gratefully. 'I'm sorry—my mind was somewhere else.'

They crossed the road, Claire still holding Rory's arm.

'Aye, you must have been thinking about what old Lowther was saying. You wanted to see if I was an existentialist and would push you in front of the car!'

Clair shook his arm, 'Hey! I'm no old lady!'

They both laughed as they entered Sandy Bell's. Rory asked her what she wanted, and he got her a G&T and a whisky for himself. They sat at a table near the back. There was a fiddle and a tin whistle playing a foot-tapping reel further in.

'The first time I really noticed you…' began Claire.

'Am I that hard to notice?'

She laughed and started again, 'The first time I really noticed you was that day I was talking to Jake and you were passing by, and you two glared at each other. What was all that about?'

'He's bad news. I'd keep away from him if I were you. How do you know him anyway?'

'We were at school together.'

'What?' Rory teased, 'The same posh private school?'

'Yes, and what's wrong with that?' Claire asked defensively. 'Anyway that was before my father left Mum and she turned to booze, and then his business went bust.'

'Hey, I'm sorry. I didn't know…'

'That's OK. I'm sorry for telling you. I don't usually talk about it. Just I felt you might be the kind of person who might actually care.'

'Yeah, I'm sorry to hear that. What actually happened… with your father's business, I mean?"

'So, he ran an accountancy firm, financial advice, that kind of thing. But as far as I can make out there was mismanagement. The firm went bankrupt, and on top of that he had made some very bad investments. You know, the sub-prime mortgage thing?'

Rory looked blank.

'I thought everyone knew about that. You know, the financial crash.'

'Oh, yeah, OK.' Rory nodded, but he'd never paid much attention to that kind of thing. 'So how do you manage for money now then?'

'Oh, I work in a pub some of the time... and other stuff. Anyway, what have you against Jake?' she said, changing the subject.

'Jonathan Kenneth Hetherington. Long story short, his father's the big landowner back home and my Grandad's the local poacher—what more do you need to know?'

'Your Grandad's a poacher?!'

'Amongst other things—crofter, Christian, fast driver, ex-SAS...'

'That's some mixture! Ex-SAS?'

'Yeah, he doesn't talk about it much. But he was in Northern Ireland in the 70s.'

'Bloody Sunday and all that?'

'Like I say, he doesn't talk about it much.'

'I'd like to meet your Grandad. He sounds interesting.' She paused. 'You said he's a Christian. That doesn't seem to fit with poacher, SAS and what else did you say? What sort of Christian?'

'Are there different kinds? I thought either you were a Christian or you weren't.'

'Well, no. There are liberal Christians, middle-of-the-road Christians, American 'born again' Christians, Catholic Christians, Orthodox Christians, C of E Christians...'

'Um... Well, I suppose Grandad doesn't really fit into

any of these. In some ways he's a traditional Highland, Free Church Christian and in some ways he's not.'

'What do you mean "Free Church"? Like Methodist or something?'

'I don't really know much about Methodists, but no, Grandad says the Free Church of Scotland is really the Church of Scotland Free—free from state interference in its affairs. About half the Established Church, the Presbyterian Church of Scotland in the nineteenth century, left to form the Free Church as a protest against landowners and town councils and the Crown choosing the people's ministers instead of the people themselves. There are statues of some of the Free Church founding fathers here in Edinburgh—Thomas Chalmers on George Street and Thomas Guthrie on Princes Street...'

'Did they all have to be called Thomas?' asked Claire with a grin.

Rory smiled. 'No, there were plenty other names—like Hugh Miller, the geologist and journalist. It was really quite a radical and democratic movement.' He looked thoughtful for a moment. 'But now it's often despised. Journalists like to call it the "Wee Frees". There was even an Edinburgh band called "We Free Kings"', he laughed. 'They were a kind of folk punk band. But I don't think that was anything to do with anything.'

'Why are they despised?'

'Grandad says it's because last century it got very strict and a lot of people lost sight of what it was really all about.'

'What is it really all about?'

Rory thought, and then remembered something Dan had said. 'Well, Grandad says you can't earn God's favour by trying to be good; instead you believe in what God has done for you. He says real Christianity is summed up in one verse in the Bible.'

'What's that?'

'John 3:16, you know, John's Gospel chapter 3 verse 16.'

'I know what John 3:16 is! I'm not a complete heathen. We had a teacher in school who said something the same thing as your Grandad. How does it go again?

'God so loved the world that he gave his only begotten Son, that whoever believes in him will not perish but have everlasting life.'

'That's the one!' Claire gazed out the window, and then said, 'It sounds very simple, doesn't it? But life's not that simple, is it? I mean, what if the existentialists are right and there's no God, so everything is permitted?'

'You would need to talk to Grandad!'

'But what do you believe? What do you think?'

Rory took some time to answer. 'I don't really know. I respect my Grandad and what he believes. If I were to judge the truth on what my Grandad is like and what, say, Jake Hetherington is like, I would take what my Grandad believes every time. But as you say, it's not that simple.'

They chatted for over an hour, about the Hetheringtons and the Highlands and ceilidhs, Claire always more interested in hearing about Rory than talking about herself.

'What about the rest of your family?' she asked.

'Not much to tell. Mum met my father, they got married, moved to Newcastle. I was born. He left Mum for someone else and emigrated to Australia. We moved back north. Mum brought me up on her own.'

Rory downed the rest of his drink and, obviously wanting to change the subject, said, 'Come on, let's go.'

Claire, sensing it was a delicate subject, finished her drink and got up. She said she was heading back to her flat. Rory said he'd get her up the road. They turned right out of the pub, crossed Lauriston Place and went down Middle Meadow Walk and then Jawbone Walk. The wind was blowing drifts of dry leaves around their feet. The wind always made Rory feel a little crazy. He caught Claire's hand. 'Come on, let's run!''

Laughing and protesting, Claire tried to keep up with his frenetic pace.

'Stop! I can't breathe!'

'Of course you can breathe,' said Rory stopping, adding unhelpfully, 'If you couldn't breathe, you couldn't speak!'

Claire punched him in the midriff and for a moment it was Rory who couldn't breathe. When they'd both stopped laughing, and had got their breath back, Claire looked up at the night sky.

'Look!'' she pointed to the full moon just rising over the slumbering bulk of Arthur's Seat in the east and started singing. *'Au clair de la lune, Mon ami...'*

'What are you singing, you dafty?'

'Did you never learn French in that cheap state school? It means "By the light of the moon, my friend..." and I'm Claire, and there's the moon!'

'That's the moon all right, and you're loony!'

Claire took a swipe at him, but Rory ran off with Claire in hot pursuit. She caught up with him before they crossed Melville Drive, and they walked on together. They stopped outside a tenement door on Marchmont Road. Rory was standing very close to Claire as she fumbled with her bag. He put his arms round her.

'Hey, Loony Tunes, come here!'

Rory suddenly pulled Claire close and kissed her, tenderly at first, then strongly as she responded. Then Claire tore herself away.

'I've got to go.' She sounded breathless and confused. She found her key and unlocked the door.

'Can I come up?'

'No! I don't let boys into my flat!'

'You'd have got on well with my Granny.'

'There you go again! I'm not an old lady! Anyway, what

does your Granny say?'

'She doesn't say anything now. She's dead.'

'Oh, I'm sorry. I didn't know.'

Claire opened the door and entered. 'Anyway your Granny was right. Stay away from girls like me.' Her face which minutes before had been full of joy and laughter, now looked sad and regretful. She closed the door.

Rory was left staring at the blank door. Eventually he turned and, looking up at the sky which had now turned cloudy, obscuring the moon, he turned up the collar of his jacket against the cool night air and headed slowly back down the street.

As he walked, he tried to make sense of what had just happened. He couldn't figure out Claire at all. He suspected she had deliberately bumped into him in the lecture theatre, and she had seemed so happy to be with him. He couldn't believe that someone as gorgeous as her was interested in him. But they had got on really well and she seemed so interested in him. Then there was that strange episode at her door. He was certain she had responded when he kissed her, and she didn't seem the kind of innocent girl that would then react the way she did. And what did she mean, 'Stay away from girls like me'? Girls like me. What did that mean? What sort of girl was she?

Rory suddenly realised he was madly attracted to her, and he meant to find out what sort of girl she really was.

CHAPTER SIX

After that first time, in spite of Claire's initial reluctance and due in no small measure to Rory's persistence, they were getting together most days over the next few months, usually after lectures when they'd go for a coffee or a drink in a pub and then wander round the amazing historic sites of Edinburgh: the High Kirk of Edinburgh (also known as St Giles Cathedral) with its distinctive crown spire, the Lawnmarket with its complicated narrow closes, the towering black gothic church of the Highland Tollbooth St Johns, which in 1999 was redeveloped as a performance space for the Edinburgh International Festival and renamed "The Hub"; the Esplanade leading up to the massive, imposing Castle; the quirky Princes Street Gardens with its floral clock and the skywards gothic space rocket of the Scott Monument honouring the author Sir Walter Scott; Calton Hill with its unrivalled views along Princes Street to the Castle; the Water of Leith and the stupendous arch of the Dean Bridge. Claire loved exploring the city and especially the places associated with J K Rowling like The Elephant House and Nicolson's café, where Rowling had written part of *Harry Potter and the Philosopher's Stone*, and even Abbotsford Park, the street where she had lived at one time near Holy Corner (so called because it's a crossroads with a church at each corner).

Any time Jake saw Claire and Rory together he would smile to himself and, when he met up with Claire for a deal, he would occasionally check up how the relationship was going, and detected she was becoming more and more involved. He was biding his time until he was sure the relationship was really serious. Then he would get a friend of his to rig up cameras to get photos of them in a 'compromising' situation. He relished the thought of the look on Dan Mackay's face when he would see the photos of Rory and Claire along with some photos of Claire in her 'professional' attire. His precious grandson with a hooker! Jake thought things were progressing nicely. He could wait patiently for the right time when he would bring pressure on Claire to take things to the next level. Revenge would be all the sweeter.

Sometimes Rory would take Claire to a gig and sometimes even to one where he was playing. But she didn't share his taste in music, especially as he was getting more and more into Celtic music, and especially the rock band Runrig who were really big at that time. Runrig had been formed in the 70s by the Isle of Skye brothers Rory and Calum Macdonald and others, but had gone on to chart fame in the 90s. Back in 1991 they attracted 50,000 people to an outdoor concert by Loch Lomond. And just the previous year in 2007 they'd recorded a live rock version of the traditional Scottish song, Loch Lomond, which went to number 9 in the UK charts. A lot of their songs have political overtones about the Highlands and Scotland in general, but are also steeped in a deep spirituality. Broadcaster and journalist Tom Morton once described their music as 'the music of loss, the music of rebellion, of the dignity of men and women who live for and by the land which they cannot possess.'

On Friday December 5th, Rory took Claire to see Runrig at the Barrowlands in Glasgow. She had never encountered anything like it and couldn't help but be caught up in the high octane fervency of the huge, all-age crowd packed into the hall (originally built as a ballroom, but now known as a major concert venue). Even the huge neon sign 'Barrowland' on the front of the building, reputed to be the largest in Britain, had astonished her on the way in. But the music was like nothing she had ever heard before—the massive pounding rock rhythms of Rory Macdonald's bass and Iain Baynes' drumming augmented by Calum Macdonald's percussion, combined with the Celtic melodies of Bruce Guthro's vocals, Brian Hurren's swirling keyboard and the soaring guitar of Malcolm Jones.

Claire liked the soul and blues-influenced music of singers like Adele, Duffy and Amy Winehouse, and she couldn't get her head round how this band, some of whom were clearly old enough to be of her parents' generation, could produce this electrifying sound that had such a huge impact on this eclectic audience. But in spite of that experience at the Barrowlands, she found she still didn't really share Rory's musical tastes.

But it wasn't just the music. Rory was frustrated by how Claire continued to keep him at arms' length. She kept saying she wasn't good for him, but he began to think she was amazingly chaste. A quick kiss was all he was allowed. She said because of her experience with the breakup of her parent's marriage, she wasn't ready to commit to a relationship. Then he began to get the impression that sometimes she was trying to avoid him. And on top of everything she wouldn't tell him what pub she worked in. She said she didn't want him bothering her there—the manager didn't like it.

Rory realised he had fallen for her completely, but he didn't really know how she felt. She wasn't rejecting him, but neither was she really committing to him.

At the end of the first semester, Rory decided to stay on in Edinburgh when his exams were finished and not return home for Christmas and the New Year. He wanted to be with Claire, and she said she needed to keep working over the holidays. Rory's Mum and Grandad weren't happy about it when he phoned, but he explained that he needed to stay on for some gigs, and his boss at Scayles, where he worked part-time, wanted him to stay on and do extra hours (all of which was true). For some reason, which he didn't completely understand, he never mentioned Claire to them.

Although Rory and Claire were both busy over the holidays, they had some lovely times when they were both off. Rory treated Claire to Christmas dinner in a smart restaurant, and he managed to get tickets to the Hogmanay concert where Paolo Nutini and Glasvegas were playing, followed by the spectacular fireworks display from the Castle. But on the 12th of January 2009, they were back to Uni.

*

On the Tuesday evening of that first week of the new term, on his way back from a band practice, Rory noticed Claire going into the Orchard and decided to catch up with her. She was dressed in her usual skinny jeans and a short coat with high heeled boots. There was a big crowd in, as there was Premier League football on the big TV screens—it was Manchester United at home to Wigan—so it took him some time to spot her. He was rather taken aback to see her talking to Jake Hetherington. He got himself a drink and waited until Jake left before going over to speak to her. She was just getting up to leave too.

'Remember what I said about Jake.'

Claire was startled to hear Rory's voice and turned round rather flustered.

'Oh, I was just waiting for a friend, but she's been held up and we're meeting somewhere else. Jake was just trying to chat me up. Why, are you jealous?'

'No, I'm not jealous of Jake,' he said derisively. "But remember, he's bad news.'

'Don't worry about me. I'm a big girl.'

'You're a big girl all the way,' he sang the line from the Dylan song.

Claire smiled, but said she was in a hurry and left. Rory had another whisky and tried to figure Claire out. He was totally in love with her, but he didn't know how she really felt. There was something that didn't quite make sense. He was left feeling very uneasy. He finished his drink and went out into the night. Somehow the darkness felt more than physical.

*

Three days later—it was Friday the 16th—Rory and Claire were in a philosophy lecture in the David Hume building in the afternoon. It was a different lecturer—Dr Winters, who was younger and trendier than old Lowther. He was talking about the philosopher the building was named after, the Scottish Enlightenment luminary David Hume, and his views on religion in particular.

Rory's mind was beginning to wander, until Winters mentioned Hume's argument concerning suffering as an argument against the traditional Christian understanding of God.

'This is what Hume says of God: *"His power we allow is infinite: whatever he wills is executed: but neither man nor any other animal is happy: therefore he does not will their happiness. His wisdom is infinite… But the course of Nature tends not to human or animal felicity: therefore it is not established for that purpose. Epicurus's old questions are yet unanswered. Is he willing to prevent evil, but not able? then is he impotent. Is he able, but not willing? then is he malevolent. Is he both able and willing? whence then is evil?"*

'However, as some more recent philosophers have pointed out, there are problems with this argument. It is based on the presupposition, the assumption, that all suffering is pointless and can serve no good purpose. But we can see a good purpose in some suffering: for instance pain warning

74

us of danger, like touching something hot. And then there is the testimony of those who say that their suffering made them better people, or somehow worked out for the best. In addition, there is the point that if, according to Hume's argument, God is infinitely powerful and wise enough to stop evil, he is also powerful and wise enough to have a good purpose, which we, who are finite, cannot see...'

Rory now was gripped. That's what he liked about Dr Winters—he presented different sides to any argument and critiqued them in various ways. He didn't just expect you to take what he said or what any philosopher said just because they were saying it. But Winters now was moving on, and Rory had difficulty in taking notes fast enough.

'Then there is Hume's view of miracles... he famously objected to miracles not because they are theoretically impossible, but because they are highly improbable. Probability rests on what can be called the majority vote of our past experiences. The regularity of Nature is based on something even stronger: a unanimous vote against miracles... In addition, if it is claimed something only happened once, like the Virgin Birth, it is infinitely improbable... However, the Oxford don and Christian apologist, C S Lewis—better known to most of you, no doubt, as the author of The Chronicles of Narnia—C S Lewis argues, "Unfortunately, we know the experience against miracles to be uniform only if we know all the reports of them to be false. And we can know all the reports to be false only if we know already that miracles have never occurred. In fact we are arguing in a circle"...

'Also, an argument from science is sometimes used against Hume. The Big Bang happened only once. That makes it infinitely improbable. But is it therefore incredible? It happened. Of course, there are some scientists, like Richard Dawkins, who have popularised the idea of a multiverse—many universes—therefore there may have been many Big Bangs. The problem with this is that there is no scientific evidence for a multiverse. It is an article of faith...

'Then there is a difficulty nearer home, nearer home for David Hume that is, the fact that this argument of his is based on the uniformity of natural cause and effect. But elsewhere he argues that there is no law of cause and effect. Just because we observe one phenomenon following another a thousand times does not mean that it will necessarily follow the thousandth and first time. The uniformity of cause and effect in a closed system is a philosophical assumption, not a scientific fact...'

Winters then moved on to deal with Hume's views on ethics, and Rory's attention was grabbed particularly by the fact that Hume argued that ethics were not based on reason but on feelings. 'Hume says, "...*morality is determined by sentiment. It defines virtue to be whatever mental action or quality gives to a spectator the pleasing sentiment of approbation; and vice the contrary.*" Of course, one of the immediate problems with this view,' continued Winters, 'is the question of how you arrive at some objective, generally agreed ethic. Hume himself includes self-denial and humility in a list of vices, whereas others would see these as virtues. If it is a matter of one person feeling something is right and another feeling it is wrong, don't we end up with complete moral relativism?...'

'However...' Winter's voice trailed away in Rory's imagination as the lecturer made further nice logical and philosophical distinctions. Rory wondered what his Grandad would make of all this. He smiled as he thought of Winters and Lowther sitting on Corrag Bhuidhe, their feet dangling over the abyss, discussing the finer point of philosophy and theology with Dan Mackay!

He was still smiling to himself when the lecture finished and for some inexplicable reason he found he was in a mad, daredevil mood. He headed out trying to catch Claire, but she was obviously in a hurry and he only caught up with her round the corner of Buccleuch Place and Buccleuch Street. She was heading into town.

'You're in a hurry!' he teased, 'Running away from me?'

'No, I'm just going down Princes Street to meet some friends at the shops.' She sounded uncertain, defensive.

'Amn't I your friend?'

'You mean "Aren't I your friend?"' she smiled in mock criticism.

'No, it's "I am" and "you are". So it's "amn't I" and "aren't you"!'

'It sound's logical, as Winters would say, but I'm sure it's not right.'

'Well, aren't you?'

'Aren't I what?'

'Aren't you my friend?' He suddenly caught her hand and said, 'Come on, Loony Tunes, let's go up Arthur's Seat!' He pointed along West Crosscauseway to Arthur's Seat looming over the city.

Although she'd been trying to resist it, she found Rory's mood maddeningly infectious, and in no time they were heading east along the narrow lane, Rory capering around her and making her laugh.

Arthur's Seat is the shattered remains of an ancient volcano around which the city of Edinburgh clusters. It is one of the unique features (among several) of Scotland's capital city which make it such a draw to visitors from all parts of the world. The origin of the name is shrouded in mystery and any connection to the legendary King Arthur is speculative. Whilst Arthur's Seat is the main imposing hill, Salisbury Crags form the most spectacular aspect. They run in a high unbroken cliff for nearly a mile, reaching a height of 150 feet above a long talus slope down to the floor of Holyrood Park, and from the airy path along the top you can look across a gulf, over tenements and spires, to the Castle around a mile away.

When Claire and Rory got to the foot of Arthur's Seat, Claire still wanted to head into town, so suggested they walk the Radical Road (a path under the Crags created by out-of-work weavers in the nineteenth century at the instigation of Walter Scott). Rory was still wanting to climb Arthur's Seat, but eventually they settled on a compromise—they'd walk along the top of the crags heading north, although Claire was a little nervous of heights (something she wouldn't dream of admitting to Rory). It was dry, but cloudy and cold, with a gusty wind blowing from the south-west.

As they climbed onto the ridge they started talking about the lecture they'd just heard—at least Rory started talking about it and Claire mostly listened.

'What did you think of Winters today? That was quite something. Just like Lowther last semester. I'd never realised that the way people think and live now is because of what people wrote last century or the one before or the one before that. Just think! How many people around us think that because there's no God, everything's permitted? "You can do what you like..."'

They had just reached the highest point of the crag looking across to the Castle. And an angry red sun was sinking down into grey clouds in the west, giving the scene a warmth that was not in the air. They were standing very near the edge, which was not at all to Claire's liking, when Rory remembered what Winters had been on about.

'Or what about Hume? No cause and effect! So I could just jump off the Crags here, and if it was the thousand and first time, I might just float down. Maybe that would be a miracle!'

Claire clutched his arm in alarm. 'Don't be stupid! Come back from the edge!'

Rory put his arms round her, and there in that high place overlooking the city he kissed her, not caring who saw them, and their long hair, dark red and dark brown, mingled in the wind.

They came down off the Crags at the north end hand in hand, and walked past the Scottish Parliament. The Parliament building was completed in 2004 at a cost of over £400 million, ten times higher than the original estimate of £40 million, and has divided opinion as to its architectural worth ever since. Architects, on the whole, think it a tour de force; whereas many of Scotland's citizens think it an expensive, confusing, postmodern concrete jumble. The Spanish architect Enric Miralles attempted to design it in a way that was sympathetic to the landscape and materials of Scotland, using leaf and boat shapes in its design, and utilising granite, oak and steel in its construction. The impression, however, is that these materials are appended to a grey-white concrete base.

While Claire thought the Parliament building was exciting and modern, Rory thought it was a mess. 'Just look at those big shapes in black granite fixed to the outside of the walls. Some people think they look like hairdryers! But I think they look like heads that have the tops of their skulls taken off. They remind me of lines in Howl, you know that poem by Allen Ginsberg:

'I saw the best minds of my generation destroyed by madness, starving hysterical naked… What sphinx of cement and aluminum bashed open their skulls and ate up their brains and imagination?'

'That's gross! I think I prefer the hairdryers!'

They laughed and walked on up the Canongate, High Street and Lawnmarket (the long continuous road known as the Royal Mile leading up from the royal palace of Holyrood House to the Castle). They were about to go their separate ways outside the High Court at the corner of the

Lawnmarket and Bank Street but, as he put his arms round Claire to kiss her, Rory suddenly became aware of the massive statue behind her.

'Look, there he is!'

'Who?'

'David Hume! Look!' he whirled Claire round. 'I've passed it dozens of times and not really looked at it.'

The statue portrays Hume, not as described by a contemporary as a corpulent 'turtle-eating alderman', but as a rather noble classical philosopher complete with toga.

'What's that slab he's holding out?' asked Claire, momentarily forgetting she needed to get to the shops before they closed. 'And there's another one—look, under his foot. No', she said, seeing Rory looking at Hume's right foot with its shiny bronze toe, 'Not that one that philosophy students rub for good luck! The other one.'

Rory stared at the left foot, and a new enlightenment suddenly filled his soul. 'They're not slabs! They're tablets!

'No, not handheld devices!' he added, seeing the look of incredulity on Claire's face, 'And not pills! Tablets—like the tablets God gave to Moses on Mount Sinai!'

The look on Claire's face was hardly less incredulous.

'What? They never taught you about Moses in that public school... or is it a private school? I can never remember.'

'Of course I know about Moses! And the proper term is public school. But Moses' tablets had the Ten Commandments on them, didn't they? These are blank.'

'But don't you see? That's the whole point! Whoever made this statue really understood.'

'Stoddart, I think, Sandy Stoddart.'

'Well, he understood. Don't you see?'

'Um, I'm not sure, what do you mean?'

'You said it yourself. The tablets are blank! This new enlightened Moses has come down from the mountain and his tablets are blank! Not only that, but he has put one under his feet. That must be the first table of the law—our responsibility to God. Of course! Hume believes God's existence is highly improbable, so he can be left out of account. But the other table—our duty to our fellow human beings—is being held out to us, and it's blank. You can write your own laws. As Winters said, "If it is a matter of one person feeling something is right and another feeling it is wrong, don't we end up with complete moral relativism?..." Everything is permitted! It all leads back there!'

'I see, or at least I think I see. But who's right? Dostoyevsky or Sartre? Hume or C S Lewis?'

Then from somewhere in the back of his mind came the memory of something his Grandad had told him about, something an Edinburgh minister had said when he was Moderator of the Free Church General Assembly, a couple of years back. Rory had then read it online and the opening paragraphs had stuck in his head. It was about a contrast between this statue of David Hume and another statue nearby.

'Come on, Loony, there's another statue we've got to see!'

Ignoring her protests, he grabbed her hand and led her across Bank Street, down onto North Bank Street, high above Princes Street Gardens, and then up Mound Place to New College. As they were going Rory was trying to explain to Claire what he had read, but she wasn't paying too much attention as she was still eager to get to the shops, and Rory wasn't making too much sense in his excitement. Then they turned into the quad of New College and there towering above them stood the statue of the Scottish reformer John Knox.

'Now! Don't you see?' Rory almost shouted. When Claire looked blank and shook her head, he tried to explain.

"You see, this minister was saying that Stoddart captured the essence of Hume's philosophy—Hume is seated,
passive, looking down, and he's holding out a blank tablet;
whereas this sculptor has captured the essence of Knox—
he is standing, active, pointing heavenwards and holding a
Bible under his arm with his finger in the place he's preach-
ing from! He said they were the two big influences on the
Scottish psyche and culture, as well as religion.

'Yes, I think I see,' said Claire hesitantly, 'Knox had
a source for his authority—God speaking in the Bible,
whereas Hume seemed to be saying there was no source of
authority apart from the individual's own ideas.'

'Exactly! You know it reminds me of something my
Grandad said. It was one of those rare occasions when he
talked about the SAS. This wasn't about something he was
involved in. It was at the end of the Second World War. He
told me something I'd never heard before. It was the SAS
that were the first Allied troops into Bergen Belsen—you
know, the infamous Nazi concentration camp.'

'I never knew that either.'

'The SAS men would never forget the sight and the smell
that met them, as long as they lived. There were still 60,000
prisoners crammed into that camp and 13,000 bodies lying
all around the site. They even saw guards still beating and
shooting the prisoners. Grandad said that a lot of people
asked: how could anyone do that to other human beings?
And then he said something that's stuck with me. He said
the Nazis had ceased to believe that human life was sacred—made in the image of God—and they had ceased to
believe that they would ever have to face the judgement of
God.'

'Without God, everything is allowed,' said Claire quietly.

They stood for a moment uncertain in the quiet of the
old stone quad, and in Rory's imagination he saw the two

massive statues of Hume and Knox towering over the city in perpetual opposition and mutual rejection.

Claire's voice wakened him from his vision, 'I've got to go. The shops will be shut.'

Suddenly coming back to reality, Rory said, 'Hey, Loony, let's go out tonight. Let's see a film or go to a gig or something.'

'Sorry, it's Friday. I always go out with the girls on Friday night.'

Rory pulled a face. 'So you prefer the girls to me...'

'On Friday nights, yes!'

'Can I come?'

'No! Well, only if you're a girl!' She laughed and ran off, leaving Rory standing disconsolately.

After a few moments, he turned and walked back up to the High Street. He crossed and headed down Old Fishmarket Close to the Cowgate, this canyon of nightclubs, music gigs, student flats and homeless shelters in old sandstone and modern concrete. After passing under South Bridge, he turned right into Niddrie Street South and up a close. Up a short flight of stairs he reached his flat which he shared with several musician friends.

His room was bare and untidy. The only thing that gleamed was his guitar—the black Fender Stratocaster. He picked it up, switched on the amp and, standing at the window, blasted a few rocking chords into the night. Gradually a melody emerged and he started to play lead—long searing notes that wanted to fly up into the vast darkness above the sandstone and concrete canyons, into a wider northern sky. They howled and screamed his longing and emptiness and confusion into the darkness. Lost in the music for half an hour, his fingers eventually fumbled and the tune died. He stuck the guitar back on its stand, and his eyes fell on the Bible lying beside his bed. It was a gift from his Grandad when he first went to Uni. He picked it up and pulled out a piece of paper that was inside the front cover. It was a copy of the eulogy from his Granny's funeral that he'd got from his Grandad. He scanned it, and some of the phrases stood out, the ones recited by his Grandad when they sat on the Corrag Bhuidhe pinnacles.

She felt keenly the injustices of those days...
But her sympathies were not limited to past ages...
She knew herself as a sinner who needed a Redeemer...
She was looking for a better country...
They shall mount up with wings as eagles...

*

Rory cooked some pasta. He took a phone call from his Mum, but didn't feel like talking and was a bit uncommunicative. He said he had to go as he had a band practice later. She said she would phone again next week.

To pass the time till the band practice, he tried to read some philosophy, but it seemed cold and stale. He couldn't settle to anything, so he told one of his flatmates he was off out to get some fresh air. It was cold and dark. He turned south onto The Pleasance and wandered aimlessly up to St Leonards. He was just thinking about taking a quick walk into Holyrood Park and up Arthur's Seat, when, as he passed the entrance to Montague Street, he saw a white BMW pull out from in front of Kings Antiques and head west. The registration plate was unmistakeable—B16 TAM. A sudden feeling of revulsion came over him. If Claire was in contact with Jake, and Jake was involved with Tam Moncrieff, and Claire was acting strangely and being secretive about things, maybe he needed to warn her more seriously than he'd done before. He looked at his watch. He was supposed to be back at the flat for his band practice, but he decided he might catch Claire before she left her flat. He headed west along Montague Street. He pulled his scarf more closely round his neck and pulled his beanie well down on his head against the biting January wind.

He turned left along South Clerk Street and then right into Hope Park Terrace and then onto the path in the Meadows that ran beside Melville Drive. He had just reached that section of the path between Middle Meadow Walk and Jawbone Walk when he caught a glimpse through the trees of a young woman crossing Melville Drive and disappearing into the trees at the start of Jawbone walk. He registered that she was very attractive and dressed quite provocatively, but wouldn't have paid her more attention as he was hurrying to catch Claire before she left, if he hadn't glanced in her direction as she emerged from the darkness under the trees into the light of a street lamp. He stood stock still. It was Claire, but not as he'd ever seen her before.

Her long dark red hair was pulled up in some fancy new style. Even from where he stood, he could make out that she was heavily made up. She was wearing a blue leather jerkin, very short black skirt, sheer black nylons and shiny black stiletto heeled boots. Rory stared and his mouth opened in a silent intake of breath. She didn't look as if she was dressed for a night out with the girls! He almost shouted and ran after her. But for a few moments he stood stunned. Then hardly knowing what he was doing, he stumbled after her. What was going on? Should he catch up with her and ask her? Then he suddenly made up his mind and decided he'd follow her and see where she went. He was going to find out one way or another what was going on. If she was meeting up with her girlfriends, he'd just head back to the band practice.

He had to be careful not to be seen, and walked on the grass beyond the light of the lamps on the path. It felt a bit funny, as if he was stalking Claire, and he almost decided he was being stupid and that he should go back to his band practice. But something seemed to compel him to carry on.

Once they reached Forrest Road, it was easier as there were more people around, but down Candlemaker Row past Greyfriars Kirk it was more difficult again and he had to hang further back behind a group of students. Down in the Grassmarket, he crossed to the other side of the wide street, passing the Covenanters Memorial, a large, low, circular structure composed of grey granite setts with a cross of red granite setts. The Memorial commemorates the seventeenth century Covenanters executed on that very spot for their opposition to the Stuart kings' tyrannical interference in the government of the Presbyterian Church of Scotland. Rory gazed at the red cross for a moment before hurrying on, trying to keep Claire in view. But as he walked, memories involuntarily flooded back of things his Grandad had told him. He remembered him saying that the Stuart kings believed the king's word was law; whereas the Covenanters believed God's law was king. One of them, Samuel Rutherford had written a book *Lex Rex*, the literal translation of which is 'The Law is King'. Rory's Grandad had also told him that Rutherford on his deathbed was summoned to answer a charge of treason, and he answered, 'I have got summons already before a Superior Judge and Judicatory, and I behove to answer to my first summons, and ere your day come I will be where few kings and great folks come.'

Rory felt a strange shiver pass over his body as he thought of the Covenanters, many not much older than himself, who had been cruelly executed at this very spot for opposing tyranny and remaining true to the one they regarded as the King of Kings—the Lord Jesus Christ. Many regarded their self-sacrifice as futile and misguided, but within a few years after their deaths, the tyranny was ended and the arbitrary power of the monarchy was abolished.

Rory wondered who today would be prepared to endure torture and cruel execution, sacrificing their lives for a cause they held dear. His thoughts drifted to the One who gave his life on a red cross, red with his own blood, to redeem a world lost in evil. And as he passed along the Grassmarket, a new steel seemed to enter his soul and somehow the thought of these things strengthened his love and determination to save Claire from whatever evil influences she had fallen under.

He kept her in view from behind trees and parked cars along the Grassmarket. Thankfully, up the West Port there were more people. He saw Claire stop at a doorway and press an intercom. After she went in, Rory approached slowly. The sign hit him and sent his mind into a tailspin — PARADISE SAUNA & MASSAGE. He pulled off his beanie and ran his hand through his hair. He went to press the intercom, but then didn't. He turned and walked blindly across the street, nearly getting run over by a car which blared its horn at him. He headed into the nearest pub at the corner of Bread Street and Spittal Street.

Rory ordered a large whisky and sat down in a corner leaning forward, staring at the whisky in his hands. He downed the whisky. He went back to the bar for another. He sat down again, but this time he sipped his drink more thoughtfully.

So that's what it was all about. That explained everything. Claire's strange behaviour, her friendship with Jake, Jake's connection to Tam Moncrieff, and no doubt Moncrieff Properties owned the Paradise. It was tearing up his mind. He'd been taken for a fool. He felt like crawling out of there, broken, beaten, mocked. It must have been all an act. But for what reason? Somehow Jake's sneering face rose up before him. How he wanted to smash that face. Jake! They must have been in it together! It was some sort of cruel joke. Forget her! She's not worth it.

But something burned inside him. He knew that he and Claire had something special. It wasn't some pretence on her part. And he loved her and couldn't stand the thought of what she'd gotten into. He didn't know how or why, but somehow she'd been manipulated, corrupted. Then like many of his fellow Highlanders before him, the long, cold hurt and bitter defeat were suddenly consumed in a blazing anger. He downed the rest of his drink and strode out of the pub. He crossed the street and went straight to the door of the 'Paradise' and pressed the intercom.

A female voice with an affected Edinburgh accent crackled through the speaker, 'Paradise. Can I help you?'

For a moment Rory's mouth went dry. 'Uh—I need to see a girl...'

'You've come to the right place, dear. In you come.'

The door clicked open, and Rory lurched in.

PART 2
THE HAMMER

CHAPTER SEVEN

Sail Mhor, Garbh Choire Beag, Garbh Choire Mor, and the peaks of An Teallach, stood dark across An Loch Beag, silhouetted against the angry sky of a setting sun. The dark grey clouds were lit from below by the red sun going down beyond the Western Isles. The rough slopes of Beinn nam Ban were glowing. A man and a dog were coming down towards Cill Donnain. The man was bent, using a long shepherd's crook, tired but still walking steadily. The dog paced quietly beside him.

Dan and Fleet were heading home after a fruitless day on the hill searching for some lost sheep. Someone had said they thought they had seen sheep at the back of Beinn nam Ban, and Dan wanted to make sure all his flock were gathered in to the lower ground as he felt that winter wasn't done with them yet. It was Monday February 2nd 2009.

They crossed the local road leading to Badrallaich and took the old track by An Crasg leading down to the croft at Cill Donnain. As they neared home in the gathering dusk, they passed among the scattered ruins of the original township of Cill Donnain from where twenty families were evicted to make way for a sheep farm in the mid nineteenth century. Dan felt a great melancholy creeping over him as he thought of all the similar communities destroyed, all the lives blighted, and the straths and glens emptied of people. And in spite of all their hard work, crofters like himself struggled to make ends meet and cling on to use the bit of land they had.

As they got nearer the house, Dan saw a light in the window and two cars parked out front. 'That's Fiona's car, boy, and the minister's car,' Dan remarked to Fleet, 'I wonder what they're doing here. There's something wrong.' Fleet looked as solemn and wise as only a dog can.

As Dan came up to the front of the house, his daughter Fiona and Neil Cameron came out the front door. Fiona ran towards her Dad and let out a wail.

'Dad! It's Rory!' She threw her arms around Dan and a great sob burst from her throat.

'What is it, *a graidh*?' asked Dan reverting to his native Gaelic in his fatherly compassion.

'He's dead! He's dead! Rory's dead!'

Stunned, Dan looked for confirmation to Neil, who just nodded.

'No! How? What happened?'

'The police told Fiona something about drugs—a drugs overdose.'

'What!?'

'That's what they said. I don't understand. You don't think...'

'No! Not Rory! He maybe drank too much sometimes—but drugs? No, I don't believe it.'

'Oh Dad, what are we going to do? Maybe it's a mistake. But I've been trying to get him on his mobile, and it doesn't even ring. Maybe he's got it switched off, but I tried last week as well... He wouldn't have it switched off that long, would he? There's definitely something wrong. So maybe it is true... They say we have to go and identify him.'

'Maybe it's not Rory. Maybe there's been a mistake.'

Neil looked dubious. 'They say they're pretty sure. Someone found his wallet eventually and handed it in to the police. That's how they were able to contact Fiona.'

'Oh!' Dan paused. 'Come on. Come in.' He ushered them towards the house, his arm around Fiona.

'I know. I'll phone Jim Matheson. He'll know what to do.' Dan turned to Neil, 'You know Jim, he's is a police superintendent in Inverness—an old friend.'

Neil set out some mugs and boiled the kettle for tea. Fiona sat twisting a hankie in her hands, and trying to dry her eyes. Apart from her teaching, Rory was all she cared about in the world. Fleet came up and put his head in her lap. She stroked his head and started crying again. Dan was on the phone.

'Could you put me through to Superintendent Jim Matheson, please? It's urgent... It's Dan Mackay. He'll know who it is.'

Neil looked at Dan as he waited for them to put him through. Dan stared out the window into darkness and his jaw was set, the muscles of his lean face tight.

'Jim—aye, it's Dan. Aye... aye... listen Jim, we've had terrible news.'

Jim Matheson was standing by his desk in Police headquarters. He had been just about to leave the office. The colour drained from his normally ruddy face as he listened to Dan.

'No! Oh, man! What happened?'

Jim listened as Dan clearly and simply gave him the little information he had. Jim paced up and down beside his desk.

'You just have to ask. You know that... I'll find out what I can. I don't have many contacts in Lothian and Borders now, but I'll see what I can do. I'll get back to you as soon as I can... Right... right... I hope they're wrong... Give my love to Fiona... I'll speak to you soon. Bye.'

Neil handed Dan a mug of steaming tea. 'He's going to phone back,' Dan said simply. Then turning to his daughter, 'Come on, Fiona, take your tea. It'll do you good.'

He handed Fiona the mug of tea. She took it reluctantly and began to sip, then put it down and started crying again.

Dan sat down beside her and put his arm round her.

There was the sound of a vehicle outside. Neil went to the door. He returned with Muhammad. Dan rose to meet him.

'Oh Dan, my friend!' He gripped Dan's hand and put his arm on his shoulder. 'I was in Ullapool and I just heard. It's not true, is it?'

'We don't know, Muhammad. I'm just waiting a call back from Jim Matheson. It doesn't look good. But thanks for coming. You'll have a cup of tea?'

Muhammad accepted the tea poured by Neil and sat down. There was a silence. All were burdened down by the unthinkable. The phone rang. Fiona started. Dan moved like a cat pouncing and lifted the phone.

'Jim... yes... aye...

There was a long silence as Dan listened. His bronzed features seemed to turn as grey as his hair.

'No doubt?... No... Ah well... Thanks, Jim. No, you've done what you can. Many thanks, Jim... *Moran taing... Oidhche mhath.*'

Dan put the phone down. He felt his heart turn cold — cold as stone. He couldn't speak.

'Dad,' Fiona wailed. 'What did he say?'

He sat down beside Fiona on the sofa and put both arms round her.

Eventually his voice came back, but it was like the voice of the dead, coming from a great distance through stony ground. 'I'm afraid it's true. They're sure. It's Rory all right. They have his photo. They faxed it through and Jim confirmed it. There can be no doubt.'

'No! No! No! It can't be.'

'Shhh, *a graidh*, my darling.' Some emotion had returned to Dan's voice. 'Oh my darling girl.'

'Aw, Dan and Fiona, I'm so sorry,' said Neil, finding his voice, 'I thought... maybe... But what happened? Did Jim know?'

'Well,' Dan's voice sounded dead again, 'He wasn't able to find out much. But he confirmed what the police said to Fiona. It was a drugs overdose—heroin.'

'Heroin!' cried Fiona, 'But that's impossible! Rory would never...'

'O my dear friends! What tragedy!' exclaimed Muhammad. 'All I know is that heroin is rife in Edinburgh. I have relatives there, and it is said among them that some of our own people are involved in this evil trade.'

'It's certainly rife,' added Neil, 'I know someone in the church there who works for a charity for people with addictions.'

There was a silence apart from the sound of Fiona weeping. She burst out, "But Rory wasn't a drug addict!"

"No, he was not", said Dan, through clenched teeth, something of his old fire returning. "There is something very, very wrong about this, and I'm going to get to the bottom of it."

He turned to Neil, 'Will you say a word of prayer for us?'

'Surely.'

Fiona clutched Dan's hand in her lap.

Struggling with his emotions, Neil began. 'Our loving heavenly Father, help us. We are devastated. We don't know where to turn. To whom else shall we go? You have the words of eternal life. You have a Father's heart. You know what it is to lose a Son, in that darkness of Calvary. Yet out of the darkness there came great light, for he gave himself for us. Oh Lord, have pity on us! Shine on us that light in our darkness. Grant us hope in our misery.'

An hour later, Dan was saying goodnight to first Muhammad and then Neil at the door. As Muhammad drove off, Dan walked the minister to his car. He hesitated, struggling with his emotions.

'You know, Neil,' he paused, 'Rory… I don't know if he had faith…'

'Maybe before the end he found it. There's some lines from an old poem that say, *"Betwixt the saddle and the ground, was mercy sought and mercy found."'*

'Aye. Maybe he did. God grant it was so. Goodnight and thanks.'

Dan watched the tail-lights of Neil's car until they disappeared in the distance, then he turned back to the grey house.

Half an hour later, Fiona, Dan and Fleet emerged. Dan had packed a small bag and he was carrying another plastic bag with Fleet's water bowl and some dog food. They were heading to Ullapool for Fiona to pack a case, before heading south in the morning. They had decided to take Fiona's car.

CHAPTER EIGHT

Early the next morning Dan and Fiona were heading to Edinburgh to identify Rory. The temperature was hovering around freezing, and the light wind from the east made it feel bitterly cold.

Fiona had hardly slept all night. She had lain awake for it seemed like hours, going over everything in her mind. One minute she felt there must be some terrible mistake and that Rory was alive; the next minute the appalling possibility that it was all true—all that the police and Jim Matheson had said—overwhelmed her. She felt as if something was grabbing her by the throat, trying to stifle the life out of her. She sobbed her heart out, but then exhausted, she'd fallen into an uneasy sleep, troubled by an oppressive weight of dread in her dismal dreams. She was standing on the shore. The wind was howling in the rugged cliffs. Huge waves were smashing onto the jagged rocks, threatening to overwhelm her. She felt she was drowning, being tossed around like a rag doll. Suddenly she awoke, to discover her father was gently shaking her shoulder. She had been screaming in her sleep. She sat bolt upright and stared at him with wild eyes, until he put his arms around her and spoke tenderly to her. It was all a bad dream, she had said. Rory—it was a bad dream? But her father had shaken his head. He couldn't speak. She saw the grief etched in his haggard face, and she let out a wail that cut to her father's heart, and she sobbed her heart out yet again as he held her close.

But now they were on the long road south. The sun hadn't risen yet—it was only 7am—but the sky was clear and as they drove along the shore of Loch Broom on the A835, there were still wisps of mist on the water.

Fleet lay on the back seat. Dan was driving Fiona's car. It was a VW Polo and he didn't like it.

'It's not got much power. What size of engine is it?'

'I don't know. It's powerful enough for me.'

'We should have taken the van!'

'We couldn't take that old thing down to Edinburgh. Anyway if you don't like it, I'll drive.'

'You're in no state to drive.'

Fiona, knowing her father was right, lapsed into silence. Every so often they tried to speak of Rory and to make sense of what the police had said, but they couldn't find the words to express their true feelings or to reconcile what they'd been told with what they knew of Rory, and so they drove most of the way in uneasy silence.

In spite of Dan's misgivings, they made good time. In twenty minutes they were at Loch Glascarnoch, a man-made loch created as part of the hydro-electric schemes in the 1950s. Looking in the rear-view mirror, Dan caught a glimpse of the jagged snow-clad peaks of An Teallach slumbering in the pale light of the northern dawn, and he thought of the time he and Rory had sat talking on the Corrag Bhuidhe ridge.

The roads were quiet at that time in the morning and in no time they were through the village of Garve where the A835 crosses the Inverness to Kyle railway line at a level crossing. A few minutes later they were through Contin and on to the Black Isle (which isn't an island at all, but a peninsula between the Moray Firth and the Cromarty Firth, although now joined by bridges to Inverness to the south and to Easter Ross, Sutherland and Caithness to the north). At Tore in the Black Isle they joined the A9 which is the main road which originally ran all the way from Edinburgh to John O' Groats on the north coast, but in the south it has been replaced by the M90 motorway from Edinburgh to Perth through Fife, or the M9 motorway and A9 dual carriageway via Dunblane. In the north it now terminates at Scrabster Harbour near Thurso, the gateway for ferries to the Northern Isles—Orkney and Shetland. In 2009 it was still composed of mainly single carriageway with some stretches of dual carriageway.

Dan and Fiona were over the Kessock Bridge and past Inverness, the 'Capital of the Highlands', in less than an hour after leaving Ullapool, and fifteen minutes later they were at the Slochd, a narrow rocky ravine and the high pass between the straths of the Findhorn and the Spey, between Moy and Badenoch, which carries both road and railway traffic between Perth and Inverness.

'There's the Soldier's Head...' said Dan, pointing with his chin to a cliff on the left where there was a formation in the rock shaped like a soldier's head with a grey helmet and pink face. 'Rory used to love that...'

'Now he'll never see it again...' Fiona's voice was broken, and she felt tears running down her cheeks.

Dan spoke through his teeth, 'No. He won't.'

Not long after 11am, after a stop at a café for a bite to eat, they were nearing Edinburgh. As they approached the Forth Bridges, Dan thought they looked like two grim dinosaurs lying across the Firth. The Forth Bridge with its distinctive three red steel cantilevers, carrying the railway north to Perth, Dundee and Aberdeen, was completed in 1890 and had the longest single cantilever span in the world at that time. The Forth Road Bridge is a two tower steel suspension bridge, and when it was opened in 1964 it was the longest suspension bridge in the world outside the USA. But none of the bridges' impressive grandeur and history registered with Dan and Fiona that day.

As they entered the city, it all seemed grey and bleak and somehow constricted after the wide open spaces of their drive though the Highlands and Fife. The sky was dark and overcast and a bitter east wind was gusting along the city streets. Dan took a route into the city that he'd discovered in the past. It avoided getting caught up in traffic jams in the centre of town. He took Queensferry Road, which was the main road into the city from the Forth Road Bridge, but only as far as the turn off for Craigleith Crescent, a twisty switchback road that leads to the leafy suburbs of Ravelston. Then through Roseburn and past Murrayfield, the national rugby stadium, he joined the West Approach Road heading into the city from the west (part of it had been constructed on the bed of an old railway line).

They were heading for the City Mortuary in the Cowgate in the Old Town. The centre of Edinburgh is divided into the Old Town and the New Town. The Old Town clusters around the Royal Mile, the road running from the Castle in the west to the Palace of Holyrood House in the east, and preserves its haphazard medieval layout and many Reformation era buildings. The New Town, incorporating the world famous Princes Street and lying to the north of the Old Town, was by contrast a planned development in the late eighteenth and early nineteenth centuries.

*

Dan had thought it strange that they had been told to head straight to the Mortuary and not to the police station first. But Fiona had been assured that police officers would meet them there.

Dan parked in the multi-storey car park on Castle Terrace, just below the Castle towering above, and then they went down steps to King's Stables Road and walked through the Grassmarket and along the urban canyon of the Cowgate, with Fleet at Dan's heel. The buildings and bridges towered oppressively high above them. There was something about the sandstone tenements that reminded Dan of the red sandstone cliffs of An Teallach, but they seemed more threatening somehow. They stopped outside the grey-brown brick and concrete box of the City Mortuary and, after some difficulty, found the entrance. They were admitted and, as they were a bit early, they were told to wait in reception for the police officers to arrive. They sat. Fleet lay on the floor, head on his paws, ears down.

After a few minutes, a casually dressed man and a policewoman in uniform entered. The man was medium height and build with longish blond hair. The female police officer was small and pleasant looking with short black hair, dark eyes and a ready smile. They checked at reception and then came over and introduced themselves to Fiona.

'Ms Williams? I'm DS Reid and this is the FLO.'

'Family Liaison Officer,' the woman explained, 'Constable Barclay.'

'Yes, I'm Fiona Williams and this is my father.'

'I'm sorry about this, but it is necessary that you identify the deceased,' said Reid.

Dan thought, 'He doesn't sound very sorry.' But he said, 'Yes, we understand. We want to be sure ourselves.'

'You see, we can't understand,' said Fiona, 'Rory didn't do drugs. Are you sure there's not been some ghastly mistake?'

'Uh... so...' Reid seemed to be stumbling over his words, 'I suppose the only way to be sure is to view the body. You'd better come through then.' And he added, 'But I'm afraid your dog will have to stay here,' when he saw Fleet getting up to follow. He went to pat Fleet on the head, but Fleet backed off and growled.

With a word from Dan, Fleet reluctantly lay down again. The officers led the way to the mortuary proper. A body lay under a sheet. An attendant pulled back the sheet from the head.

101

Fiona stared in disbelief at the cold, pale face revealed, and she felt her throat constrict as she gasped, 'No! It is Rory!' She felt numb. All her hopes had crumbled. She couldn't reconcile herself to the fact that this cold, still body was her beloved son, once so full of life and promise. She felt her knees almost give way.

Dan took her in his arms and stroked her hair. 'O Fiona, my darling. O Fiona...'

He was aware of the officers looking at them, and he looked at DS Reid and nodded.

'Yes, it's Rory all right... Could you let us have a minute alone?'

The officers and attendant withdrew. Dan comforted his daughter, but he also pulled back the sheet and looked intently at the bruises on the side of Rory's head and arms and at the needle marks on his left arm.

'What can have happened? Dad?' Fiona sobbed.

Dan was grim-faced. 'That is what we're going to find out.'

Dan and Fiona walked slowly out, Dan's arm tightly around his daughter.

'Well, thank you for coming, Ms Williams,' said DS Reid, trying to sound business-like, 'It's not easy. I'm sorry...'

Dan cut him short. 'Who's in charge of the investigation?'

'Ah... well, Mr Williams, there isn't really any further investigation now...'

Dan saw Fiona was going to correct Reid about his surname, and he quickly frowned at her with an almost imperceptible shake of his head and said. 'No investigation?' And he thought to himself, 'That's good, he doesn't know my real name.'

'What I mean is, our enquiries are complete... didn't you get told? I thought the local boys would have passed on the information.'

Fiona was distraught. 'All we were told was it was a drugs overdose—heroin. But we don't understand—Rory never did drugs in his life.'

'I'm afraid it's true, Ms Williams. There was no doubt. The SOCOs' report...'

'That's the Scene Of Crime Officers...' put in Constable Barclay helpfully.

'Aye, Scene of Crime—and the report was submitted to the PF...'

'That's the Procurator Fiscal...' interjected Barclay again.

Reid glared at her. 'And the PF had the pathologist's report—extremely high level of heroin in the blood. A massive dose. All the gear was there...'

'Who was the senior investigating officer?'

'Uh, that was DI Lawson.'

'Well, I want to see him. There are some questions I'd like answered.'

'Ah... right... OK... I'll just phone up to St Leonard's and see when he can see you...'

He took out his phone and headed out. The others followed.

*

An hour later, Dan and Fiona parked in St Leonards Hill at the back of the Edinburgh Police Headquarters in the Southside, a honey-coloured brick building with a slate roof that attempted to complement the nearby old sandstone tenements. Dan told Fleet to stay in the car, and he and Fiona headed round the front to the entrance and into reception. After a short wait DS Reid came out and took them along to DI Lawson's office. Lawson got up from behind his desk as DS Reid led in Fiona and Dan and introduced them.

'This is Ms Williams and her father.'

DI Lawson shook hands and indicated for them to sit

down. 'I'm very sorry about your son, Ms Williams. It must have been a great shock to you.'

Fiona nodded dumbly.

'I understand from DS Reid,' said Lawson, adopting a business-like approach, 'That you want to find out more about our investigation.'

'Yes, we know hardly anything,' said Dan, doing the talking for his daughter, 'Like, when did it happen? Where was he found?'

'Oh right... ah... so you haven't been told anything? Well, he was found by a dog walker... that was the Sunday was it, Jack?' he asked Reid.

'Yes, that must be right,' said Reid, 'Sunday the 18th... The pathologist said he'd been dead two days...'

'But that was over two weeks ago!' burst out Fiona, 'Why weren't we told until yesterday?' But all she could think of was her only son, lying dead and undiscovered for two days, and then lying cold in the mortuary for two weeks.

'Ah, well, it took us some time to find out who he was. Someone handed in his wallet over a week later. It had been found in the Park. There was no money in it, but his student card enabled us to identify him, and then the university had your contact details...'

'So he could have been mugged,' said Dan.

'It's more likely someone stole his wallet when he was already dead. It would be unusual for a mugger to inject someone with a lethal dose of heroin...'

'Point taken,' said Dan, although he didn't like Lawson's tone of voice, but he pretended to play the innocent.

'In any case,' continued Lawson, 'He actually still had the syringe in his hand.'

'That would be in his right hand? I noticed the needle marks were on his left arm."

'Yes, that would be right. His right hand. Your point being...'

'My point,' said Dan, 'is that's suspicious right away.' Dan paused so what he said next would have major impact, while Lawson and Reid looked rather nervously at him.

'Rory was left-handed!'

For a heartbeat Dan thought Lawson's suave façade slipped, before he quickly recovered. 'Of course, but your grandson did play the guitar, isn't that right? We found a guitar in his flat. He could have had good dexterity in both hands.'

'Possibly,' replied Dan, 'but still suspicious.'

'Believe me, Mr Williams, we looked at all possibilities, but there were no other fingerprints on the syringe and other gear but your grandson's.'

'Where was he found?' asked Dan, having made his point and realising Lawson was adept at explaining things away.

'He was in Dumbiedykes, just on the edge of the Park, not far from here in fact.'

'Aye,' put in Reid, 'It's a well-known haunt for druggies.'

'But that's what we don't understand. Rory wasn't a drug addict. The last time he was home—there were no marks on his arms.'

'I'm afraid it all seems to have happened in the last few months. People in his flat said he had become a bit of a loner. They hardly saw him. He seemed to have been particularly depressed that night.'

'Right enough, Dad,' said Fiona. 'He didn't come home over Christmas, and we hardly heard from him this last while… not really since New Year.' She stopped. 'But now I remember, I phoned him… it must have been a fortnight ago. Yes, it was about teatime on the Friday, after I came home from school, and it's true. He didn't seem his usual self. Something seemed to be bothering him, but when I asked, he said everything was fine. You know the way boys are.'

'That's true, but I still can't believe...' Dan paused. 'And what about the bruises?'

'Ah... um... yes, bruises... the pathologist put that in his report. He was found behind an old stone wall. He could have fallen over the stone wall when he climbed over it, or he could have been beaten up by someone—it happens with addicts and dealers—but the pathologist was quite clear, that was not the cause of death. That was the heroin—a high dose of very pure heroin. He may not have known, but it is possible he knew.'

'What are you saying?' Dan's tone was sharp.

'Well, in his depressed state of mind, feeling low, he could have done it deliberately. It happens, you know.'

Dan's voice was quiet but very strong. 'It may happen, but Rory would never have taken his own life.'

'I'm sure you knew your grandson best, and anyway the PF's report says it was an accidental death, by drugs overdose.'

'What about yourself, Inspector? You don't feel there was anything suspicious about it?'

'No. There's no doubt about it. All the evidence points to it being a self-inflicted drugs overdose. I'm sorry but there it is.' And he hurriedly added, 'Now, Ms Williams, I'm sure you'll want to collect your son's personal possessions...

'Yes, of course. Thank you.'

'We have the clothes he was wearing and some personal possessions here—the keys for his flat as well. You'll find it all in that box.' He pointed to a cardboard box on a side table. 'You'll know the address of the flat in South Niddrie Street.'

Dan went over, opened the box and looked inside, lifting some of Rory's clothes. 'No mobile phone?' he asked.

'Uh… no…that's all he had on him. As I say, his wallet was found later. It's there too.'

DI Lawson stood up, as Dan and Fiona prepared to leave. DS Reid opened the door for them. Just as he reached the door, Dan turned. Fiona realised his smouldering anger was about to erupt.

'So any young person can pick up drugs in this city and there's nothing the police can do about it? You know who these guys are—the drug dealers—the suppliers—the drug barons, and yet there's nothing you can do about it.'

Lawson was rather taken aback. He had mistakenly taken Dan for just an old teuchter from the sticks. 'Uh…yes… well, we have our suspicions, but we need evidence, you know. And of course no one's prepared to talk—too scared mostly.'

'Amazing!' Dan's eyes burned. 'We can split the atom. We can send men to the moon. We can take out a terrorist car a thousand miles away with a guided missile, but we can't clean up our own capital city!'

Dan turned on his heel and walked out. Lawson and Reid exchanged glances and Lawson rolled his eyes heavenwards.

As Fiona and Dan went round to their car, Dan noticed Constable Barclay, the Family Liaison Officer, about to get into a car. He opened the car for Fiona, put the box on the back seat and then went over to speak to Barclay.

'I wonder if we could bother you to show us where it was that Rory died? I understand it's not far from here?'

Barclay glanced at her watch and looked round a little nervously. 'I'm sorry but I'm just on my way out to another appointment…'

'It would mean a lot to us,' Dan interrupted. 'My daughter's devastated. It might help.'

Barclay looked a little uncertain. 'It really should be one of the CID…'

'They don't strike me as very sympathetic.'

She smiled, 'No, detectives aren't noted for their bedside manner.' She paused. 'Well, OK then, but I'll just move the car first. If you walk along the street here to the corner with Bowmont Place, I'll meet you there.'

In a couple of minutes Dan and Fiona and Fleet met her on the corner, and she led them towards a little path into a wooded area. This tumbled wooded area lies between the main part of Holyrood Park, which encompasses Arthur's Seat and Salisbury Crags to the east, and the sandstone tenements of St Leonards and the concrete blocks of Dumbiedykes (locally pronounced Dummiedykes) on the west.

Fleet became very excited and started whining and sniffing around in the grass at the edge of the road. Suddenly he was off, and although Dan shouted, Fleet kept going down the path and into the trees.

'There are rabbits in the Park,' smiled Barclay.

'Hmm,' frowned Dan, 'He would stop if it was just a rabbit.'

They followed as best they could over some rough ground, and then they spotted Fleet as he stopped for a moment and looked back, but then he was off again, head low to the ground.

'That's very strange,' said Barclay, 'He seems to be heading straight for the place where they found your grandson!'

In a minute they came upon the remains of a low broken-down wall, and Fleet was sniffing all around and whining.

'It was just here they found him... Well isn't that amazing? Your dog seems to have followed his scent.' She looked nervous. 'Will you be all right now? I really have to go. I'm sorry.'

Dan watched her retreating figure, and then turned to Fiona who was softly weeping. He put his arms round her and held her close.

'What a horrible place for him to die," she sobbed, "All alone, and so far from home.'

Dan gazed up at the grey-red volcanic cliffs of Salisbury Crags and found the words wouldn't come. Eventually he released Fiona and started to look around.

'This all gets more and more suspicious. That wall isn't high enough for someone to fall over and get the head injury Rory had. And the bruises on his arms weren't from any kind of fall. They were made by hands gripping them.'

'What are you saying, Dad?' asked Fiona, wiping her eyes which were red from weeping.

'Just this – the police are lying through their teeth.'

*

Dan and Fiona with Fleet at their side walked back down the Pleasance past the Flodden Wall on the right. The Flodden Wall is around 24 feet high and 4 feet thick, and is so called because it was built in expectation of an English invasion after the disastrous Scottish defeat at the Battle of Flodden in Northumberland in 1513—one of many battles in the long defeat after the Wars of Independence in the fourteenth century, culminating in the end of Scottish independence in the Union of 1707.

As Dan gazed at the wall, a gloom seemed to descend on his spirit. He couldn't help but be reminded of the plaintive lament played on the pipes at the funerals of Scottish soldiers—'The Flowers of the Forest'—commemorating the fall of the flower of Scotland's nobility and soldiery at Flodden.

They turned left into the Cowgate, past the Mortuary, and then left again up the narrow lane of Niddry Street South, just before South Bridge crossed high above. The old tenements towered darkly above them. They stopped at a door and tried one of the keys, but found the door just pushed open. They entered and walked up a short flight of stairs. Dan tried the bell, and then when no one answered, he knocked. No response. He tried first one key then the other. The door opened and they entered.

They found themselves standing in a dark corridor. The only light came through a slightly open door on the right side. They looked in some of the rooms. There was a lot of musical equipment. Everything was shambolic. The rooms on the left were dark and windowless, the ones on the right had windows. This is because the tenements there rose up several storeys from the level of the Cowgate before they fronted on to South Bridge which crossed high above at right angles to the Cowgate. They entered the last room on the right. Fiona pointed at Rory's black Stratocaster lying on the floor.

'Strange,' said Dan, 'He would never leave it on the floor. He'd always put it on the stand. This place has been searched.'

Dan picked up the guitar, set up the stand and put the guitar on it. Just then Fleet's hackles rose and he growled. They heard a noise of someone moving about. They turned and a young man shuffled into the doorway. He had a mop of tousled blonde hair, he was barefoot and wearing only a pair of skinny jeans. He looked as if he'd just woken up.

'Eh, everything OK? Are you the police or what?'

Fleet growled again, more loudly.

'Lie down, boy,' commanded Dan, and Fleet instantly obeyed.

'No. I'm Rory's Mum,' said Fiona, 'and this is his Grandad. This is Fleet,' she added. 'It's all right, he's quite safe.'

'Oh, right. Hi. I'm Steve. Hey, that was really bad about Rory. I'm sorry…'

'Thank you,' Dan responded. 'Do you know anything about what happened?'

'Not really. We were all really shocked, man. I mean,

Rory liked a few whiskies, but H, man... no way. It don't make no sense.'

'He wasn't depressed?'

'No... not really. He had some chick. He was really up about life... although sometimes he was a bit moody lately. But come to think of it, that last day... he seemed out of it. We were supposed to practice for a gig. He just wasn't into it. He split.'

'This girlfriend—do you know her?'

'No. Saw her a couple of times at gigs. That's all. Can't even remember her name... something beginning with L... Lou...?'

'Lucy?' Fiona offered, 'Louise?... Lulu?'

Steve shook his head.

'Well if you remember, give me a ring. This is my mobile number...' Fiona wrote her number on a bit of paper and handed it to Steve.

'Yeah, OK. Eh, hope you get things sorted out.'

As he was about to turn to go, Dan asked, 'You never thought it strange when Rory never turned up?'

'No, not really, because Rory texted that night and said he was going to be staying with his girlfriend.'

'He texted that night? When?'

'Uh, it was late... It was only when the police came round last week that we realised something was wrong. I'm sorry.'

'Could you check on your phone and see what time that text was sent?'

'Sure.' He pulled his phone out of his back pocket, and after thumbing a few keys, he said, 'It was 11.32.'

'Ok, if you think of anything else, give my daughter a phone.'

'Sure. Sure.'

As Steve shuffled off, Dan started looking though some books and notebooks on the table.

'Hey, look at this!' he said softly and showed Fiona some writing among some scribbles and doodles on the cover of a notebook: "LOONY TUNES" followed by several apparently random letters.

'Do you think that's her, Rory's girlfriend?' asked Fiona.

'Let's ask Steve.'

'No!' said Dan firmly. 'There's something not right at the bottom of all this. And I don't want anyone knowing we're on to something—especially the police. I don't trust that Lawson and his sidekick. I have a bad feeling about them.'

He paused, frowning. 'But, you know, I think these letters are a code.'

'How? What do you mean?'

'Well, remember how Rory was always fascinated by letters and numbers. Remember we used to play games sometime? Now, one of the simplest codes is to allocate letters to the first twenty-six numbers, so A=0, B=1 and so on up to Z=25, and of course CF can be the same as Z, that is 25, or 2,5.'

'You've lost me already.'

'OK, let's see. A, so that's 0. H, that's 7. J, that's 9. X, that's 23...' It was a mobile number, and in no time Dan had deciphered it. Fiona wanted to phone the number right away on her mobile, but Dan said no. He wanted to find a phone box.

*

Back in the car, they headed out along Dalkeith Road and they were arguing about looking for a phone box. Dan kept checking the rear-view mirror.

'We don't need a phone box,' insisted Fiona. 'I can use my mobile. The phone boxes are all vandalised anyway.'

'No,' Dan was emphatic. 'Mobiles can be traced. We don't know anything about this girl yet.'

After trying several kiosks that weren't working and

tempers getting frayed, Dan turned off Old Dalkeith Road onto Walter Scott Avenue and there in front of some shops Dan spotted a phone box.

Dan turned in, parked the car in front of the shops and got out. The phone box was empty and working. He dialled the number.

A young female voice answered, 'Hello?'

There was traffic noise in the background.

'Hello. Is that Loony?'

'No. Sorry.' The voice sounded scared. 'Wrong number...'

'I'm Rory's grandfather. His mother and me were wondering if we could speak to you.'

Silence.

'His mother just wants to understand what happened to him. We can't make sense of it.'

Still silence.

'Are you still there? It would mean a lot to us.'

There was a pause, then, 'Three questions. One: What were you doing in Northern Ireland?'

Dan hesitated, then said, 'I was in the SAS.'

'Two: have you ever broken the law?'

Dan realised what she was doing. 'Well, I shoot the occasional beast that needs shooting. Some would say that was breaking the law.'

'Three...' there was a pause, then, 'John three sixteen'.

Dan smiled, 'For God so loved the world that he gave his only begotten Son, that whoever believes in him shall not perish but have everlasting life'.

'Good answers. OK. I believe you're Rory's Grandad. You sound a bit like him anyway—the way you speak.'

'Aye, I suppose I do. Can we meet?'

'Have you been to the police?'

'Yes. We had to identify Rory.'

'Are you being followed?'

'No. I'm an old hand at that sort of thing.'

'OK. Do you know Salisbury Crags?'

'Yes, in Holyrood Park.'

'OK. I'll meet you there in half an hour. Come on your own—just you.'

'I'll have my dog with me, if that's OK? He's big and grey, and he's called Fleet.'

'OK, that's cool. I like dogs. Walk along the top of the Crags. Stop at the highest point. I'll call you Grandad. What are you wearing?'

'My name's Dan. I have grey hair, it's longish, and I'm wearing jeans, black boots, black leather jacket.'

'Doesn't sound like any Grandad I know!'

Dan smiled grimly, 'I'm like no Grandad you're ever likely to know!'

'No, I don't believe you are.'

*

As Fiona was exhausted and depressed by all that had happened, Dan dropped her off at the Guest House they'd booked in Newington. He got her settled in and poured her a whisky from the mini-bar in her room. Half an hour later he and Fleet were climbing along the edge of Salisbury Crags to the highest point where the vertical cliff of dolerite and columnar basalt rock stands at 150 feet. He looked west over the city, the gusty wind tugging at his clothes and blowing back his long grey hair. Fleet stood beside him, nose to the wind, scenting the strange smells that wafted up from the city. Dan felt the wind chill was freezing his very bones. Perhaps the cold explained why there were very few people around.

The wind reminded him that Edinburgh was called 'the Windy City' and described as 'east windy, west endy', but historically was better known as 'Auld Reekie' from the smoke that hung over the town. Now the only reek was the distinctive malty smell from the breweries on the west of the city.

Dan looked down at the grey concrete blocks of flats in Dumbiedykes that someone had called Stalinist chic (Dan thought the Stalinist bit wasn't far off the mark, but wondered about the 'chic'), and beyond to the older sandstone tenements and church spires, and further, over a wide gulf of air, to the Castle, grey and formidable, looming over the city. He took in the University buildings, St Leonards Police station, desirable residences and deprived schemes. From the Castle his eyes swept down the Royal Mile leading to the new Scottish Parliament building and the Palace of Holyrood House, just out of sight beneath the crags. He felt that in Edinburgh, perhaps more than most cities, wealth, power, culture and religiosity lived next door to poverty, powerlessness, desperation and Godlessness. And under the historic and cultural façade, there surged in its dark underbelly a rottenness and corruption. Edinburgh: the Athens of the North and the Drugs Capital of Europe.

His eyes lifted to Edinburgh's hills. He counted them as he swung clockwise—Blackford, Braid, Craiglockhart, Corstorphine, Castle Hill, Calton and, behind him to the east across a deep valley, the improbable bulk of Arthur's Seat towering over the city—seven hills. Like Rome, Edinburgh was built on seven hills. Rome, the eternal city— but, thought Dan, no city was eternal, not Edinburgh, not Rome. All the cities of the world would crumble to dust. Only what St Augustine had called the City of God would endure.

Dan was startled out of his reverie by a voice calling, 'Grandad!' He looked down the grassy slope on the side hidden from the city and saw a girl beckoning to him to come down, which he did. As he approached her, he was trying to assess this girl in skinny jeans and short jacket, her long dark red hair falling in long waves around her beautiful face.

'Loony?'

'Yes. My real name is Claire. It was Rory's little joke... you know—"Au Claire de la Lune"?'

'Ah... I'm Dan.' He held out his hand and, after a moment's hesitation, Claire took it and found her small delicate hand held firmly in a very strong but not painful grip. She looked up into his craggy weather-beaten face and his dark green eyes and felt that this old man's appearance belied some hidden strength within him. Dan held her hand for a few seconds and looked her in the eye, still trying to gauge her. He sensed she was frightened, very frightened.

'Are you all right? You're shivering.'

'Yes. Fine. It's just this cold wind.'

'And this is Fleet,' said Dan releasing her hand. Claire stroked Fleet's head. 'Hello, Fleet.' And Fleet responded, licking her hand.

They walked off together down the slope, Dan conscious of the quick nervousness with which Claire walked, and Claire conscious of Dan's sure hill-man's stride. After a bit they found shelter in a hollow among some rocks and sat down.

Dan smiled at her, 'Thanks for agreeing to meet me.'

Claire blurted out, 'Look, do you know what you're getting into here?'

'Yes, we just want to know the truth. It doesn't matter supposing it's hard.'

'That's not what I mean. It'll be hard enough to accept, but it's not that. Let me put it like this: If certain people were to find out that I'm telling you what happened, I'm dead.' She pauses. 'And they'd kill you too.'

Dan smiled grimly. 'A few people have tried that—harder men than whoever you're talking about.'

'Maybe, but that was a long time ago—and you don't know Big Tam.'

'Big Tam? Who's he?'

'Big Tam, Mr Thomas Moncrieff, is responsible for half of the corruption and crime in this city, all behind an apparently legit property management business. And he has the police in his pocket too—or at least some of them.'

'Ah, that explains why we couldn't get anywhere with Lawson and his sidekick.'

'Doesn't surprise me. They were there that night—Lawson and Reid—the night Rory was killed.'

'Killed! So it wasn't an accident or suicide?'

Claire lowered her head and whispered, 'No, it was murder.'

'How did it happen? And how were Lawson and Reid involved?'

Claire became more agitated. 'Look, I've agreed to meet you and tell you what happened. I owe it to you for Rory's sake. But that's it. I'm never going to repeat this again to anyone else. And you're not going to like what you hear, and you're going to hate me. You're going to blame me for what happened.'

'If you tell me the truth, I'm not going to hate you or blame you. I'm going to thank you.'

'All right. We'll see.' She paused and took a deep breath. 'OK, for starters, I work some nights in this place owned by Tam Moncrieff. Only I didn't tell Rory about it, because I knew he wouldn't approve. And I don't suppose you'll approve either. It's a sauna—you know?'

'Ah,' Dan nodded, 'Yes, I know what Edinburgh saunas are. But why on earth would a lovely intelligent girl like you get involved in that?'

'I never thought when I came to Uni I would end up doing that, but my father's business went bust and I had to work nights in pubs. Then I started taking uppers to keep me awake because I was burning the candle at both ends. And then someone said they knew of some work where I could make a lot more money. This turned out to be The

Paradise, owned by Tam Moncrieff, and he is one very scary man.'

Claire sighed. 'Anyway, that night I was working there, and it so happened I was with Tam Moncrieff himself, but unknown to me Rory had followed me...'

As Claire tells her story, Dan sees the scenes come vividly to life before his eyes.

CHAPTER NINE

Tam is pouring champagne into two glasses Claire is holding. Music is playing. Claire seems so slim and slight beside Tam's bulk. Claire is staring at the glasses as they fill. She seems far away.

'Hey! Happy faces! You're with Big Tam and everything's gonna be all right!'

Claire forces a smile and holds out one glass for Tam. He takes it and they pass the glasses round each other's arms and drink like that with linked arms. Tam is in a good mood. When the glasses are empty, Tam goes to refill, but Claire shakes her head.

'Go on, have another one! I'm going to give you a good time.'

'No, really, I'm OK.'

Tam swears and comes up to her with the bottle of champagne. 'When I say you'll have another drink, you'll have another drink.'

He puts his thumb over the top of the bottle, shakes it and squirts it into Claire's face. She shrieks and half turns away, but not before he sprays it over the front of her dress. She runs to the other side of the bed, but he chases her spraying her with the champagne. He catches her and throws her on the bed and starts licking the champagne off the front of her dress and neck as she struggles. At that moment the door bursts open and Rory stands for a split second in the doorway. His eyes are blazing. Then he launches himself at Tam.

119

'What the …' gasps Tam.

Before Tam can struggle up, Rory's fist smashes into his right side just about his kidney and, as he half turns in rage and pain, Rory's left catches him on the side of his jaw and he topples off the bed.

'Come on Claire, let's get out of here.'

Claire, kneeling at the top of the bed, stares at him as if he is mad, and points to Tam who is groaning on his front on the floor.

'Come on! He's not going to hurt you anymore. He's finished. I know he's connected with Jake. And I know what Jake's into. We're going to the police. Come on!'

'Don't be stupid! The police aren't going to take your word against Mr Moncrieff's!'

'I don't mean the local lot, I know a superintendent somewhere else. Come on!'

At the mention of 'superintendent', Tam shakes his head and looks up with a snarl of fear and anger on his face.

Rory grabs Claire by the wrist and drags her off the bed. Tam struggles to his knees and lets out a roar as Rory drags Claire towards the door, but Billy King, Lawson and Reid suddenly rush in. They stop dead at the sight of Rory.

Rory realises his only chance is surprise and goes straight for Billy. He is so fast, he kicks Billy in the nuts and sends him sprawling into Reid, and he almost makes the door, but Lawson grabs him and they all pile into him. Claire catches Lawson's arm and screams, 'Let him go! He doesn't mean any harm!'

Lawson sends her flying with a swipe from his arm. Rory is still putting up a struggle when Tam hits him on the back of his head with the champagne bottle. Rory crumples on the floor and Reid sticks the boot in. Lawson sees Rory is out cold and pulls him back.

'Hey! Hey! We don't want a body on our hands.'

'Body! I'll break his bloody body!' shouts Tam.

'Not a good idea. You don't want a murder pinned on you or on this place. Who is he anyway?'

Tam, only slightly calmer, snarls, 'I dunno who he is!' He turns to Billy and Reid, 'Get out there and calm things down!' (Rory had opened a few doors before finding the right one.)

Tam turns to Claire who is sitting on the floor in the corner, crying. He grabs her by the hair and pulls her to her feet, then pins her to the wall with his hand round her throat and jaw.

'Now, listen to me, you bitch. A man I know will pay me a lot of money if I put you on a Russian freighter in Leith tonight bound for St Petersburg. I hear they do interesting things to bitches like you in brothels over there.' He pauses. 'So, who is he?'

'Rory... Rory Williams. He's nobody... just a student on my class. I've seen him a few times. But he started getting too heavy... Jake knows him...'

'I'm not interested in your love life, bitch. I want to know where he comes from, and why was he talking about a police superintendent?

'I don't know. He comes from out West somewhere... and I don't know anything about police... except...'

'Except?'

'He did talk about some friend of the family—a superintendent or something. I don't know anything more.'

Sharon enters in a state. 'Tam! Tam, what are you doing? You're hurting her!'

Tam glares. 'Shut it! And get this bitch out of here.' He puts his face close to Claire's. 'And remember... Russia...'

Tam pushes Claire in Sharon's direction, and Sharon puts her arm round her and leads her out.

*

Tears were rolling down Claire's face as she sat with her head bowed beside Dan behind Salisbury Crags. 'That was the last time I saw Rory... I'm sorry...'

Fleet put his chin on her lap, and she stroked his head. Dan gave her his hankie. 'You're not to blame. There was nothing you could do.' He paused. 'Was Rory still alive when you left?'

Claire nodded. 'Yes. He was still alive. Sharon—she's the receptionist there—she told me what happened after she got me to leave. Only... she swore me to secrecy, so you've never heard what I'm going to tell you. She'll deny everything.'

Dan's face was set like flint. 'What happened?'

Claire looked out into the distance over the Firth of Forth and Fife and took a deep breath. 'This is what Sharon told me...'

*

Tam comes out into the foyer trying to get reception on his mobile. Sharon is behind the desk. Tam glares at her. He is still enraged.

'How did that bampot get in here?'

'Tam, he just said he wanted a girl. He sounded OK, so I let him in, and he just went through here like lightning and started opening doors...'

'Just don't let it happen again!' Tam snaps. 'Now get everyone out of here.'

'The clients have all gone. This sort of thing's not good for business...'

'You don't need to tell me that. Tell the girls to go home, and take an early night yourself. We'll lock up.'

As Sharon leaves the desk and heads towards the lounge, she overhears Tam on the phone.

'Jake? You've been careless! Get over here right now—Paradise—and bring some gear... Yeah, the works. Pure stuff, none of your usual crap. It's for a special client...'

Sharon sees Claire and the other girls off. Claire doesn't want to go, but they all persuade her that Tam will kill her if she doesn't let it drop, and she reluctantly goes. Sharon closes the outside door, collects her coat and bag behind the desk and heads back through to the lounge. She moves quietly, looking over her shoulder, unlocks a door and lets herself into another smaller room. It's dark inside. She doesn't put on the light and closes the door. She stands for a minute to let her eyes adjust. It's a room that Big Tam used to blackmail some clients.

She moves to what looks like fitted wardrobe doors. She opens a door. She is looking through a two way mirror into the room where Tam, Billy, Lawson and Reid are standing around Rory's motionless body. She turns a volume knob down low, presses a switch and Tam's voice comes through.

'Right, you two better make yourselves scarce. Me an' Billy'll deal with this. We don't want to compromise the arm of the law. Remember, you'll get an anonymous tip off. Make sure you don't mess this one up. As I said, it'll be worth your while.

Lawson on his way out says, 'Don't worry about us. Just make sure nothing can be traced. See you later.'

When Lawson and Reid have gone, Billy turns to Tam. He doesn't seem very happy.

'You sure about this? I mean, it's one thing giving him a good shoeing, but this is something else. I don't like it. What if something goes wrong?'

Tam is still seething. 'Nothing's going to go wrong! And think about it. We can't let this little shite go to some polis high heid yin. If he's been watching this place and following that little tart around, who knows what he's seen? And he knows Jake for another thing. We don't need any heat just now. We've got competition. And no' everyone in the polis is like Lawson and Reid, are they?'

'I still don't like it.'

'It's got to be done. Trust me. You saw him. He's no' the

sort you can reason with, is he? You're no' going all soft on me, are ya?'

'It's no' that. I've just got a bad feeling, like.'

'You've just got a bad feeling 'cos he kicked ya in the balls!'

They turn at the sound of a cough from Rory who is coming round.

'Get a hold of him and make sure he doesn't kick ya again!'

Just then they hear the buzzer, and Tam goes to answer it. Billy kneels over Rory who is moaning and looks completely out of it, his eyes rolling, and says, 'I don't think you're going to be kicking anyone for a while.'

After a few minutes, Tam returns with Jake who's wearing latex gloves, holding a syringe and looking extremely nervous.

'Is that him?' Tam points to Rory.

'Yeah, that's him, all right. He's the one who's been pestering Claire.'

At the sound of Jake's voice and Claire's name, Rory seems to become more alert. He tries to focus his eyes on Jake and his speech is slurred.

'Claire... where's Claire? Jake?... What... what...'

'Eh, are you sure about this?' Now Jake is looking terrified. 'I mean...'

Tam shouts an obscenity. "Get on with it, or certain people will find out what you've been up to!"

Tam and Billy lift Rory onto the bed, take off his jacket and roll up his sleeve. All the time Rory is mumbling and groaning and keeps repeating Claire's name. When he sees Jake approach with the syringe full of liquid, he starts to struggle, but Tam and Billy hold him down as Jake ties a strap tightly round his arm.

Sharon puts her knuckle in her mouth to stifle the scream she wants to let rip as the scene unfolds before her.

Jake's hand is shaking as he sticks the needle in a vein in Rory's arm.

'Where's Claire?' gasps Rory.

'Oh, you don't need to worry about her,' smirks Tam. 'We'll take good care of Claire. Perhaps I'll give her to Jake here.'

Rory summons up his last strength, 'One day, you'll pay...' His eyes stare darkly at each of them in turn as his pupils dilate. Then he mumbles, 'But it's all paid... paid in blood', before his head slumps onto his shoulder, his eyes gazing blindly into an infinite distance.

Tam laughs. Beads of sweat are forming on Jake's brow as he sticks the syringe into a plastic bag. But Billy stares briefly at the collapsed figure of Rory with a frown on his face, before putting on a grim smile.

Sharon turns away her head, tears streaming down her cheeks.

'Right, Billy, get your car round the back. Jake, go to the cupboard through the back and get a big plastic bag, you know the kind mattresses come in.' Tam is brisk and matter of fact.

Billy leaves, and Tam and Jake wrap Rory's limp body in the large clear plastic bag and carry it to the door.

Sharon waits about 15 minutes until everything is quiet. She then closes the wardrobe door, exits the room and leaves the Paradise by the front door.

*

Claire was sitting on a rock, tears on her face. Dan leant across and put his hand on her shoulder.

'You really cared for Rory, didn't you?'

'I'm so sorry. It would have been better if he'd never got involved with me.'

'None of this is your fault, Claire. None of it. You're as much a victim as Rory was.'

The generosity and forgiveness of Rory's Grandad are

too much for Claire, She sobbed bitterly, and Dan sat beside her and put his arms round her, as he would if she had been his own granddaughter. They sat like that for a time, Claire's head buried against Dan's shoulder.

When Claire was calmer, Dan asked, 'Claire, do you know what time Rory died?'

'Uh... I think Sharon said it was about half past nine.'

'So he couldn't have sent a text at half past eleven.'

'What?' Claire looked shocked.

'Someone used his phone to text his flatmate to say Rory was staying with you. Did Rory say he was going to stay with you?'

'No! I never asked him to stay with me! Believe me, we never slept together!'

'I believe you, Claire.' Dan paused and then asked the question he feared he already knew the answer to, 'Who's this Jake?'

'Jake? He actually knew Rory. Jake Hetherington. You'll know him...'

'Jake Hetherington! I know him all right!' Dan stood up, his knuckles white as he closed his fists, his face a mask of anger. 'I told him once what would happen to him if ever he hurt Rory again.' Slowly he mastered his emotions. 'Claire, you've got to go to the police—you and Sharon.'

Claire shook her head miserably. 'They have the police in their pocket. You know that now. If we ever lived long enough to testify, they'd have the best lawyers. They'd get off and it'd be Sharon and me that got put away for some drugs offences or something, and we'd never leave Cortonvale alive.'

'But I know someone—the policeman Rory told you about—not in Edinburgh...'

'It's no use. I'm not going to put Sharon through it. She's terrified as it is. You don't know what they do to women like us. We'd just disappear—end up being abused in some

Russian brothel—or worse.'

'That's not going to happen. I can protect you. You could both come away with us.'

'And how long would it last? They'd find us. "You can run, but you can't hide..." If you want to do something, why don't you shoot the bastards? You were in the SAS, weren't you? You could do it and no one would ever know.'

'Maybe I could. But that wouldn't be justice—just revenge.

'What would it matter? The scum would be off the street anyway.'

'It would matter to me. I want them to face up to what they've done, and I want to look them in the eye when they realise justice has finally caught up with them.'

Claire looked at Dan who seemed transformed before her eyes. She sensed a deadly power in him. She shivered and got up.

'I'm sorry. I'd want to help you for Rory's sake, but I can't. I hope you see that. I'm weak. I'm no good.'

She walked off down the hill, and Dan stared bleakly after her.

*

Twenty minutes later he was in Fiona's room in the guest house. He recounted the main points of what Claire told him.

Fiona was trying to come to terms with it all. 'I still don't understand why we won't go to the police. Surely there's something we could do. You should speak to Jim Matheson again.'

Dan sounded tired. 'It would do no good. You need witnesses, Fiona, and neither Claire nor Sharon will testify.'

'But why not? Surely they know what happened was wrong. Have they no feelings? I wish I could talk to them.'

'It would be no good. They're too scared, and I don't

blame them. We're talking about ruthless men here.'

'You still haven't told me who these people are. Did Claire tell you?'

'She told me, but I'm not telling you. The fewer people that know the better. And I don't want you put in any danger.'

'And why would I be in any danger?'

'Fiona, if they killed Rory because of what he suspected, they wouldn't give a second thought to taking you out if you start making a fuss. You would never know. One night there'd be an accident—your brakes would fail, or your car would be found on a lonely stretch of road and you'd have disappeared...'

'That kind of thing doesn't happen in the Highlands!'

'No? I can think of several unexplained accidents and disappearances and shootings in the Highlands the police have never solved—the Inverness woman Renee Macrae and her three year old son Andrew in 1976, and the Nairn banker Alistair Wilson in 2004. You know it's true.'

Fiona fell into a sullen silence.

'But there's one thing I am going to do before I leave Edinburgh', said Dan quietly, "I'm going to see the Procurator Fiscal'.

CHAPTER TEN

Dan got off the Number 7 bus on South Bridge. A bitter north-east wind was sending grey clouds scudding across the sky. He was a bit early, so as he walked back up the street he paused to look over the bridge down into the canyon of the Cowgate and remembered something he'd heard or read about the bridge.

South Bridge is a large nineteen arch viaduct built in 1788 across the deep ravine of the Cowgate to link the Old Town around the High Street with the university area in the Southside. Only the arch across the Cowgate is now visible; the others, called The Vaults, are all concealed by buildings, but in the early years after the bridge's construction, they were used for all sorts of nefarious purposes, including prostitution and illegal distilleries. After that they were filled in with rubble and lay forgotten for many years until rediscovered in the 1980s by former Scottish rugby internationalist, Norrie Rowan, when he found a tunnel leading into them. It was this tunnel he used to help Romanian rugby player Cristian Raducanu escape the Romanian secret police and seek political asylum just weeks before the Romanian Revolution of 1989.

Dan smiled grimly to himself. It was a pity that there had been no one to provide an escape route for Rory.

Dan then turned right up Chambers Street. On the right were various University buildings. On the left towered the massive Old College Quad with its huge green copper dome topped by the Golden Boy. Dan couldn't help a little smile as he remembered what a friend had told him about a student prank of many years before. As a dare for St Andrews Day, some students climbed the dome and tied a kilt around the Golden Boy. Unfortunately the kilt they had brought was too small, not realising the statue had been based on a giant of a man, reputedly a boxer called Anthony Hall. The kilt looked more like a tartan apron!

It was a memory of more innocent times, thought Dan. Now students were involved in more dangerous forms of rebellion against authority.

He passed the Museum of Scotland with its impressive façade of intricate Venetian arched windows, and saw further up its blunter modernist extension with its cylindrical tower, although the latter did remind him somewhat of the ancient cylindrical buildings in the north of Scotland known as brochs. Then near the top of the street he arrived at the Crown Office and Procurator Fiscal Service. In Scotland, the procurator fiscal is responsible, among other things, for the investigation of all sudden, suspicious or unexplained deaths.

Dan found Constable Barclay, the Family Liaison Officer waiting for him. She'd arranged for Dan to see the person who had dealt with Rory's death. A few minutes later they were led into the room of the fiscal depute. He introduced himself as Julian Carruthers. It took Dan only moments to sum him up. He was middle aged, with thinning brown slicked-back hair, very definitely overweight, a fact not concealed by the expensive tailoring of his grey suit. His small, round eyes seemed to dart from one place to another as if scared to focus too long on anything. 'Shifty', Dan said to himself.

'Ah yes," said Carruthers in his plummy Edinburgh private school accent, 'You've come about the tragic death of your grandson, I believe, Mr Williams. Your daughter wasn't able to come?'

'No. She is too tired and upset. And in any case she had to look after our dog.'

'Ah, you have a dog', purred Carruthers. 'Well, that's something we have in common.'

Just about the only thing, thought Dan.

'What breed is it?' asked Carruthers.

'Fleet's a cross between a Collie and an Alsatian, although there might be a little bit of deerhound in there somewhere.'

'Oh', said Carruthers, slightly amused. 'Ours is a pedigree Shih Tzu.' Dan couldn't help but notice the note of superiority, and thought the dog was appropriately named, and that Fleet could probably eat it for breakfast and not notice. But he said, "Mr Carruthers, I've come to find out exactly what happened to my grandson, and what investigation has taken place'.

'Yes, yes, of course'. Carruthers opened a file on his polished oak desk and shuffled some papers. 'So what would you like to know exactly?'

'I'd like to know who murdered my grandson.'

'But', Carruthers stammered, 'there was no question of murder, Mr Williams! The forensic report and the pathologist's report are quite clear. There was no indication of foul play. The post mortem revealed your grandson, eh... Rory', he added, referring to his papers, 'Rory had a massive dose of heroin in his blood, very pure heroin. That would have been fatal without the combination of alcohol. Not a very high level of alcohol—but enough to put him over the drink-drive limit. No, I'm sorry, but there is no question that your grandson's death was anything other than self-inflicted.'

'But as I said to the police', said Dan as patiently as he could, 'Rory did not do drugs. Yes, he would have a whisky or two, but not drugs. Never.'

'But the evidence...'

Dan cut Carruthers short. 'I don't doubt that Rory died of a drugs overdose, Mr Carruthers. What I don't believe is that it was self-inflicted.'

'Um, ah, I see.' Carruthers seemed flustered. 'But neither the investigating officers, nor forensics, nor the pathologist found any evidence of foul play. The only fingerprints on the syringe found by the body were your grandson's.'

'That could be arranged. And then there's this...' Dan played his trump card. 'The needle marks were on Rory's left arm, yes?'

'Um... let's see...' Carruthers turned some pages. 'Yes, that's right—left arm.'

'And the syringe was found in Rory's right hand, yes?'

'Eh... ah... yes. Nothing unusual about that, is there?'

'Just this—Rory was left-handed!'

'Oh!' For a moment, Carruthers appeared flummoxed, but he quickly recovered—too quickly, Dan thought. 'Eh... yes... I seem to remember there was something about that. Let me see. Yes, here it is. A note that's part of the police report. Yes... when the police searched his flat, they noticed the guitar was left-handed. So that did raise some questions, but they add that guitar playing requires dexterity in both hands, so the syringe in his right hand was not considered evidence of foul play.'

Dan realised right away that Carruthers had been nobbled by Lawson, but he wanted to let him know that he knew. 'And when did you receive that note—this morning?'

'Mr Williams!' responded Carruthers indignantly. 'I don't know what you're implying! This note is part of the original evidence.'

'Ah, yes, of course,' said Dan with just a trace of sarcasm in his voice. 'But what about the injuries, the bruises? They didn't seem self-inflicted or accidental to me.'

'Are you a medical man, Mr Williams?' asked Carruthers

rather too smugly.

'No, but I've served in the Forces, and I reckon I've seen more trauma injuries and dead bodies than you have, or even your pathologist.'

'That may very well be, Mr Williams', Carruthers retorted rather stiffly, 'But I have to go with the professional medical and forensic opinions of those who are experts in the field.'

Barclay, who had sat quietly until then, could see that Dan was about to explode, and hastened to calm things down. 'I'm sure Mr Carruthers didn't mean any disrespect, Mr Williams. But, Mr Carruthers, isn't it possible to conduct further enquiries, perhaps re-examine the evidence, order a second post mortem?'

Carruthers glared at her and then pursed his lips. 'Technically… technically it is possible, but I would need some new evidence to justify the inevitable expense', hastily adding, seeing Dan's agitation, 'and of course I couldn't release the body for funeral arrangements and so on, until all that was complete—and that would take months.'

Barclay saw her chance to make things easier for Dan. 'Why don't you discuss all this with your daughter, Mr Williams, and then let Mr Carruthers know?'

Dan took a deep breath and exhaled slowly. 'Yes, I suppose you're right, Constable.' He rose. 'You'll be hearing from me, Mr Carruthers.' Barclay accompanied him out of the room and right out of the building onto Chambers Street.

'What do you make of it all, constable?' Dan asked her.

She looked up and down the street, and then said, 'You'll want to check Rory's flat and make arrangements for his stuff to be collected', adding in a lower voice, 'We can talk more freely down there.'

Dan readily agreed, and they walked on down Chambers Street, across South Bridge and onto Infirmary Street, then down Robertson's Close, left onto the Cowgate and left again up the dead end of Niddrie Street South. On the way, they talked generally about the city, the traffic, the tourists and the buildings until they were in Rory's room in the flat. There was no one about.

'I thought it best to come here.' Barclay sounded nervous. 'If anyone happened to see us, it wouldn't arouse any suspicions that I'm accompanying you to Rory's flat.'

Dan eyed her. 'Why would it arouse any suspicions?'

She hesitated. 'Well… because of what I want to say to you. And remember, you never heard this from me.'

'Aye, all right, but that's not the first time I've heard that,' said Dan rather wearily.

She glanced keenly at him, but as he was not about to elaborate, she went on, 'For what it's worth, I completely agree with you. From what I understand, there ought to be further investigation.'

'Well, that's worth a great deal to me, Constable.'

'I'm glad. And please call me Louise.'

'Thank you, Louise. And call me Dan. But am I right in thinking that there's a "but" coming?'

She smiled in embarrassment. 'You don't miss much, do you, Dan?'

Dan laughed, 'No', but added in a tone that sent a slight shiver down the young policewoman's spine, 'Not once I've got it in my sights!'

'Anyway, this is what I wanted to say. You may be completely right about what happened to Rory, but you're not going to get anywhere.'

'Why not?' Dan's tone was even, but Louise felt steel in it.

'Because… well I have no proof of this but, to put it bluntly, because of corruption. There, I've said it!'

Dan eyed her steadily, 'What you say doesn't surprise me, Louise. As soon as I met Reid and then Lawson, I knew there was something not quite right. And a minute with Carruthers convinced me there's someone with his snout in the trough.'

Louise nearly choked as she tried to stifle a laugh. 'I'm sorry, Dan, but do you know what people call him behind his back?' She paused for effect. 'Miss Piggy!'

Even Dan had to smile at that, but he quickly turned serious again. 'But surely that can be investigated?'

'Yes, there's the Complaints Department of C Division for the police and the Professional Standards Committee for fiscals, and if there's a question of criminal wrongdoing, there's the Serous Crime Squad. But the problem is: who's going to be the whistle-blower? You see, it begins with low-level stuff. You make any complaint or even question something or show that you're not very happy with what's being done, and you quickly get labelled as "difficult" and get passed over for promotion or, even worse, get framed for some misconduct yourself. But it's not just that. People's lives can be made hell with intimidation and bullying. Now I'm not saying the whole force or the whole legal profession is like that, far from it, but there are definite corrupt networks and even links to organised crime. And various people have tried to tackle it with little success. You see there's too much drug and vice money sloshing around in this city.'

Dan was silent for a long time, so Louise said, 'I'm sorry, it's not right, but you're not going to get anywhere with taking any of this further. I don't want to prolong the agony for you and your daughter, and in the end get nowhere.'

He sighed. 'No, I can see that. I don't know if Fiona could stand it—not having Rory's body released for his funeral for months and months, and all for nothing.' Dan stood with his head bowed. He was not used to coming up against things that he couldn't sort out, and this institutional evil seemed way beyond his capacity to deal with.

He suddenly felt very old and tired.

'But thank you,' he raised his head and looked down into Louise's worried face, 'Thank you for being so honest with me. And,' he added, 'I hope when the time comes you'll have the courage to stand up for the truth.'

They said their goodbyes, Dan stayed in the flat to pack up Rory's things to be collected later, and Louise set off back to St Leonards.

Later that day, after a long emotional discussion with Fiona, Dan phoned Carruthers and asked him to arrange for the release of Rory's body. The next day he collected the death certificate and contacted his home undertaker, and they made arrangements with an Edinburgh undertaker that had been recommended by Neil Cameron. Dan and Fiona then collected Rory's things and set off on the long road north.

CHAPTER ELEVEN

Dan stood at his bedroom window looking out on the scene unfolding below. He was wearing a black suit, white shirt and black tie. The dull light of an overcast winter's day caught his mane of grey hair and the side of his face, highlighting the long scar on the side of his neck. It was a strong face, lined with unspoken pain and browned by long years of exposure to the North-west winds and weather. His moist green eyes stared down at the long black hearse and the gathering dark-suited men hunched against the penetrating cold.

His attention turned to the framed photograph he held in his hands. It was a picture of Rory kneeling down stroking Fleet and laughing. Dan smiled through his tears and then his jaw set in a grim line as he put down the photo and wiped away his tears. He turned from the window, his shoulders bowed with more than the weight of years. It was Wednesday 12th February—the day of Rory's funeral.

He stepped slowly down the stairs and entered the living room. Fiona and a few relatives and neighbours were sitting and standing around. Fiona went up to him and straightened his tie.

'We'll need to go, Dad.'

'I know, Fiona, I know,' he spoke tenderly. 'But there's something we must do first.'

Dan looked around the room. He addressed the oldest man present, a Church elder, 'Donald Ruadh, will you say a word?'

THE FORGE

The old man stood, bowed his head slightly and, in a way characteristic of many Highland men of his generation, he put his left hand across his brow, fingers on one side, thumb on the other, as he began to pray.

'Eternal and ever blessed One, with you a thousand years are as one day, and one day as a thousand years. You are immortal, eternal. But we are creatures of time....'

As Donald prayed various scenes flashed briefly before Dan eyes.

Rory as a small child saying 'Again! Again!' as Dan throws him up in air.

Rory as a boy helping in the hayfield, manfully lifting bales of hay as big as himself.

Rory as a teenager playing football for the school team, and although he is smaller and slimmer than many of the others, he could hold his own.

'O Lord, bless our friend Dan and his daughter Fiona in their sore loss. May they know the comfort of the One who sympathises with us in our weakness, the One who wept at the grave of his friend Lazarus...'

By the time Donald Ruadh concluded his prayer, it wasn't only the women who had tears in their eyes; many strong men were wiping their weather-beaten cheeks with the backs of their hands.

People moved out to their cars. Dan was the last out. Fleet came up and nuzzled his hand. Dan stroked his back. He spoke softly, but firmly. 'Well, Fleet. You've got to stay, boy. You can't come.'

Fleet whined and looked disappointed.

Fiona turned. 'I think he wants to come.'

'I know. He loved Rory, and Rory loved him.'

They got into the old green Transit van and drove off after the hearse. The few slow miles passed with them both deep in their own thoughts and memories. At the Church they were greeted by Neil Cameron who led them to their seats at the front. It was a traditional Highland church building—stone-built with white plastered internal walls, wooden panelling to around window height, and a wooden ceiling. The windows were high gothic arches. There was a balcony and facing it a high wooden pulpit. Everything was plain and unadorned. It was a large building. It could seat 500 people, and the church was full, with many young people standing at the back.

Rev Cameron welcomed them all and announced the first Psalm – the Twenty-third Psalm, not the old traditional version, but a modern one that had quickly caught on in the Highlands because it was sung to an adaptation of a traditional tune called Tarwathie. It was a favourite of Rory's.

The precentor stood up and led the praise. His voice was strong and mellow. In his younger days he had been in great demand at local ceilidhs.

The LORD is my shepherd; no want shall I know.
He makes me lie down where the green pastures grow;
He leads me to rest where the calm waters flow.

After the first few notes, the congregation joined in, the notes rising and swelling with an aching longing, there was even the suggestion of the unique waterfall effect of the traditional Gaelic Psalm-singing where each singer put in their own grace-note harmonies.

My wandering steps he brings back to his way,
In straight paths of righteousness making me stay;
And this he has done his great name to display.

The precentor now took the lead in a quieter, more restrained tone, as if bowed under the threatening cliffs of the valley of shadow, then rising in volume and confidence towards the end of the verse.

Though I walk in death's valley, where darkness is near,
Because you are with me, no evil I'll fear;
Your rod and your staff bring me comfort and cheer.

As he led the last verses, the precentor's voice exuded faith in the God of covenant love who provided and guided and gave hope of glory.

In the sight of my enemies a table you spread.
The oil of rejoicing you pour on my head;
My cup overflows and I'm graciously fed.

So surely your covenant mercy and grace
Will follow me closely in all of my ways;
I will dwell in the house of the LORD all my days.

The minister rose to speak.

'There are many things that are hard to bear. One of the hardest is to live to see your son's or your grandson's death. Our deepest sympathy is with Fiona and Dan today.

'There is one thing I must say at the outset. Don't believe everything you may hear about Rory Williams. We all know Dan Mackay, and Dan says there are many unexplained things about Rory's death. And what Dan says is good enough for me...'

After giving a eulogy for Rory, he opened the Bible and read from 2 Corinthians chapters 5 and 6:

We know that as long as we are at home in the body we are away from the Lord. We live by faith, not by sight. We would prefer to be away from the body and at home with the Lord... We must all appear before the judgment seat of Christ, that each one may receive what is due to him for the things done while in the body, whether good or bad...

If anyone is in Christ, he is a new creation; the old has gone, the new has come!... God was reconciling the world to himself in Christ, not counting men's sins against them... We implore you on Christ's behalf: Be reconciled to God. God made him who had no sin to be sin for us, so that in him we might become the righteousness of God... Now is the time of God's favour, now is the day of salvation.

Neil Cameron then urged all present to heed the inscrutable providence of God in the death of one so young—none of us knew how long we had in this world—and whether young or old, death comes to us all. Are we ready to 'appear before the judgement seat of Christ? Then he pled with everyone to respond to the loving invitation and command: Be reconciled to God. No one left that church in any doubt that the invitation was genuinely and passionately given.

The service closed with the singing of Psalm 103 verses 13 to 15 in Gaelic to the tune Kilmarnock. The precentor rose and led the large congregation in this utterly unique style of spiritual praise in which the precentor 'gives out the line'—singing each line quickly and then the congregation joined, repeating the line more slowly. Many of those present did not speak or understand Gaelic, but no one was unmoved by the elemental, ethereal music that conjured up the sighing of the sea, the wind in the hills and the longing of the human soul.

Amhlaidh mar ghabhas athair dàimh
is truas da leanban maoth,
Mar sin da fhìor luchd-eagail fhèin
Dia gabhaidh truas gu caomh.

Oir 's aithne dhàsan agus 's lèir
ar cruth 's ar dealbh gu ceart;
Gur duslach talmhainn sinn air fad,
is cuimhne leis gu beachd.

An duine truagh, a ta a làith'
amhlaidh mar fheur a-ghnàth;
Mar bhàrr na luibh' air machair fòs
a ta e fàs fo bhlàth.

*

At the graveyard, Dan, Jim Matheson, Muhammad, and others lowered Rory's coffin into the open grave beside his grandmother's grave. The headstone on her grave was inscribed with the words MARY MUNRO MACKAY, BELOVED WIFE OF DAN MACKAY, 1944-1998, "WITH CHRIST WHICH IS FAR BETTER". They stood back. A large crowd was gathered round in a rough semicircle. Neil Cameron stepped forward and read some verses from Psalm 103, including the verses sung earlier in Gaelic:

As a father has compassion on his children, so the Lord has compassion on those who fear him; for he knows how we are formed, he remembers that we are dust. As for man, his days are like grass, he flourishes like a flower of the field; the wind blows over it and it is gone, and its place remembers it no more. But from everlasting to everlasting the Lord's love is with those who fear him, and his righteousness with their children's children — with those who keep his covenant and remember to obey his precepts.

*

It was dusk on that winter's day at Cill Donnain. It was still not completely dark; although the waning moon had not yet risen, a few stars were beginning to appear in the gaps in the clouds. Everything was very still and quiet. There was no light in Dan's house. In the distance a vehicle could be heard getting nearer. Then Dan's van appeared along the road and drove down to the house. He cut the engine, stepped out and walked towards the door. He was alone. He stopped and looked out over the still landscape, over the leaden surface of the loch reflecting the dying light, up to the massive bulk of the lower ridges and outliers of An Teallach, and then round east to the ridge of Beinn nam Ban. He took a long time. Everything was completely quiet again—apart from the eternal sigh of the sea rising to the heavens. His eyes returned to the house. Its dark unlit windows stared blindly out. He turned and put his hand on the doorknob. He paused, took a deep breath and then went in. The door shut—a door that was slightly the worse for wear, the dull dark green paint peeling in places.

*

The brass plate on the highly polished hardwood door with shiny brass fittings said MONCRIEFF. The impressive door befitted the house. It was a palatial villa in the Grange, a very exclusive area on the south side of Edinburgh between Morningside to the west, Marchmont to the north, Newington to the east and Blackford to the south. The area was known as St Giles' Grange from as far back as the twelfth century, and the owners of the original mansion house in the nineteenth century, the Dick Lauder family, sold off a considerable area of land for redevelopment and many large Victorian villas were built there, with extensive gardens surrounded by high stone walls.

Lights blazed from nearly every window of the Moncrieff residence. Several expensive cars were parked in the driveway. The sound of laughter and music came from within. In the distance a vehicle was approaching. The security gates opened automatically and lights appeared coming up the drive. It was Tam Moncrieff's BMW. He saw that Reid and Lawson's cars were there, and Carruthers' Mercedes and several others that belonged to influential people that Tam had in his pocket. He parked, stepped out, smiled, straightened his cuff links and headed for the door. Before he could get there, the door opened and his wife, Gayle, stood to greet him. A very pretty blonde in her late-thirties, she was expensively dressed in a tight turquoise silk dress and jacket and matching high heels, her face and hair immaculate. She'd been a dancer in her younger days, but now no longer as slim as she used to be. There was a slight tiredness about her eyes. She was holding a glass of white wine, and it didn't seem like her first.

'You're late, dear.' Her tone was a kind of mock scolding. 'All your guests are here!'

'Someone's got to earn a crust about here—to keep you in the manner to which you're accustomed!' Tam kissed her briefly on the cheek and brushed past her. She heard him greeting several people in his usual hale-fellow-well-met style followed by more laughter. She stood for a moment looking wistfully out at nothing, then draining the glass, she closed the door.

CHAPTER TWELVE

Four months had passed since Rory's death. Somehow the fire had gone out of Dan Mackay. People were saying, 'He's not the old Dan Mackay we used to know. He took his grandson's death real bad.' Dan felt cold, numbed; he couldn't be bothered to engage with people, although Neil Cameron and Jim Matheson and Muhammad and others tried their best to take him out of himself. Dan had busy times, feeding hay to the sheep in what remained of a cold wet winter and early spring, and the lambing in early April, but on the whole he couldn't settle to things. Everything was a weary slog. He just gritted his teeth and got on with it. People would see him on the hill, his head down battling into the rain and wind, with Fleet beside him looking as weary and downhearted as himself.

Occasionally Dan would phone Claire to see if she was OK, and to see if there was any way she and Sharon would be prepared to go to the police. Understandably neither of them was, and although Dan was disappointed, they always ended their conversations on good terms. But the calls only increased his depression and feeling of uselessness.

However, his daughter Fiona was much worse. She was completely shattered by Rory's death and the whole injustice of it. She couldn't go back to work and was signed off by the doctor who put her on antidepressants. But she started drinking more heavily than usual, and the combination of the medication and alcohol set her on a downward spiral. To begin with, her colleagues from school and other friends would visit and try to get her to go out, but they found her obsession with Rory and his death overwhelming and gradually the visits tailed off.

Dan had tried to help, but because of his own state of mind, he wasn't able to do much good. Rory's death had increased Fiona's bitterness against God, and Dan, out of his own powerlessness and frustration, would get angry at her, which only exacerbated their estrangement. But he did ask Neil Cameron to visit her, and to everyone's surprise she invited him in and he spent many long sessions listening as she poured out her bitterness and anger. Neil wisely didn't say much, but gradually he won her confidence as he listened sympathetically to her life's history—the heartbreak of her marriage breakup, the early loss of her mother, the cruel death of Rory. In the end he managed to persuade her to see a counsellor from a charity called Road to Recovery whom he knew. By late May she was beginning to make some progress, although it was slow. She started going out again, and even went to church, which amazed everyone, not least Dan.

*

The street in Leith was deserted in the small hours of the morning and poorly lit. Two figures in black hoodies approached a close door in a tenement. They were each concealing something under their jackets. They entered. The street was quiet, apart from the wind rustling in sweet wrappers and takeaway cartons on the pavement, and the sound of the occasional vehicle on Leith Walk.

Suddenly the two figures emerged from the close, running. As they pelted down the street, the hood of one of them flew back. It was Mark Fulton.

When they were far down the long street, a window high up behind them burst, and flames and smoke poured out.

'Bloody hell! I didnae ken it would be that quick…'

There were screams and the sound of people shouting. But Mark and his mate didn't hear them. They were far away. The flames burst out of another window. People started emerging from the close door in their nightclothes. The sound of sirens filled the night air. Three fire engines screamed up and fire-fighters poured out. Some went straight in the door. Others went up on the ladders with hoses. A police car arrived.

When the fire was eventually extinguished, a fire-fighter approached a policeman.

'That was no chip pan fire. There was a smell of petrol up there. You'd better get the SOCO boys here. They've killed a whole family, the bastards.'

'Who were they, d'you know?'

'A neighbour said they were Asians. Name's Hussain, I think.'

*

Two days later, Dan got news that shook him out of his depressed state of mind. He met Lachie MacLean, the game-keeper from Dundonnain, on the road, who asked him if he'd heard about Muhammad's bad news. Seemingly he was in an awful state. Dan got straight back into his van and roared off.

When he got to Muhammad Hussein's shop in Badcaul, he found Muhammad stacking some shelves and looking a pale reflection of his former self.

'I came as soon as I heard. What happened?' Dan put his left hand on his friend's shoulder and gripped his right hand in his.

It was all Muhammad could do to keep his voice from breaking altogether. 'Oh Dan, my friend, come away through.' He led Dan into the back shop.

'It is the family of my cousin's son in Edinburgh. There was a fire. The police say it was started deliberately. The whole family were killed including three children...' Muhammad finally broke down and started sobbing.

Dan put his arm round him to comfort him. 'Oh, man! Was it one of these racist attacks?'

'No, somehow that would have been easier to bear. No, seemingly my cousin's boy was mixed up in drugs. The police seem to think it was something to do with organised crime. But the children...'

'Drugs... organised crime... children...' Dan spoke half to himself.

There was a pause while Muhammad composed himself. 'You are familiar with death, my friend. First Mary your dear wife, and then Rory in tragic circumstances. How do you manage to carry on?'

'Well, to tell you the truth I've been struggling. But it was more the injustice of Rory's murder, because that's what it was. But underneath it all, I have hope. Death is not the end.'

'No, we too believe death is not the end, but... then there is the Judgement, when our deeds will be weighed, to see if our good deeds outweigh our evil deeds, and we hope they will...'

'Yes, we will all have to answer at the Judgement Seat. But my hope doesn't lie in getting what I deserve, because if it did, I'd be finished! My hope lies in redemption.'

'You always talk of redemption, my friend, but I do not understand.'

'Well, imagine I was told never to go near the Dubh Lochan bog, you know the one up from Corrie Hallie, and I did, and I was sinking in it and I couldn't get out. And you went in after me and managed to get me onto solid ground but you yourself sank. You would have saved my life at the cost of your own. That's redemption. That's what Jesus has done for us.'

'I am still not sure I understand...' Muhammad sounded doubtful. 'I know we call Jesus a prophet and the Messiah, but our scholars disagree about whether the Qur'an teaches that Jesus was crucified or not. It is all rather puzzling to me.'

But then Muhammad went on to speak of his cousin's family, about the children, how old they were, and how their father had become involved in drug dealing. After an hour they parted, with Dan promising to come back and see him.

*

That evening Dan was on the phone.

'Claire? Hello. It's Dan. We haven't spoken for a while. How are you? Are you OK?...'

'That's good. I'm fine. Well, not good, to tell the truth. Have you heard about that Pakistani family that died in that fire?...

'Aye. Well, they were cousins of a good friend of mine... Someone was involved in the drugs scene... So what does that suggest?...

'Claire, have you thought about what I said? Will you go to the police now?...

'I understand... No, I don't think that... No.'

They talked for a while about Fiona and Sharon and Claire's studies, but eventually their conversation died.

'OK... Well, goodnight Claire. Take care. Goodnight.'

Dan sat in the old armchair by the fire and stared unseeing into the glow and the little tongues of flame licking round the peat. He put his head in his hands. Conflicting thoughts swirled around in his mind. He could understand why Claire and Sharon wouldn't speak out. But was no one going to stop the Tam Moncrieffs of this world? Why weren't the authorities doing anything? Why didn't God do something? He'd appointed the authorities as his servants to punish the evildoer. But what do you do when the authorities are corrupt?

THE FORGE

*

Dan and Fleet were climbing the roller-coaster ridge of An Teallach—Sail Liath, Cadha Gobhlach, Corrag Bhuidhe, Sgurr Fiona and finally Bidein a Ghlas Thuill. Dan had just felt he had to get away out on to the high tops, to see if he could get a different perspective on things. He sat near the summit, looking north and west and ate his lunch, feeding Fleet pieces of sandwich.

It was one of these unusual days in early summer in the North-west Highlands when the air is astonishingly clear and you can see over vast distances. All the peaks of the north were visible—from Foinaven towards Cape Wrath, Beinn Mor Assynt in the heart of Sutherland, the full whaleback ridge of Suilven, the pinnacles of Stac Pollaidh and the bulk of Beinn Mor Coigach. And out west, Dan could see the Hebrides from the Butt of Lewis to the Cuillin of Skye. At first Dan sat in silence overwhelmed with the immensity of the creation. But then his mind turned back to what had eaten at his mind over the past months.

'Remember the last time we were here, Fleet—with Rory.'

Fleet looked up into Dan's face as if he understood.

'Rory won't be coming here again. He had to climb a different mountain. He came face to face with evil men. And he didn't stand a chance.

'He'll never stand here again. But they're still walking around—walking around the hard city streets—hard men, destroying everything that's good and beautiful, creating a desert. And now a whole family's been burned to death. And no one can touch them. Too scared... or too corrupt.'

Fleet looked as wise and compassionate as only a dog can.

'You wouldn't be scared, boy, would you? No. But you're not a poor young girl or a frightened woman who see the future and see only death, disfigurement or depravity unless they toe the line.

'It's too much to bear!'

Dan rose suddenly and stood looking along the cliffs, his fists clenched. Then as Fleet nuzzled against his leg, he slowly relaxed and stroked Fleet's head. He packed up the rucksack.

'Come on then, boy.'

They started moving off down towards the ridge of Glas Mheall Liath and the steep descent to Loch Toll an Lochain.

*

In Tam Moncrieff's office, Gina was putting on her coat. Tam was looking disgruntled.

'Come on, Gina! You know you want to. A weekend in the best hotel.'

'You know I can't. Jonnie won't be off-shore for another week, and I'd need to get someone to babysit the kids. Anyway, you should be off home to your own wife.'

'Her! She's a cold bitch, you know that. I need a real woman—warm, loving—someone just like you.'

'Aye, right!' said Gina over her shoulder, making a hasty escape.

Tam looked disconsolately at the door that she'd just banged. He checked his watch. He went to the wall behind his desk and removed a picture, revealing the door of a wall-safe. He spun the combination knob and opened the door. Amongst various papers there were a few small bundles of bank notes. He pulled out one bundle, pocketed it and closed the door.

Just then the buzzer went. Tam answered the intercom and pressed the entry button. A few seconds later, Red Billy entered. He was clearly agitated.

'Mark Fulton's dead! They found him wi' his throat cut.'

Tam blazed, 'What! If they want war, I'll give them

war.'

'That's exactly what the polis want...'

'The polis! What are we paying Lawson and Reid for?'

'Tam, it's way beyond Lawson and Reid. Torching that flat was way out of line...'

'You're not going soft on me, King Billy, are you?' Tam's tone was menacing.

'Naw, it's no' that. It's just it's stirred up a hornets' nest. We're going to have to lie low for a while.'

'Lie low! How do you think we're going to do that? We've got a few million pounds of heroin to shift amongst other stuff. How are we going to lie low on that?'

'I don't know—but we've been through hard times before—we can do it again.' Billy headed for the door. 'See you tonight.'

Tam looked round the office in frustration. Then he suddenly kicked a chair and sent it crashing across the room.

*

That evening Sharon was at the reception desk in the Paradise Sauna. The sound of muffled raised voices and indistinct sounds came from along the corridor. Sharon looked concerned. She moved quietly part way along the corridor and listened. There was the distinct sound of a struggle and furniture falling over, a slap and a woman's scream.

Sharon rushed to the door of the room and burst in. Tam Moncrieff had caught Claire and was about to hit her again.

'For God's sake, Tam...'

'Who asked you to stick your fat nose in?'

'Tam! Tam, think of the noise! You'll scare the clients. We can't afford to lose business...'

Tam exploded with an obscenity and grabbed her by the neck. 'Get out of here!'

He sent her flying out the door and slammed it hard. Sharon's head hit the opposite wall with some force and she crumpled on the floor, crying, but trying to stifle her sobs.

Billy came along the corridor, stuffing his shirt into his trousers. 'What the...? Sharon! What's happening?'

'It's Tam!' Sharon sobbed softly. 'He's off his head. He's beating her up.'

'Who?'

'Who do you think? Billy, you've got to stop him. He's going to kill that lassie.'

Billy listened at the door. 'It's OK' he grinned. 'Normal reception seems to have been resumed. Come on. Let's get you sorted out.'

Billy helped Sharon to her feet and led her back along the corridor and into an empty room. He looked at her cheek and neck which had red marks and her mascara was running.

'Ye'd better sort yer makeup, hen.'

'Sharon looked in the mirror, touched her cheek and neck gingerly and grimaced. 'Billy, what's got into Tam? He's always had a nasty streak, but this is different.'

'Och, it's just woman trouble.'

'It's not that. He's always had woman trouble. There's something else. What is it?'

'No' much you miss, Sharon, is there? Och, there's business problems. Competition, like. You know what I mean?'

'Aye, I think I can guess. But you see if you can have a word with him. It's no' right what he did. He won't listen to me.'

'Aye, right. I'll see what I can do. And no' a word about what I just said, by the way.'

'What do you take me for?'

Billy retreated. When he'd gone, Sharon continued to feel her head and neck. 'I swear to God that's the last time Tam Moncrieff ever lays a finger on me.'

Late that night Dan received a call from Claire. He listened grim-faced for a long time. His heart was breaking for her, but he didn't know what to say. It seemed a hopeless situation, because still neither Claire nor Sharon would go to the police. But he was particularly interested to hear that Tam Moncrieff was having business difficulties, and before Claire rang off, Dan said he had the beginning of an idea. He wouldn't say what it was, but he'd be in touch.

PART 3
THE ANVIL

CHAPTER THIRTEEN

A few days after that late night call from Claire, on Sunday 21st June, Dan heard a sermon from Neil Cameron that shook him to the core. He was sitting on his own near the back of the church. He still wore his black suit, white shirt and black tie to church. His head was bowed. The church was not nearly as full as it had been for Rory's funeral.

The minister gave out his text: 'Second Kings, chapter 9, verse 20 — "the driving is like the driving of Jehu the son of Nimshi; for he drives furiously."'

A young boy grinned at his wee brother, swerved an imaginary steering wheel from side to side and pointed across at Dan. Their mother dug him in the ribs with her elbow and half frowned, half smiled.

Neil Cameron's face, which was usually so jovial and friendly, looked severe.

'There comes a time when the patience of God runs out. He is slow to anger. All day long he holds out his hands to a disobedient people. But that does not mean he is a soft touch. If we refuse to respond to his grace, there comes a day of judgement, a day of reckoning…

'That day had come for the royal house of Ahab and Jezebel. That day is drawing near for our own nation, and for every one of us who refuses to listen…

'God's judgement may come in different ways. In Jezebel's day it came in the person of one man, Jehu. Jehu drove furiously…'

Dan raised his head and looked intently at the minister.

THE FORGE

'King Ahab and Queen Jezebel had power and authority and they ruled by manipulation and corruption. If they wanted a vineyard, they could have the owner framed and condemned to death. If they wanted to silence the word of God they could slaughter his prophets. They thought they were untouchable. They thought they were hard. But God raised up someone harder still. Jehu drove furiously...'

*

That evening Dan was standing at the window of his bedroom holding a picture in the fading light of the midsummer sun. The face he'd loved more than any other smiled back at him. It had been taken when his late wife Mary was younger, when she was strong and lovely, long before cancer had ravaged her body (but not her spirit). There were tears in his eyes, he shook his head and sighed.

'Oh Mary, what am I going to do? I can't accept it! I can't just let them get away with it and carry on ruining people's lives. But what can I do? It's another world down there...'

He looked round the room, the room that once had held so much joy, where they had made love, but now it felt so empty. He turned from the window and returned the picture to its place on the dressing table. He picked up his wife's wedding ring, which was lying on a little china dish, he looked at it tenderly and then pulled out a drawer to put it away. That's when he noticed the red box again. He opened it, picked up the large eastern necklace and sat on the bed. The large central stone glowed blood-red in the lamplight. After staring at it for a minute, the memories came flooding back, and he looked up at a picture hanging on the wall. It was of a man in the uniform of a Major in the 93rd Sutherland Highlanders. He looked formidable with his whiskers and his high bearskin hat with red and white flashes, red coat, green tartan kilt and basket-hilt Highland broadsword. As Dan looked at the picture, he heard his late wife's voice as clear as if she was in the room with him.

'That's my great-great-grandfather, Major John Munro, of the 93rd Sutherland Highlanders, who fought in India at the time of the Mutiny. It was there he risked his life to save a Muslim princess.'

Mary's voice made the words come alive as they had done when he first heard her tell the tale.

*

Major John Munro's company was on duty that night. They had been expecting the Princess and her guards to arrive before sundown, but they hadn't come. The Major led four men out to investigate. They were skilled at moving quickly and silently in rough country. After about an hour they came on a scene of carnage.

John Munro gazed in horror at the scene before him. The Princess's guards were all killed, and the Princess herself stood helpless and terrified surrounded by ten soldiers of another British regiment, who made it very clear what their intentions were. In the shadow of the trees there were four lookouts posted. John Munro signalled to his men to draw their dirks and dispatch the four lookouts. That was quickly done, and then they fixed their bayonets and waited the signal. John Munro cocked his pistol and stepped out into the clearing.

'What in the name of God is going on here? Throw down your weapons, and stand away from the lady. My men have you surrounded.'

The men turned, a look of terror in their eyes. They knew there was only one punishment for what they had done. But then the ringleader, Sergeant Tom Miller, looked around and saw only the Major. He grabbed the Princess, standing behind her and holding his bayonet to her throat.

He sneered, 'It's only a damned kiltie, boys. Do you know why they wear skirts? It's because they're women! We know how to sort that lot out—like we did at Culloden. 'You'd better throw down your weapons, if you want your precious Princess to survive.'

John Munro spoke evenly, 'If you weren't so ignorant, you'd know that the Sutherland men did not support the Young Pretender. But neither did we approve of the cruelty of your Butcher Cumberland and his like.' He paused. 'I am telling you for the last time, stand away from the lady! You're going to die. Either you're going to die at the end of a rope, or you're going to die here. If you let her go, I can give you a quick death.'

Miller laughed, 'I'll see you in hell first!'

'No, I don't think you'll see me there, sergeant.'

The Major's pistol cracked and the ball tore right through the sergeant's right elbow.

The sergeant screamed and fell; the princess struggled to get free.

John Munro faced three of the soldiers who were charging towards him with fixed bayonets. Four shots rang out, and four of the soldiers fell, but only one of those who were advancing on Munro. He swept out his Highland broadsword, parried the bayonet thrust of the first and cut him down with his sword. He caught the bayonet of the second in the hilt of his sword and snapped it off, before sweeping his dirk out and stabbing him.

Munro left his men to take care of the others, and went straight for the sergeant who was lying on the ground struggling to reach his fallen bayonet with his good hand, but he couldn't do that and hold on to the Princess at the same time, and she tore herself free. Munro put his foot on the sergeant's wrist and put the tip of his sword against his throat. Three of the Highlanders gathered round.

'We've seen to the others, but one of them killed young Rob Mackay.'

John Munro looked with grief at the fallen boy. He spoke in cold anger to Miller, 'That young boy's mother is waiting in far Strathnaver, waiting for her son who will never now come home. And all because of you — your greed and your lust.'

He drew back his sword and the sergeant thought his hour had come. But the tip of the sword stopped a fraction of an inch from his throat.

'It would be just to kill you. But I'll not touch you. I'll leave you to the hangman's rope.'

The men bound the sergeant, while John turned to the Princess, who rose and bowed low before him. She was only a young teenage girl. He took her by the hand and raised her up. They set off back to the fortress. Ahead marched the sergeant at bayonet point, howling and complaining about his smashed arm, and behind came the other two Highlanders carrying their fallen comrade.

The Princess's father, the Nawab, was overjoyed to see his daughter alive. He praised Major Munro and presented him with a piece of jewellery of great worth. It had a large central stone in an ornate gold and diamond setting. It shone blood red in the lamplight.

The Nawab wrote a letter thanking Major Munro, in which he said, 'This jewel was paid to my father for rescuing a Russian merchant. The central stone is a rare Alexandrite, mined in the Ural Mountains. But I consider it a small price to pay to the man who has redeemed my daughter. You are a man of honour and great courage. You have stood by the way of God and not the way of man. May this jewel bring you and yours blessing for ten generations, and if need be, may it redeem many lives.'

Dan took a long brown envelope out of the drawer. He pulled out the papers inside, one of which was yellow with age. It was the Nawab's letter. He read it through, and the last words echoed in Dan's mind like the sound of the great Highland bagpipe. 'If need be, may it redeem many lives.' He stood up and gazed alternately at the jewel in his hand and out the window, other words resounding in his brain:

'...waiting for her son who will never now come home. And all because of you—your greed and your lust...'

'Sometimes you've just got to stand up to evil...'

'One day you'll pay...'

'...the driving is like the driving of Jehu the son of Nimshi; for

he drives furiously...'

'They thought they were hard... But God raised up someone harder still...'

. *'Redeem many lives... One day you'll pay... He drives furiously...'*

Suddenly Dan's fist closed tight on the blood-red jewel in his hand.

CHAPTER FOURTEEN

Over the months since Rory's death, from time to time Dan had mulled over all the possibilities of how it might be possible to bring down Tam Moncrieff and his criminal empire. Everything that had happened since then confirmed him in his belief that there was no hope of the police and the law doing anything and, if anything was to be done, it was going to be up to him. The problem was that up until now he had oscillated between a feeling of hopelessness and burning anger. The unbearable grief and depression of his only daughter, the devastation of Muhammad's family, and his own deep sense of the loss of his grandson all played on his mind. His occasional phone conversations with Claire only added to his broken-heartedness.

But in that moment as he stood there at his bedroom window, clutching that precious jewel, he knew exactly what he had to do. The beginnings of a plan had been forming in his mind ever since his last phone call from Claire, and now all the uncertainties were blown away, and he was his old decisive self again. But he knew that he must remain deadly calm.

The first thing he had to do was phone Fiona. He ran down the stairs like the Dan of old. He picked up the phone and dialled.

'Fiona... yes... how are you?... That's good ...

'Fiona, there's something I want you to do for me. It's very important...

'I have to go away for a few days, and I don't want any-

163

one to know. Now, I know this is sudden and doesn't give you much notice, but I want you to come and stay here for a few days and look after Fleet...

'I know, I know... but the weather is looking fine for the rest of the week—you'll be able to get out for walks...

'The sheep will be fine. They're all out on the hill. We'll do the clipping after I get back...

'I'm leaving early tomorrow morning. Could you come tomorrow?...

'OK, Fleet will be all right till you get here...

'No, I can't say just now. I'll be in touch. There may be a couple of visitors, so make up the spare beds...

'I'll let you know. All I can say is that I'm doing this for Rory. It was something he started, and I'm going to finish it...

'Right, *a ghraidh*. Yes. *Oidhche mhath*.

Dan rang off and dialled an Edinburgh number. It was for a hotel he'd seen advertised in the newspaper. It was described as 'an exclusive bijou hotel'. He made his booking and then phoned Jim Matheson.

'Jim. How are you? Sorry to be disturbing you so late on a Sunday night...

'Jim, can I see you tomorrow morning?...

'I'll be leaving early. What time are you in the office?...

'Right. I'll see you then—first thing. I'll explain when I see you.'

Lastly, Dan phoned Claire.

'Loony?... Aye... Are you alone? Can we speak?...'

'I'm coming to Edinburgh... Tomorrow... I'm going to deal with our mutual friend... No, no police... I'll do it myself... He'll never hurt you or anyone else again...

'Claire, can we trust Sharon absolutely?... OK, can you speak to her and persuade her to meet me?... I'll let you know once I'm in Edinburgh. I'll have a cheap mobile, so if you see a number you don't recognise it should be me.'

*

At midsummer it hardly gets dark in the North of Scotland. And if there is a clear sky it doesn't get dark at all. There is a nautical twilight of around four hours when dusk blends slowly into dawn. Such was this night. There had been rain earlier in the day, but the pressure was rising and the sky was clearing. It was half past ten and the sun was just sinking in a bed of cloud in the north-west beyond the Minch and the Western Isles, and a light breath of wind was rippling the water of the loch.

With Fleet in attendance, Dan came out of the house and headed to the shed. He opened the door and reached for the light switch. Fluorescent light flickered into life and flooded the big space. Dan's van was at one end. There was a work bench, with various tools and bits and pieces of wood and metal lying around. On one wall there was a gun cabinet with a rifle and two shotguns inside.

Fleet lay down beside the bench. Dan cleared things off the bench and sorted out some tools. He went to the gun cupboard, unlocked it and very carefully, almost reverently, took down the two shotguns. They were an 'over and under' design where one barrel is on top of the other one. He handled them lovingly as he laid them on the bench. He picked up one of the shotguns. The polished walnut stock and the long barrels gleamed in the fluorescent light. On the intricate rose-and-scroll engraved side were the words '*J Purdey & Sons*'.

These very expensive shotguns had been presented to him on retiring from the army by his commanding officer who belonged to a wealthy landowning family. In his letter to Dan, he had written, "Because the work of the SAS is top secret, those who have displayed conspicuous bravery are seldom decorated. One of the greatest injustices was the refusal to award Paddy Mayne the Victoria Cross in World War II, even although the medal recommendation was

165

signed by Field Marshal Montgomery himself. However, be all that as it may, I will be eternally grateful for your act of bravery in saving my life. I know you are a countryman, so please accept these guns as a small token of my undying gratitude.'

This referred to an incident which Dan had not thought much of at the time. Due to false intelligence, the Q car he was driving, with Colonel Fitzgerald in the passenger seat, was ambushed by the IRA. A van was blocking the road and another vehicle came in behind. The Colonel was hit in the upper chest. In one searing moment, Dan pulled the Colonel down, and gunned the car straight at one of the gunmen standing between the van and a wall. The gunman went right over the roof of the car and Dan was round the next corner before the others could even aim an accurate shot. A car pursued them, but Dan soon left it far behind. The car he was driving looked like an ordinary Ford Escort Mark II, but in fact had an RS 1800 powertrain. Dan took the Colonel straight to hospital where he was operated on and made a full recovery.

Dan smiled grimly at the memory as he disassembled the gun after carefully scribing a mark on the barrels near the wooden fore-end. He took a deep breath and fastened the barrels in the vice. He looked down at Fleet who regarded him with a sombre eye.

'Well, boy, it's got to be done.'

He picked up a hacksaw and very deliberately and carefully began to cut off about two thirds of the length of the barrels. He laid the cut-off barrels down and then started to smooth the edges of the remaining barrels with a file. He then reassembled the gun. He now had a sawn-off shotgun less than two foot long. He then did exactly the same with the other gun. When he had finished, he wrapped them up carefully in newspaper and placed them in a small holdall, which he then put in the back of the van. He also loaded a few other items, including a couple of old sacks, a plain rounded chair-leg, a short rolled up umbrella and an old camouflage jacket that had a roll of gaffer tape and a coil of snare wire in the pockets. His second best shepherd's crook also got put in the back of the van. The horn handle was not as ornate as his best one, but it was a heavier stick.

He next turned his attention to the Transit itself. He opened the bonnet. The engine, by contrast with the rest of the van looked very clean—the word 'COSWORTH' stood out brightly across the camshaft cover. The van was an ordinary rear wheel drive, short wheelbase Transit van, but Dan, with the help of a mechanic friend, had put a modified 3 litre V6 Cosworth engine in it some years before, together with a 6 speed gearbox. They'd also lowered and strengthened the suspension, and fitted powerful disc brakes all round.

Dan checked the oil, brake fluid and coolant levels. He closed the bonnet and checked the tyre pressures. The wheels were large and the Bridgestone tyres were very wide—235/50 R18, 101Y.

The last thing Dan did that night was to pack his old suitcase with a few clothes, and he put the red jewel case and the accompanying brown envelope in the inside pockets of a long brown coat. Those pockets were very deep 'poacher's pockets'.

*

Early the next morning Dan emerged from the front door of the croft house. He was wearing a green tweed suit, checked shirt, green tie and his long brown coat. On his head was a brown leather Indiana Jones style hat, and he carried an old battered suitcase, a brown briefcase and his shepherd's crook with the ornate horn handle. Fleet tried to push out, but Dan stopped him.

'No, Fleet. You've got to stay, boy. The city is going to

be no place for you—not this time. Fiona will be here soon. Good boy.'

Fleet looked at him with a mournful eye, as Dan shut the door.

Dan walked over to the shed and opened up the big double doors. He opened the rear doors of the van and stuck his cases and stick in and then got behind the wheel. The van started with a purr and a cough and then gained a steady beat. He drove out, closed the shed doors and then stood for a moment surveying the land. The early morning mist was now beginning to break, and the northern outliers of An Teallach were towering out of the mist. Dan drove up to the side road that led from Badrallaich to its junction with the A832, turned east and drove slowly down past Dundonnain Lodge. When he hit the A832, he headed east and opened out the Cosworth engine. A few miles further on, at Loch Glascarnoch, he caught the last glimpse of An Teallach in the door mirror, the morning sun catching the cliffs and turning them the colour of old blood.

Less than an hour after leaving his house, Dan arrived at Police Headquarters, Inverness, having covered over 60 miles on the twisty Highland roads. Inside, he had only to wait a moment at reception before Jim Matheson came through to welcome him and escort him to his office.

'Dan! How are you?'

'Fine. Fine, how's yourself?'

'Just grand. All the better for seeing you.' He looked quizzically at Dan's tweed suit. 'Going somewhere special?' he laughed.

Dan smiled. 'Oh, aye. No, not really. Just got to see a man about some stock.'

'Landed gentry, is he?'

'Aye, something like that.'

Jim sat behind his desk and indicated a chair for Dan. 'So, what can I do you for?'

Dan laughed, kind of embarrassed. 'Well, aye... it's just this... you know you once said you'd do anything for me and Mary...'

'Well, I'd have done anything for Mary.'

'Aye,' laughed Dan, 'you always had a soft spot for her. Well, there's something you can do for me now—and I know it's something Mary would have wanted... Look, I know this'll sound stupid, but an enquiry is going to come into the station here... an enquiry about me...'

'What sort...'

Dan stopped him, holding up his hand. 'That's not important. Look, I'll be straight with you. I'm going down to Edinburgh to find out more about how Rory died. An enquiry is going to come here about me from Lothian and Borders—criminal record, that sort of thing. I want you to make sure that that enquiry gets passed on to you personally. Now, I don't want you to tell any lies for me. I just want you to paint the worst picture you can...'

'That shouldn't be too hard!'

'You know, rumours of poaching on an industrial scale, but suspicions of darker deeds, a hard man, different irons in the fire, selling a lot of stock, came into a big inheritance when his wife died, got contacts all over the North in the farming and fishing communities—that sort of thing...'

'What are you up to?'

'I'm going down to Edinburgh to rattle a few cages. I might just flush out the truth.'

'And you might just get flushed down the pan!'

Dan smiled ruefully, 'I might just, at that. But there's something else. I need a clear run on the A9 later this week.'

'More than my job's worth! Anyway, these things are decided weeks ahead.' Jim nodded to a chart on the wall as he rose. 'You'll take a cup of tea. I'm sorry I haven't anything stronger, but you're driving anyway.'

'Aye, a cup would be good,' said Dan rising, as Jim went to get some tea organised. Dan moved to the wall chart and scanned the information about patrol cars and mobile cameras and saw one night that week was clear. 'Thursday night to Friday morning... it'll be tight,' he said to himself.

*

Heading up to the Slochd on the dual carriageway section of the A9, Dan's opened out the Cosworth engine and overtook everything including a rather sleek Mercedes sports car whose occupants gazed in amazement at the ease with which the battered old van cruised through the Slochd, over the bridge and receded into the distance against the background of the Cairngorms, blue in the summer haze.

Dan left the A9 at Perth and headed south on the M90, but quickly turned off east onto rural roads. He saw the sign to Auchtermuchty and smiled at the thought of the home of two Scottish icons: the late great Jimmy Shand, accordionist extraordinaire, and The Proclaimers, the folk rock band famous for 'Sunshine on Leith' and '500 miles'. But he turned off at Strathmiglo and, by Falkland and the A92, headed to Kirkcaldy.

As he drove, he thought of the man he was going to meet—Harry Brown. Dan had first encountered him when he was in N Ireland with The Det, although then he was known as Sean McGuiness. While engaged in a surveillance operation on a property in West Belfast, Dan discovered that Sean McGuiness was meeting with known active members of the IRA, and he also discovered that McGuiness was cheating with the wife of one of the IRA men, and Dan had photographic evidence of the affair. He was then able to blackmail McGuiness into becoming an informer for British intelligence. When it became clear the IRA were becoming suspicious of McGuiness, he was smuggled out of Ireland and given a big pay off and a new identity in Kirkcaldy.

Dan parked in a small car park off the Esplanade on the shore of the Firth of Forth, and as he walked towards the High Street, he mused on the fact that Kirkcaldy is known by the rather prosaic name of 'the Lang Toun' in Scots, whereas it has a much more romantic Celtic etymology. In fact the names of the great majority of towns and even of all the cities in Scotland (apart from Edinburgh which is Anglo-Saxon) derive from Celtic languages (and some from Norse).

Kirkcaldy is an old town. Its first mention in a historical document is by King David I in 1130 AD in the form Kircaladin. Scholars dispute the meaning of the name, but the most likely explanation is that the suffix is not the Anglo-Saxon 'Kirk', but the Celtic 'Caer' referring to a fort, and the second part of the name ('caladh') refers to a harbour or haven. It certainly was an important trading port by the sixteenth century, and in the fifteenth century Ravenscraig Castle had been built there, possibly on the site of a previous fort. Dan smiled grimly to himself at the irony that it was that same King David who had furthered the Anglicisation of Scotland started by his mother Queen Margaret.

Of course in Dan's childhood, Kirkcaldy was famous for the production of linoleum, but in the 21st century employment is mainly in the service sector.

Leaving those musings, Dan walked along the High Street carrying his brown briefcase until he reached a pawnbroker's shop with the classic three golden balls hanging outside. He entered.

The place was empty, apart from a young man behind the counter.

'Good morning. Can I help?'

'Aye, hello. Is Harry around?'

'I'll check. Who will I say is asking?'

'Dan Mackay. He'll know who it is.'

The young man went through the back and some moments later emerged with a short smartly dressed man in his fifties, with a cup of coffee in his hand and looking rather nervous. He had grown a moustache and his hair was different from when Dan had seen him last. But Dan would never forget those cold blue eyes.

'Ah, yes, Mr Mackay, isn't it?' He spoke with barely a trace of an Irish accent. 'What are you after?'

'And nice to see you too, Harry. Just a word in private— through the back.'

'I'm rather busy at the moment, actually.'

Dan laughed, 'Well, that's a change.' He turned to the young man, 'You wouldn't believe what he was like when I first knew him. I remember...'

'Oh, all right,' Harry interrupted quickly, not knowing what Dan might come out with, 'Just a few minutes then. Come through.'

'Is everything all right, Mr Brown?' asked the young man nervously.

'Yes, yes. Fine. You just mind the shop.'

Harry ushered Dan into the back shop. The place was dingy and untidy. Lots of papers and boxes were lying around. There was a desk and also several big safes.

'What the hell are you doing here?' Harry's Irish accent was becoming more noticeable by the second. 'You know the deal. I gave my information. Just because the Troubles are over, doesn't mean there aren't some who would settle an old score.'

'No, no, nothing like that, Harry. I just want you to pawn something for me.'

'Pawn something?' Harry sounded slightly relieved. 'What is it?'

Dan reached into the pocket of his coat and took out the dark red jewellery box. He laid it on the table and carefully opened it, displaying the exotic piece of jewellery.

'Where the hell did you get your hands on that?' Harry's eyes goggled.

'Don't worry about that. Perfectly legit. It belonged to my late wife. It came originally from India. I have the provenance here.' He took out the brown envelope.

Harry inspected the contents of the envelope as he sipped his coffee. 'What do you want for it?'

'I'll be reasonable. I want to pawn it for ten grand.'

Harry choked on his coffee. 'Ten Thousand Pounds!' he spluttered. 'You're off your head. I haven't got that kind of money!'

Dan spoke quietly and reasonably. 'As you can see from those papers, that stone,' he pointed to the large deep red central jewel, 'is an Alexandrite. It was first discovered in Russia in the nineteenth century and named after the Tsar of the time—Alexander II. You can see it's a genuine Alexandrite if you move it from daylight to incandescent light. In daylight it's green and in electric light or candlelight it's red. Look.' Dan took the necklace to a window and Harry followed him.

'See, now it's green... and if I take it back to your desk light... it's deep red.'

'Wow!' even Harry was impressed, but he went to his desktop computer and typed in "Alexandrite" after checking the spelling from the provenance Dan had given him. He whistled. 'You're right. That piece is worth a fortune.'

Over his shoulder Dan said, 'That stone alone is worth £20,000—we had it valued, as you can see from the other paper there. The whole piece, with provenance? The sky's the limit.'

Harry was shaking his head. 'I'm afraid it's out of the question. If this went wrong, I could lose my business.'

'Lose your business? You could lose your life.'

Harry stared at him, his mouth open.

'As you said,' continued Dan dryly, 'There are some

who'd like to settle an old score. Some people don't like being betrayed.'

'You bastard!'

'Ten thousand. I'm sure you've still got a bit of the cash you were given. Ten thousand—in twenty pound notes. And I'll be back in a week to redeem it. If not, you can keep it. You can't say fairer than that.'

Harry turned pale, as pale as the grubby sheets of paper on his desk. He bit his lip, then went to one of the huge metal safes, reached round the back and then swung the safe out from the wall, revealing a wall safe behind.

Dan laughed, 'Very clever!'

Harry ignored him. He spun the knob, part opened the door, reached in and, after fumbling around, took out five bundles of £20 notes. Dan quickly checked one of the bundles of 100 notes, opened his briefcase and placed them all inside.

'Now the receipt,' said Dan evenly.

Harry sat down at the desk and wrote out the receipt. They both signed it. Dan folded up his copy and put it in his pocket. He picked up his briefcase and headed for the door.

'Nice doing business with you, Harry.'

Along the street, on the way back to the van, he stopped to buy a cheap Pay As You Go phone.

CHAPTER FIFTEEN

Arriving in Edinburgh, Dan stopped at a supermarket and filled up the extra-large petrol tank of the transit and then parked on a quiet side street in Newington on the Southside where the parking was free. He put on his long brown coat and hat, and taking his suitcase, briefcase, holdall and best stick out of the van, he walked to the corner and waited for the taxi he'd called. Anyone who knew Dan would have been surprised how bent and cripple he seemed to be.

The taxi delivered him to a small hotel not far away—the Kilgraston Hotel on Craigmillar Park—where he'd booked a room earlier. Kilgraston Hotel was one of several small hotels and guest houses on this long, straight stretch of the A701 which changes name from Minto Street to Mayfield Gardens to Craigmillar Park heading south out of the city. The Kilgraston was a lovely Victorian building of honey-coloured sandstone and roofed with dark blue slate. Dan had picked it because it was small but quite expensive.

Once settled in his room, he picked up his new mobile and tapped in a number.

'Loony?... Aye... I'm in Edinburgh... Look, Claire, have you persuaded Sharon to meet me?'

'Great! I'm at the Kilgraston Hotel. Are you both free this evening?...

'No? OK, what about tomorrow?...

'All right, come for lunch here tomorrow... say about one o'clock. I'll meet you in the lounge...

'And listen Claire', he laughed. 'Sharon's my niece and

175

you're her young friend... Oh and what size does Sharon take? ... All shall be revealed tomorrow! ... And what's her favourite colour? ... Yes, OK... And by the way, I'm in tweeds, I'm limping and using a stick...'

'Aye, something like that!' he laughed again.

*

That evening, after an excellent dinner of Scottish-French cuisine, washed down with an expensive claret, Dan spent hours poring over maps and sketching out plans on a notebook. The next morning he walked along to Cameron Toll shopping centre where he bought a pile of newspapers, a packet of computer printing paper and a guillotine. He later took a taxi into town and bought an expensive cashmere ladies jumper and, as he wandered back towards his hotel, he noticed something in an antique/junk shop on Causewayside that caught his eye. It was an ornate little wooden box that turned out to be a solitaire game. He bought it. Later he booked a table for lunch on the following day in a high end restaurant in town.

At 12.45, he was sitting at a small table in the hotel lounge bar with a large whisky in his hand, staring out the window at the busy traffic and longing for the peace and quiet of Cill Donnain.

Claire and Sharon arrived five minutes later and went straight to his table. Claire was in her student garb, but Sharon was dressed in a smart blue suit and high heels, but not quite succeeding in looking matronly—her bleached hair and make-up didn't quite fit. Dan stood to greet them.

'My wee niece Sharon, and looking as lovely as ever!'

'Oh Uncle Dan, stop it. But you're looking awful thin. I hope you're looking after yourself.'

Sharon put her arms round him and gave him a hug, but once she had her arms round him, she didn't want to let go. She kissed him on the cheek.

'Me? Never better!' said Dan extricating himself. 'And

who's your young friend?'

'Oh this is Claire, she works with me.'

'Nice to see you, Claire,' he said, giving her a hug too. 'Now ladies, what can I get you?'

'A vodka and lime for me and a G&T for Claire, please.'

Dan went to the bar, limping and using his stick. Sharon looked wide-eyed at Claire.

'You didn't tell me he was so gorgeous!

'Now, Sharon, behave! He's your uncle, remember!'

Sharon rolled her eyes.

When they'd finished their drinks, they went through to the dining room for lunch and chatted merrily but disjointedly about his trip down and his impressions of how Edinburgh had changed, and how he was looking to make some investments while he was in town. When lunch was over, Dan said, 'Come on up and see my room, you'll like it."

'Are you sure your reputation can stand it?' whispered Sharon, smiling.

Dan chuckled, and they were soon in his room. Dan and Sharon sat in the two armchairs and Claire sat on the bed.

'So neither of you will go to the police?'

'You know we can't,' Sharon shook her head.

'I know.' Dan paused. 'Right, are you willing to help me? I'll deal with him my own way, but I need your help.'

'You know we want to', said Sharon, 'but we're scared. It's not right what he's been doing—the way he's treating Claire—and that family—and your grandson... that was evil.' Her voice started to break and she felt tears welling up.

'I'm going to get you both well away before anything happens. So if anything goes wrong—which it's not— you're both going to be safe. You know I can do it.'

'Yes, I believe you can,' said Sharon drying her tears with a tissue.

'But when Tam Moncrieff goes down, his whole empire goes down with him—including The Paradise. You understand that?'

Sharon and Claire both nodded, and Claire said, 'That's a price we're happy to pay'.

Sharon added, 'Anyway, my heart's not in it anymore, if it ever was.'

'Right,' said Dan, 'tell me everything I need to know about yourselves and about Tam Moncrieff, Billy King and Jake Hetherington. And then I'll tell you what we're going to do.'

Dan learned, among many other things, the important information that Sharon's father had been in the army around the same time as himself and had served in Northern Ireland where he'd been killed by the IRA. Dan took copious notes. He then outlined to them exactly how they were all going to proceed.

After a couple of hours, Sharon and Claire got ready to leave, but not before Dan presented Sharon with a gaily wrapped parcel. When she opened it, she found an expensive cashmere jumper in her favourite shade of fuchsia pink and the right size too!

'When you speak to Billy later on,' said Dan, 'be sure you're wearing it and don't be shy about telling where you got it!'

*

That evening, Sharon was at the reception desk of the Paradise Sauna, and she and Billy were chatting.

'You know how you were saying business was a bit slow for Tam just now?' she ventured.

'Yeah, what of it? I hope you haven't been blabbing.'

'Don't be silly. No, it's just that there's this man I know. He and my Dad were in the army together. He tried to save Dad that time in Ireland. Of course he didn't manage, but…

'And?'

'Well, he's in town just now. He's from up North, somewhere near Inverness—has a farm, and he's loaded. I mean he's just throwing money around. He's staying in this posh hotel and he treated me to lunch there today. And look at this cashmere jumper he bought me. That costs at least £200.'

'Very nice, but so what?'

'Just this. He's got a real chip on his shoulder. He's always been anti-authority, anti-establishment. He says people like my Dad and him risked their lives and for what? What thanks did they get?

'Well, he's finally come into some money and he's looking to make some more. He started talking about the amount of money people could make in the drugs scene and he asked me if I knew anyone. Of course I said no.'

'Clever girl! It could be some sort of trap. But I'll mention it to Tam and we'll see. In the meantime say nothing to this guy, a'right?'

'Don't worry—I don't want to get involved. But I'm sure it's not a trap. He's not that sort of man.'

Billy made a quick exit. Outside he got into his car—a black Jaguar S-type. He took out his phone and made a call.

*

In the early hours, Sharon was locking up, switching off lights. She put on her coat, set the alarm and had a last look round before going out the front door. She locked it and looked up and down the street. It was deserted. She set off up the street. Her flat wasn't far and she enjoyed the walk home when the streets were nearly deserted. It was just this first street that was a bit dark, but after that she'd be on the main streets.

There were several parked cars on her side of the street and, a few cars back, one pulled out but did not go past. She could hear its engine just behind her. After a few yards, she became convinced it was following her. She looked round nervously, but couldn't see who was driving because of the blazing headlights.

She stopped and fumbled in her bag for her phone. The car stopped too. She couldn't immediately lay her hands on her phone and she panicked. She set off at a quicker pace but, restricted in her tight skirt and high heels, she couldn't move fast. The car followed. She broke into as near a run as she could manage, her stiletto heels clicking out a staccato rhythm on the pavement.

Suddenly the car surged forward and stopped in front of her. She saw the number plate—B16 TAM. The passenger door opened.

'It's you, Tam! What a fright you gave me!'

'Get in!'

'How nice of you to offer me a lift home!' she said getting in and trying to sound normal.

'I can do all sorts of nice things for people who are nice to me,' shot back Tam.

'Oh aye?'

'And I can do all sorts of not so nice things to people who aren't nice to me. You with me, Sharon?'

'Oh aye, Tam.' She tried to smile, while on the inside she was in turmoil.

'How long have you known this guy? The guy you told Billy about. What's his name?'

'Eh, it's Dan, Dan Mackay. I haven't seen him for a year or two, but I've known him since before Dad died, and after—he used to come and check if Mum was OK—until she died. I used to call him Uncle,' she laughed. 'But Dad thought the world of him. He said he was really hard, but there's no one you'd want more on your side when the chips were down.'

'Can I trust him? Can I trust you, Sharon?'

'You can trust me all right. You know that. And he's always been straight with me. I don't think he's got anything to do with the police, if that's what you mean. In fact, quite the opposite—he can't stand them. I just thought it might help...' her voice trailed off.

'How do we get in touch with him?'

'He's staying at the Kilgraston Hotel in Newington. I had lunch with him there earlier.'

'Hmm, very posh. What does he look like?'

'Well, he's quite old and bent now. He's got long grey hair. Walks with a limp—he got hurt in the same blast that killed my Dad. Wears a tweed suit.'

'A tweed suit!' Tam smirked. 'OK. We'll deal with it. You don't let on.'

Tam stopped outside Sharon's flat. She was just fumbling with the seatbelt release when Tam's hand came down on hers, pinning her. He leant across her so his face was inches from hers.

'I'm taking a big risk on this one, Sharon. It better no' go wrong. Remember I can be nice...' He pressed his lips lightly against her cheek, 'Or not so nice...' He suddenly bit her on the neck, making her squeal.

'So you'd tell me if there was anything wrong with all this, wouldn't you, Sharon?'

'Of course. You don't need to frighten me, Tam Moncrieff. We go way back.'

He chuckled, released her and unfastened her seatbelt.

'Night, night, Sharon. Pleasant dreams.'

Sharon got out of the car, smiled and waved at Tam as he drove off. She stumbled up to the door feeling her neck with her hand. She was fighting the sobs that rose in her throat as she fumbled with her key and let herself in.

*

The following day, after a big breakfast, Dan asked the receptionist to call a taxi for him. He was going into town. He

181

was wearing his green tweed suit, shirt and tie, but he left his coat as it promised to be a hot day. He had his long grey hair tied back with a green tartan ribbon and had his brown Indiana Jones hat on his head. When the taxi arrived, Dan went out and noticed a blue Mazda parked down the street with several occupants. He couldn't make out who was in it, as the rear of the car was towards him and it was too far away. Dan got into the taxi and told the driver he wanted to go to the top of the Royal Mile. As he passed the Mazda, he noticed the driver was getting ready to pull out. Dan manoeuvred himself so that he could get a good view in the door mirror, and saw the Mazda was following.

Dan got out on the Lawnmarket, up near the Castle, and paid the driver. He took a look round, looking up at the buildings as if he was a tourist, but also clocking that the Mazda had stopped further down and a small balding man in a grey suit and a dumpy woman got out. Dan went into one of the expensive shops, limping and leaning on his stick, and Dumpy Woman followed him in. Dan bought a cashmere jumper for Fiona. It cost £210. As he came out of the shop, the Grey Suit was looking in the window of another shop nearby. Dan limped further up the street and as he came to the roundabout near the Castle, he gazed around at the impressive buildings—the back of the Church of Scotland Assembly Hall, St Columba's Free Church and most impressive of all, the church building that was now known by the prosaic name of The Hub, but once had a name befitting it's prominent position and gothic grandness—the Highland Tollbooth St John's. As he looked both ways for the traffic, he noticed Grey Suit was following him.

Dan looked as if he was struggling up the slope of Castlehill among the crowds of tourists heading towards the Castle. He went into The Scotch Whisky Experience and looked around at the various expensive malt whiskies, until he noticed that Grey Suit had come in and was pretending to examine the whiskies, but was clearly embarrassed when an assistant asked him if he needed help. Dan bought a 25 year old Macallan and didn't bat an eyelid as he counted out several hundred pounds of £20 notes, making sure Grey Suit saw it all. Dan left the shop and walked up to the Castle Esplanade, where he enjoyed the expansive views over the city and across the Forth to Fife.

Neither Grey Suit nor Dumpy Woman seemed anywhere in sight, but a younger smartly dressed blonde woman nearby was taking photos with her phone and seemed to be including Dan in her photos. She was so close he could smell her sweet exotic perfume. After that, she disappeared in the crowds and Dan went back down towards the Lawnmarket, but just as he was passing The Scotch Whisky Experience, he smelt her perfume again and he stopped suddenly. Exotic Perfume Lady collided with him and stumbled, clutching her knee.

'Oh, I'm most terribly sorry!' exclaimed Dan solicitously.

'No, no, it was entirely my fault,' said the young lady as she limped a few steps to sit on the stone parapet in front of the building between two flower boxes. As Dan followed to see if she was all right, he had a chance to get a good look at her. She was wearing a pink and white flowery dress with a little white jacket and white stilettos. Her golden blonde hair was pulled back in a ponytail and she had a pretty face, but there was just something about her makeup that just didn't seem to match the image her clothes were trying to portray of an innocent young woman.

As Dan came up, she had crossed her legs, pulled up her dress and was examining her rather shapely knee. Dan decided to play along with her little game. 'Oh dear, you've hurt your knee. Let me see.'

'Oh, it's nothing. It sometimes happens when I get a

jolt,' she smiled sweetly up at him.

Dan knelt down with some difficulty, and she offered no resistance as he pretended to examine her knee. Then he suddenly pressed hard on the patellar tendon causing her lower leg to kick out in a reflex reaction.

'Oh my!' she exclaimed, 'You've fixed it. The pain has gone! How did you do that?'

'It's just an old trick I learned in the Army.'

'You were in the Army? When was that?

Very soon they were chatting away. Then Dan said, 'Look I'm just going for lunch here at the Witchery next door. Let me treat you to lunch. It's the least I can do.'

She needed no persuasion, and they were very soon seated at the table Dan had booked earlier for himself in this high class restaurant, but the waitress had no difficulty in placing another setting at the table. The young lady said she was Gina, and Dan said he was Dan, and they shook hands and laughed. Dan ordered the three course lunch. He had mackerel ceviche, followed by collops of venison, and that great Scottish favourite, sticky toffee pudding, for desert. Gina struggled with knowing what some of the dishes were, but with a little help from Dan she chose haggis with pineapple chutney, followed by duck with hazelnut parfait, and the apple and almond crumble for dessert. Dan ordered a bottle of Cloudy Bay Sauvignon Blanc from New Zealand, and ensured that Gina drank most of it.

Their conversation began with Gina asking Dan all about himself, and he played up the rich farmer bit, telling her he was in town to clinch a business deal, and how he had bought an expensive cashmere jumper for his daughter (after buying one for his niece yesterday) and an even more expensive bottle of malt whisky for a good friend back home. Gina insisted on seeing the presents, but was more impressed with the cashmere jumper than with the whisky.

But when Dan started asking her all about herself, she was much less forthcoming at first. She just said she had a boring job in an office, working for a property services company, and when Dan casually asked her what it was called, she hesitated momentarily and then said it was Morrison & Co. But as she got a little tipsy, she began to open up more and when Dan asked if her boss was nice, she giggled, 'Oh yes, although he does have wandering hands!' She immediately blushed and said, 'Look I'll need to be getting back. I was running an errand for my boss before lunch and he'll expect me back.'

Dan insisted on paying the bill and escorting her out of the restaurant. He even offered to see her to her office, but by this time Gina was rather flustered and said she had to run, and off she minced down Castlehill, her stiletto heels clicking rapidly on the pavement. Dan followed at a leisurely pace and saw her heading down Johnstone Terrace towards where Claire had told him Tam Moncrieff's office was.

Dan smiled to himself, walked down the Lawnmarket, hailed a taxi and headed back to his hotel. After resting on his bed for about an hour, he decided to go out for a stroll round East Suffolk Park to stretch his legs. On returning to the hotel, the receptionist said, 'Oh, Mr Mackay, there's a message for you. Ah, here it is,' and she handed Dan a small brown envelope addressed MR D. MACKAY.

Dan asked, 'Do you know who left it?'

'Sorry,' the receptionist said, 'He didn't give a name. Said he was a friend of yours. We chatted for a wee while. He said you liked the high life and asked if your taste in wine was as expensive as ever. I thought he was getting a bit cheeky, so I said I'd see you got his note.'

'What did he look like?'

'Very non-descript, really. Small, balding... he was wearing a grey suit.'

'Oh, aye—now I know who it was.' Dan went off grinning.

Back in his room, Dan opened the envelope. The note, like the address on the envelope was typed. It read: IF YOU WANT TO DO BUSINESS, BE AT BOSWELL'S PUB AT 8 TONIGHT. He smiled and nodded to himself as he looked out the window. He then made a call.

'Loony? Hello… Well I've had an interesting day. Been followed up and down the Royal Mile! ... Someone's checking up on me! … Anyway, it's on… Tonight at 8… Where about is Boswell's Pub?... Ah right… Ok, just make sure you keep Jake away from Boswell's tonight'.

Dan then phoned Jim Matheson and told him to expect that inquiry from Lothian and Borders Police that night shortly after eight o'clock. He stressed that Jim should make sure he got the name of the officer making the enquiry.

*

That evening Claire was walking through the Grassmarket towards Paradise Sauna, speaking on her mobile.

'Jake—hey—it's Claire. Can you bring me some stuff tonight?...'

'Jake! I'll make it worth your while!' she replied teasingly.

'No really, I mean it… No, not tonight, 'cos I'm working. I'm booked up. But definitely later in the week…'

'Come on, I need it, Jake. Can you bring it to work at 8?...'

'Ooh, thank you, Jake. I'll make sure it's memorable.'

She called off and smiled a twisted smile.

CHAPTER SIXTEEN

Dan got out of his taxi outside Boswell's Pub in the New Town just before eight o'clock. He was dressed in his tweed suit, check shirt and tie, his long brown coat and his leather Indiana Jones hat, with his hair tied back with the green tartan ribbon. He was carrying his brown briefcase and was leaning on his stick as he limped towards the pub. He spotted the white BMW with the B16 TAM number plate parked along the street.

Dan entered slowly and had a good look round. It was an old fashioned pub with plenty brass and leather and various hidden corners and no TV screens. Several people stared at this odd looking old guy in tweeds with a shepherd's crook, but Dan looked at each in turn with steady eyes, and they looked away. He went up to the bar.

'What would you like, sir?' asked the young brunette behind the bar.

After surveying the shelf of malt whiskies, he said, 'A Clynelish—a large one.'

She had difficulty identifying the whisky. Dan had to point it out. She was about to put ice in the glass when Dan stopped her.

'No ice, thank you! Don't put ice in a malt whisky,' he smiled. 'Have you a bottle of spring water...? Just perfect— a wee drop of that brings out the flavour.'

'I'm sorry... I'm new... I don't know much about whiskies.'

'Don't worry! There's a lot of people more experienced

than you who don't know that! You'll be one up on them now, won't you?'

He paid her with a twenty pound note and told her to keep the change. Her eyes opened wide and she said, 'I think you've made a mistake, sir. This is a twenty pound note!"

'No mistake,' said Dan, 'I like you. Anyway there's plenty more where that came from.'

He moved over to an empty table, and sat with the briefcase under his chair. He noticed someone who fitted Sharon's description of Billy King observing him, but pretended not to. He took a good mouthful of the whisky, squashed it in his mouth and swallowed. He breathed out a long sigh of contentment through his nose, enjoying the surprisingly exotic spiciness of this northern malt. He took a round dark wooden box out of his pocket. It had an ornate mother-of-pearl pattern on the lid. He put it on the table and opened it. It was the pocket solitaire he'd bought the day before. He started to play, removing the ivory pegs one by one.

Gradually people lost interest in him, and he checked Red Billy getting up and disappearing through the back. Dan took a sip of his whisky and returned to the solitaire.

The barmaid came up to his table as she was collecting empty glasses from other tables. She bent down, pretending to wipe his table.

'Excuse me, but a gentleman would like to have a word with you in the back room.'

'Oh aye?' said Dan, not looking up. 'What's he want?'

'Don't know,' she looked nervously towards the back of the pub. 'He just said to go through now.'

'All right. Tell him I'll be through in a minute.'

'It's opposite the Gents. Says "Staff Only" on the door.' Then she added in a lower voice, 'But I wouldn't keep him waiting if I were you.'

Dan looked up briefly and smiled. 'But you're not me, are you, love?'

The barmaid returned to the bar and Dan returned to his game, relishing another mouthful of his whisky.

In the back room, Tam was sitting at a card table, shuffling a pack of cards and smoking a big cigar. He was dressed in suit and tie. Red Billy entered rather agitated.

'He's still sitting there—just sitting there playing some game in a wooden box—I think it's solitaire—and drinking his whisky. He's got some nerve.'

'Calm yourself, my man. I like a man with bottle. Anyway, it may show he's genuine—not too eager.' He added, 'But just you stand behind that door and be ready. We don't want to be caught napping.'

'I don't think there'll be a problem. There are no other strangers in the pub—just regulars.'

Dan finished his game leaving one peg in the middle. He downed the last of his whisky, and then replaced all the pegs, closed the lid and placed the solitaire carefully in his pocket. He got up with difficulty, picked up his case and stick and headed through the back.

In the back room Tam and Billy heard the tap, tap of a stick getting louder. There was a knock. Billy was behind the door. Tam waited, shuffling the cards. Another knock. Tam still waited. Then there was the tap, tap of a stick moving away from the door.

Tam looked up with a smile of appreciation on his face and indicated with his thumb for Billy to open the door, which he did. Dan turned.

'Ah, I thought I was in the wrong place...'

'Depends what you want,' said Billy.

'I was told someone wanted to do business, but maybe I was misinformed...' He turned to go.

'Billy, that's no way to treat a guest!' exclaimed Tam smoothly. 'Come away in, Mr Mackay.'

Dan limped into the room and Billy closed the door behind him.

'I'm sorry, but Mr King here is not renowned for his manners. Just one other thing, though—he'll just check you in case you're carrying. I can't be too careful.'

'Certainly. I quite understand. I would do the same myself.'

Dan holds out his arms a little, staggering as he loses the support of his stick.

Billy, standing behind him, ran his hands over Dan's coat. 'What's this then?' he said, feeling something suspicious.

'Oh aye... that's my rolled up umbrella.'

Billy came round in front of Dan and fished out a short folded black umbrella from inside his long coat.

'Can't be too careful in Edinburgh in June!' commented Dan deadpan.

Billy reached inside the other side of Dan's coat. 'But what about this then?'

'Ah, well, that's my sawn-off...'

'Bloody hell...' Billy hauled it out.

'My sawn-off chair leg.'

Tam and Billy stared stupidly at the long rounded chair leg in Billy's hand.

'You'd never believe the number of scrapes that old chair leg has got me out of! There was this guy who came at me with a knife...'

Suddenly Tam laughed, releasing the tension.

'You're one cool cat, Mr Mackay! Come and have a seat.'

Dan sat down opposite Tam, lowering himself into the chair with some difficulty and placing his case on the table between them. Billy stood behind Dan, his right hand inside his jacket.

'Well, Mr Mackay, I understand you're looking for some

business I might put your way.'

'I am that. Let's put it this way. I have a lot of money to invest. And I want to invest in your product for two reasons. First, the high return, of course, but second, I want to keep the heat off my other interests. In short, I want to open up a new market in the North. I've got people lined up all over the North from Stornoway to Elgin and from Fort William to Wick who'll take it off my hands. And of course if this deal turns out to your satisfaction, I have contacts in several of the harbours of the North and with fishermen too. So, if your lines of supply were ever becoming difficult, I'm sure I could arrange something—for a small fee, of course!'

Dan opened the case revealing the neatly stacked twenty pound notes.

'That's ten grand. Go on, you can check it, if you want.'

Tam's face could hardly conceal his amazement as he checked a couple of the bundles of the notes. He'd suspected Mackay wasn't for real somehow. He was rapidly changing his opinion.

'The thing is,' said Dan, 'this deal is worth a hundred times what's in that case.'

Tam looked up astonished. 'You mean a bloody million pounds! You're joking!'

'I never joke about money, Mr Moncrieff. A million pounds for the best Horse you've got. But I don't have time to mess around. I want it quick.'

'How quick?'

'Tomorrow. I'm heading up the road day after tomorrow. I don't want to hang around here too long and arouse any suspicions. Anyway my contacts are all waiting.'

'No can do. Even if I knew you're for real, that's impossible.'

Dan snapped the lid of the case shut and clicked the catches. 'Oh well. I thought you were the man. I've heard a lot about Big Tam Moncrieff around town. I didn't think you'd let me down. But I can go elsewhere. I hear there's others in the market now.' He stood up to go.

'Hey, not so fast. I never said I couldn't do it. I just need time to check you out, that's all.'

'You know Sharon. You can trust her. I take it that's how you contacted me. What more do you need?'

'Sharon's a good girl, but she doesn't know shit about business.'

'True. Right. OK. I'd prefer to do business with you for Sharon's sake. So if you want to check me out, here's what to do. I take it you have some tame police contacts?'

'Of course!

'Right, get them to make enquiries with their colleagues in Northern Constabulary, Inverness, about a certain Dan Mackay.'

'Should they ask for anyone in particular?'

'No, no, anyone on duty will do. I'm notorious enough!'

'Right, Billy, get Mr Mackay a drink, while I make a call. And the usual for ourselves.'

Tam went out a back door taking out his phone.

'A large Clynelish, please, Billy,' said Dan, adding, 'It's a malt whisky. The barmaid, the dark-haired girl, knows how I like it.'

Billy grunted and picked up an internal phone. 'Get Karen to do the same whisky for the old geyser, and the usual for Mr Moncrieff and me.'

Billy put the phone down, paced up and down and then looked at Dan.

'A word of advice. Don't mess with Big Tam Moncrieff. If you do, he'll take you down.'

Just then Karen came in with the drinks.

'A lot of people have tried to do that, Mr King. See this scar here?' He pointed to the scar on the side of his neck.

'This guy came at me with a knife and cut me ...'

'So your chair leg didn't help you there then.'

'Thanks, love,' said Dan to Karen, before continuing to Billy, 'That was twenty years ago—I've got the scar all right, but he's still in hospital.'

Billy gave a twisted grin.

Dan winked at Karen as she left, 'He's a surgeon.'

Billy snorted, 'Ha! Very funny. You're a funny man, Dan Mackay, but funny won't cut it with Big Tam.'

In a minute Tam returned. 'We should hear back in a wee while.' He took a slug of his whisky. 'So you knew Sharon's Dad?'

'Oh aye, we were in Northern Ireland together—the Queen's Own Highlanders. Jimmy Henderson was killed by an IRA bomb there in 1979—the same bomb that left me with this bad leg. I kept in touch with his widow Jean after that. Sharon was only a young thing then—must have been about 14 or so. Did you know the family?'

'Not really. I knew they were from Gracemount, but I only got to know Sharon after both her parents were dead.'

'Aye it was a shame that about Jean. I don't think she ever got over Jimmy's death, and then it was the big C that took her away.'

'So what is it you do, Mr Mackay?' asked Tam, changing the subject. 'You must have the readies for a deal like this.'

'Oh well, a little bit o' this and little bit o' that, you know', Dan smiled. 'Farming—I've a couple of thousand sheep—amongst other things. Poaching on a rather large scale—you wouldn't believe the money in that just now. You know the hills are just moving with deer. The estates just aren't shooting enough. I have no idea why. I'll send you down a haunch of venison, when this deal is done, if you'd like. And if you know of any high class restaurants down here looking for supplies, just let me know.'

Tam was intrigued as Dan waxed lyrical about the Highlands. Like many from his particular background, Tam was not often out of the Central Belt and rarely even to Glasgow. Anything north of Perth was a mystery to him.

After what seemed an age to Dan as he tried to spin as many yarns as he could about how good life was in the Highlands if it wasn't for the absentee landowners and the police, Tam's phone rang and he headed off to answer it.

Dan looked at Billy and asked in a friendly manner. 'Have you known Mr Moncrieff a long time?'

'Long enough. Why do you want to know?' said Billy taking a swallow of his whisky.

'Just wondering if I can trust him.'

Billy nearly choked on his whisky and spluttered, 'Trust him! You can trust him all right, trust him to bury you if you try to cross him in a deal… or set him up. The question is: can we trust you?' Billy looked meaningfully at Dan.

'No need to worry about that on my score. I've as much to lose if this gets out.'

Billy started pacing up and down again. Dan took out his solitaire.

Time dragged, but in no more than ten minutes Tam returned.

'Well, the Northern Polis have nothing on you.'

Billy grinned a kind of told-you-so grin, but Dan just nodded.

'But they'd damn well like to!' added Tam laughing. They all laughed, and Tam grabbed his whisky and clinked glasses with Dan.

'Here's to you Dan Mackay, and here's to the deal.'

They drained their glasses. Tam slammed his glass down on the table and held out his big hand. Dan took it and they shook hands.

'My friendly local Inspector contacted Northern and

they eventually put him through to someone who sounded very interested to hear that a certain Mr Mackay was raising eyebrows in Edinburgh. He said he'd been trying to collar you for years!'

Dan smiled at this description of his friend Jim Matheson.

'But I'm sorry to hear about your wife, Dan. He said she'd died a while back.'

'Aye, I still miss her. I miss her trying to keep me on the straight and narrow! But ach well, it has its compensations. She had inherited a fortune from a wealthy uncle and when she died it all came to me.'

'Aye, that's what they said.'

'But, do you know this? She also had quite a jewellery collection. You know, I sold it recently, and just one piece was worth fifty grand. It had this stone in it about the size of your thumbnail and it was an Alexandrite. I don't know if you've ever heard of it?'

'Aye, I have,' put in Billy, suddenly interested. 'I take an interest in antiques and gems in particular. It's an amazing stone—green in daylight and red at night!'

'That's the one!' said Dan.

'So you're not short of readies, Dan,' said Tam pointedly. 'You've been buying expensive presents, I hear, and treating young ladies to expensive lunches.'

Dan looked up surprised. 'What? Mr Moncrieff, I do believe you've been spying on me!'

'You can't be too careful in my line of business'.

'Well, you know, I never saw anyone. How did you do it? It wasn't that nice young lady that hurt her knee, was it?'

'She was just one of them. And her knee wasn't hurt.'

'Well, of all the… I see I'll need to sharpen up my game, if I'm to keep up with you, Mr Moncrieff!'

'Anyway,' said Tam, 'It just confirmed that you're a man

with the kind of money required.'

'You need have no worries on that score. I'll have your million for you tomorrow.'

'OK. Tomorrow it is.'

'All right—make it after midnight—say one o'clock. I like things nice and quiet. Where? Here?'

'Na. There's a little antique shop on Montaygie Street...'

*

Dan was back at his hotel before midnight. He called Claire.

'Claire? You OK?'

'Yeah, fine. How did it go?'

'We're on for tomorrow night—after midnight, one o'clock in the morning.'

'Yes! Excellent! You did it! Well done, old man!'

'It's not done yet. That's only the beginning. The most dangerous part is still to come. And less of the "old man"!'

'Sorry! But I'm so high.'

'You haven't used?'

'No! No, I'm just so excited.'

'Well, stay calm, Claire. Now, have you got hold of that student friend of yours?'

'Yes. His name is Don, Don Fraser, and he doesn't do drugs or anything like that. He doesn't know Jake at all.'

'But can he drive?

'Yes, yes. He's got his driving licence.'

'OK then. I'll meet Sharon for lunch tomorrow as arranged. I'll give her the van keys, she'll pass them on to you and then you give them to Don. Tell him to move the van so that he arrives at Montaygie Street at 6.30—that means he should get a space opposite Kings Antiques and he won't have to pay for parking. And I want him to park it facing towards South Clerk Street, not St Leonards. Then he'll find me sitting on a bench beside the tennis courts in the Meadows. He'll sit down beside me and rummage in his rucksack so the keys and other stuff fall out. I'll laugh and help him to pick stuff up. I'll pick up the keys and stick the thirty pounds in his bag. Have you got all that?'

'Eh, it's a lot to remember. Do we really need to be this careful?'

'Yes, we do. Remember I was tailed yesterday. I'll be vigilant, but you never can tell. Anyway I'll write it all down, including where the van is, and give it to Sharon to pass on.

'Now remember it's after midnight tomorrow—one o'clock in the morning. That's when you've got to set up you-know-who, but by that time you and Sharon have to be long gone.'

'I know, leave it to me.'

Remember I'm depending on you. But take care.'

'You too. And thanks… for everything.'

CHAPTER SEVENTEEN

The next morning, Dan was in his hotel room. Using a £100 note as a template, he was meticulously cutting up his newspapers and computer paper with the guillotine and putting them into small packs. He put a rubber band round each pack and put each pack in turn in his briefcase—three lengthwise in three rows. Then he stacked nine packs neatly under a hundred-pound note and finally covered them with nine solid packs of hundred-pound notes, each containing £1,000.

Dan had been to a local branch of his own bank first thing that morning and managed to persuade the girl at the counter to take pity on this old, eccentric man who wanted to see the manager about changing a large amount of money into high denomination notes. She'd checked with her manager and, while he waited, Dan noticed the Grey Suit from the day before pretending to read some leaflets. The manager came out and invited Dan through to his room. Dan explained that he'd sold his late wife's jewellery because he needed the money to pay for some new farm stock down in the Borders, but the man who bought the jewellery had only had £20 notes, and Dan wanted £100 notes as they would be easier and less conspicuous to carry. He showed the manager the pawnbrokers receipt and opened his briefcase. The manager was astonished to see the £10,000 in £20 notes and, concerned about money laundering, he checked on computer, but discovered that the serial numbers were from thirty years before and there was nothing suspicious about them. 'That's all you know,' thought Dan. The manager didn't want to just change the notes, but he finally agreed that if Dan paid the £10,000 into his own bank account, he could then withdraw the same amount in £100 notes. Dan had asked that the whole transaction be done in the manager's office, as he didn't want anyone seeing such large sums being handed over.

So Dan had walked out of the bank with two packs of £100 notes each containing £5000 in the deep pockets of his long coat. His case was now empty, but for the benefit of the Grey Suit, he carried it as if it was much heavier.

Back at the hotel, when he finished filling his case to look like a million, he checked out of the hotel and asked them to keep his suitcase and holdall until he came back for them in a day or two. They were happy to oblige, as he had tipped very generously. He was wearing his long brown coat over a khaki-coloured shirt and trousers. His hair was tied back under his Indiana Jones hat. He had light walking boots on his feet. His tweed suit was packed with his other things in his suitcase. The cashmere jumper for Fiona and the bottle of malt whisky, along with his umbrella and chair leg, were all that his old holdall now contained. Carrying his briefcase and leaning on his stick, he took a taxi into town to meet Sharon for lunch at The Outsider restaurant.

*

Mid-afternoon at the Paradise, Cheryl, one of the other girls, was at reception. She was a big girl with short spiky black hair and a plump attractive face, and she was wearing a tight red Lycra top and glossy skin-tight black leggings. She was reading a magazine. The intercom buzzed.

'Paradise Sauna… Hi, Claire.'

Claire entered carrying a large holdall. She had just come from passing on Dan's keys and instructions, which Sharon had given her, to Don Fraser.

'Hi Cheryl. Where's Sharon?'

'Called in sick. Asked me to fill in. Anyway, what're you doing in? You're not on today.'

'I know. But Cheryl...?'

'What are you up to?'

'You know Jake?'

'You mean snobby Jonathan Kenneth Hetherington?' Cheryl did her best to imitate Jake's posh accent.

'That's the one. He's supposed to be my client tonight. At half past twelve. Can I ask a favour, Cheryl? I want to get the room ready just now and leave it all set up for later. It'll be quiet tonight, so could you keep it locked?'

'You're definitely up to something!'

'If you promise to keep it a secret, I'll let you have a peek before I go.'

About half an hour later, Claire and Cheryl emerged from one of the rooms laughing.

'It'll serve him jolly well right, the stuck up snob!' chuckled Cheryl.

Claire locked the door, put the key in a little brown envelope and handed it to Cheryl. 'Right, keep this behind the desk and don't give it to him until after 12.45. He's going to be here at 12.30. Just keep him waiting. And then when he's been in the room, say you've remembered there was a phone call for him from Billy King. Just write this down,' and she dictated to Cheryl, 'Mr King phoned to say if Jake appears, tell him to be at Montaygie Street at 1 am. It's a big one. Mr King's mobile is broke.'

Cheryl raised her eyebrows and looked at Claire. 'Is this for real?'

'Of course not. It just means he'll have to high tail it and not give you any hassle. Just say you forgot about it earlier. Look, I really appreciate this, Cheryl.'

'I hope we don't get into trouble over this!'

'No chance. Jake will be too embarrassed to tell anyone. And he won't want Big Tam knowing he tried it on with me, know what I mean?'

'OK, but you owe me one—a big one!'

'I certainly do!' She hugged Cheryl and went off smiling.

Half an hour later, she and Sharon were heading north across the Forth Road Bridge in Sharon's old pink Fiat Punto. They were laughing.

'I just wish I could just see Jake's face!' giggled Claire.

'I just wish I could see Big Tam's face at one o'clock,' said Sharon, turning serious. 'I wonder what Dan's going to do?'

'I don't know. He wouldn't say. He said it was better if we didn't know. I think he'll shoot them, but he'll do it so as no one will ever know it was him.'

They stared out the window, both with their own thoughts.

*

After surreptitiously giving the detailed instructions for Don and his van keys to Sharon and seeing her off from the restaurant, Dan spent the afternoon in town, mainly sitting in a café reading a small paperback, being very careful no one touched his long brown coat or his briefcase that he had placed beside him. He then limped round to sit on a park bench beside the Meadows tennis court. All day he had been aware he was being tailed and watched, so he smiled to himself as he pulled his hat down over his face and had a nap for a couple of hours in the warm afternoon sun. His tail would be pretty bored by the time the day was through!

His vibrating phone alarm woke him at 6.20pm. By this time there were few people around, and he could see no one that might be observing him, but he went back to reading his paperback and then, when Don Fraser came shuffling along and sat down beside him, he went through with the little agreed pantomime just in case he had missed someone watching. After half an hour, he set off to have dinner at a steak restaurant on West Preston Street.

*

While Dan was enjoying his leisurely dinner, Billy King was driving to the outskirts of Edinburgh to an old run-down farm in Gilmerton. There were several old unoccupied cottages, a rather dilapidated farmhouse and several outbuildings. Billy parked the car and walked round to the barns. The farm was on its last legs. Very soon, like so many other areas in the 'Greenbelt', it would be bought up by developers for building luxury homes, and Tam would have to find somewhere else to stash his goods.

Billy found the farmer, old Nat Brewer, at the entrance to one of the barns that was stacked with straw bales. He was gazing out onto the fields and was startled out of his reverie by the sound of Billy's approach.

'Good evening, Nat. How are you?'

'Oh, it's yourself, Mr King.' His long weather-beaten face carried years of worry. 'Well, to tell you the truth, I'm not too good. The farm is finished. The supermarkets pay peanuts for milk. And the landowner wants to sell to the developers. It'll soon be all over.'

'Sorry to hear that, Nat. But you'll be glad of the little business we've put your way. In fact that's why I'm here — to collect one of the boxes I left with you a month ago.'

'Oh aye. Well, I'll not lie, I have been glad of the rent you pay for storage. It seems very generous for the little space they take up.'

'Ah, but that retro music equipment is very expensive, and I need somewhere safe and secure… and secret to store it.'

'Well, I'll just get the forklift.' Brewer went out and returned driving the tractor with the forklift on front. He removed two stacks of bales revealing several black flight cases with heavy aluminium binding and corners. Billy went in and picked up one of the cases and Brewer returned the piles of bales.

Billy waited till he finished and handed him an envelope. 'Thanks again, Nat. We'll be in touch.' He walked off back to his car, leaving Nat Brewer sitting on the tractor staring at the large bundle of notes in the opened envelope, shaking his head with a disbelieving, conflicted frown on his face.

*

In the long dusk of a northern summer evening, lights were glowing in the windows of Dan's croft house. The sound of a car could be heard approaching. Sharon's Fiat came into view and as it swung round in front of the house, the front door opened and Fiona stepped out with Fleet beside her.

Sharon and Claire got out and Fiona went to meet them.

'Hello, I'm Fiona.'

'Hi, I'm Claire and this is Sharon.'

They all shook hands. Fleet came up to Claire and nuzzled against her leg. She knelt down to stroke him.

'You'll have a friend for life, if you make a fuss of him like that!' said Fiona as she helped Sharon with their luggage.

'You found your way all right? Were Dad's directions OK?'

Claire laughed, 'We got lost a few times. Map-reading was never one of my talents!'

'Well, come away in, you'll be starving. I've been expecting you,' said Fiona, taking Sharon's small case, and escorting them inside. 'Dad phoned earlier to say you'd be coming, and that you would probably take longer than he would!'

'Is he really a fast driver?' asked Claire. 'Rory used to say he was really fast...' she broke off, realising the mention of Rory's name was painful to Fiona. 'I'm sorry... I'm sorry for everything. Please forgive me.' And she suddenly broke down in the hallway, great sobs shaking her body.

Fiona put down the case she was carrying, and put her arms round Claire, tears rolling down her cheeks. They stood like that for a long time, Sharon standing beside them with her head bowed. When Fiona finally got command of her voice, she said, 'You don't need to be sorry, Claire. As Dad says, you're not to blame for Rory's death. At one time, in my darkest hours, I blamed you. I was bitter against everyone—blamed everyone, blamed God. But I came to see that was wrong. You're a victim, Claire, not a criminal. And anything you may have done wrong, I forgive you. I've been learning a lot about forgiveness recently. There's so much I need to be forgiven for.'

*

At half past midnight Big Tam's BMW turned off South Clerk Street onto Montague Street and parked a bit past King's Antiques, facing the other way from Dan's van, but on the same side of the street. Tam and Billy got out. They were both dressed casually in jeans and trainers. Tam took a large black briefcase out of the boot (they had transferred the contents of the flight case earlier). As they were about to cross the street, they passed the old Transit van, and Billy said, 'Look at that old piece of junk! They stick wide wheels on it and they think it'll go faster!'

'They've even stuck a fancy exhaust pipe on it!' laughed Tam, as they headed into the shop. 'It's a wonder they haven't put go-faster stripes on it!'

*

Just a little earlier, Jake was heading to Paradise Sauna. He was in a hurry. But that didn't stop him checking himself in a plate glass window and smiling to himself as he passed.

Cheryl was sitting at reception, filing her nails and looking bored. The clock above the reception desk said 12.30. The buzzer sounded and Cheryl picked up the receiver.

'Paradise Sauna.'

'Who? Oh, Jonathan Kenneth! I'm afraid you're too early. Claire isn't ready.' She put the receiver down and resumed her manicure. The buzzer sounded again, longer this time.

Cheryl seemed intent on examining each red polished nail in detail. The buzzer sounded again, this time it didn't stop. She picked up the receiver.

'Paradise Sauna.'

She was greeted by a volley of expletives from Jake, to which she responded, 'You'd better apologise and change your tone, or I won't let you in at all!' She put the receiver down again.

The buzzer sounded a short ring. Cheryl picked it up again, and listened.

'Well, that's much better, Mr Hetherington. I suppose you can come in, but you'll have to wait.'

Jake came in, looking as if he might explode any minute. 'Where's Sharon?'

'Sick.'

'Funny, Big Tam never mentioned that to me earlier.'

'Oh, what does that remind me of? Can't remember. But obviously you don't get told everything! And that's Mr Moncrieff to you.'

Jake ignored this subtle attempt by Cheryl to put him is his place. 'Right, where is she?'

'At home in bed I imagine…'

'What! Claire's not here?'

'Oh, I thought you meant Sharon!'

'Not Sharon, you stupid cow! Claire!'

'Don't you take that tone with me, young man!'

Jake leant threateningly over the desk. 'Cut the crap! So where is she?'

Cheryl was unperturbed. 'You'd better start being nice, 'cos Mr Moncrieff might not take kindly to you seeing

Claire anyway.'

'You wouldn't dare.'

'Try me. Now sit down and be a good boy. She might be ready in a little while.'

Jake looked daggers at her, but reluctantly sat and looked at his watch.

*

Tam and Billy were in the back room of King's Antiques. Junk was piled everywhere, but there was a table in the middle. Tam placed his large black business case on it. Billy was restless.

'Do you think he'll show?'

'He'll show. He'd better! The only question is whether he's got the million.'

'What if he hasn't? What then? Shouldn't we've had some more heavies here?'

'No! I wanted to keep this thing quiet. Anyway, there's nothing to be worried about. I've been having him tailed. You know about yesterday. Well today he went to the bank, saw the manager and came out with his case looking a lot heavier than when he went in. Then he went back to the hotel, took a taxi into town and had lunch with Sharon. In the afternoon he read a book in a café and had a snooze in the Meadows. This evening he had a steak in that steakhouse not ten minutes from here and now he's in The Wine Glass round the corner. Wee Sammy just texted me.

'So, like I say, nothing to worry about. The two of us will be a match for that old codger. So relax, Billy boy. Anyway, it's time you went outside. Just bell me when you're sure it's all clear.' Billy exited through the front shop.

Tam sat. The old grandfather clock over his shoulder said twenty to one as it ticked slowly.

*

Jake was looking at his watch and running his hand through his hair. He jumped up and came to the reception desk.

The clock said 12.45.

'Right. That's it. I'm not waiting any longer. Where is she?'

'Well, actually' teased Cheryl, 'I think she'll be ready by now, so if you're a good boy, I'll let you have the key.'

'Key! What bloody key?'

Cheryl held up the brown envelope. 'Why! The key to Room 3, of course!'

Jake snatched at the envelope. 'Give me that!'

'Uh uh. Ask nicely. Promise to be nice to Claire.'

'I promise. Now give me the key.'

Jake grabbed the envelope, ripped it open and dashed for Room 3. He hurriedly unlocked the door and threw it open.

He was greeted by the sight of pink crepe paper tied round the large four poster bed with a ribbon and the words OPEN HERE FOR THE ONE YOU REALLY LOVE across the front.

He ripped open the paper and was confronted with a free standing mirror on the bed in which he saw his own reflection. He gaped in incomprehension which turned quickly to rage. He kicked the mirror which cracked in all directions reflecting his own shattered image. He exploded with a torrent of obscenities.

He turned and made for Reception. Cheryl was behind the desk with some other girls standing around. Jake glared at Cheryl, 'Did you know?'

'Know what?'

'Don't come the innocent with me!' he spluttered, not wanting to let the other girls hear about his humiliation.

'I don't know what you're talking about', she said superciliously, before adding, 'Oh, I've just remembered.'

'Remembered what?

'What I forgot earlier.'

Jake's exasperation was boiling over, 'What did you forget, you fat bimbo?'

'If that's your attitude, I won't give you this message from Mr King!"

Jake leaned threateningly over the desk, 'What message?' he almost screamed.

'Don't get your knickers in a twist—this one.' And she handed him the note Claire had given her earlier.

Jake stared in disbelief at the note and glanced at his watch. It said 12.50. 'You stupid bitch! Why didn't you give this to me earlier?'

He pointed a threatening finger at Cheryl as he ran for the door. 'Just you wait, you fat cow! Just you wait!' As the door was closing behind him he could hear loud, high-pitched feminine laughter pursuing him.

Jake was so angry and frustrated he wasn't thinking straight. All that was on his mind was to get to Montague Street by one o'clock. But even if he had tried to check that Billy King's mobile was out of action, it was on silent, because at that moment Billy was hiding in a close entrance screened by some cypress trees, as he checked for any suspicious activity.

Jake set off running through the Grassmarket, up Candlemaker Row, past Greyfriars Kirk and Greyfriars Bobby (the statue of the legendary Skye Terrier that was said to have sat faithfully for fourteen years by his master's grave in the nearby Greyfriars cemetery). Greyfriars Kirk was where the famous National Covenant was signed in 1638, setting the nation on a trajectory that would ultimately lead to the ending of arbitrary royal power and the establishment of constitutional democracy.

But Jake was too preoccupied to entertain any such thoughts, and even if he had, he would have dismissed them with the sarcasm he reserved for all such sentimental stories or high-sounding ideals. By the time he reached Bristo Place, he was breathing heavily; he had a stitch and had slowed to a walk. He wasn't quite as fit as he thought he was. He walked for a bit as he went across in front of the University's McEwan Hall and on to Crichton Street and West Crosscauseway, past Buccleuch Church with its high steeple pointing heavenwards. As he turned right onto St Patrick Street, he looked at his watch. It said 1.01. He started jogging as he turned left up Rankeillor Street which runs parallel to Montague Street. Near the far end he turned into a car park entrance to the left, dodged through the car park and jumped over the low wall at the back. He checked his watch again. It was 1:03.

*

A little earlier Dan had left The Wine Glass pub. The taxi he had ordered took him the few hundred yards to Kings Antiques on Montague Street. He paid and tipped the driver, asking him to return his stick to the Kilgraston Hotel, which the taxi driver was only too pleased to do, as Dan's tip was so generous. He got out and limped towards the shop entrance. He seemed tired and even more bent and lame than usual. He had spotted Billy in a darkened close, but pretended he didn't see him, but he also noticed his own van parked right where he said it should be, and Tam's BMW a little further on facing the other way. Everything was falling nicely into place. He stopped outside King's Antiques and knocked on the door.

Tam heard Dan's knock but waited till his phone buzzed. He checked that it was Billy giving the all clear and clicked it off. He went through to the darkened front shop. Dan was standing at the door silhouetted against the light. Tam opened the door to let him in and Billy very quickly came in behind him. 'All clear, Tam,' he said.

'Not trust me, Mr Moncrieff?' asked Dan with a smile.

'Oh, I trust you all right. Just making sure no one was following you.'

Tam led the way through the back, Dan limping behind

him and Billy taking up the rear.

'No stick tonight, Mr Mackay?'

'No, left it in the taxi. He was away before I realised. Stupid really. I'll pick it up tomorrow. But I've got my chair leg! Want to check it?'

'No need. What Billy's got in his pocket's more than a match for any chair leg!'

Dan laughed, 'I'm sure it is, Mr Moncrieff!'

Tam moved round to the other side of the table opposite Dan, while Billy stood slightly to one side.

Tam opened his black case so it faced Dan. It was packed with transparent packets of high grade heroin which looked as pure as snow in the fluorescent light.

'That's what a million quid looks like. But if you handle it right, Mr Mackay, it'll make you plenty more.'

Dan lifted his briefcase, laid it on the table and opened it slowly. 'And this is a million quid.'

Tam and Billy gazed eagerly at what looked like a case full of hundred pound notes. Tam was just reaching out to pick up a bundle, when there was the click of a lock and the rattle of the outside door opening through the back and Jake's breathless voice. 'It's me—Jake. Eh, there's something wrong at the Paradise…'

Tam and Billy turned towards the door leading to the back corridor as they heard Jake coming through, so they never saw Dan cross his arms and reach into the deep pockets of his coat.

As Jake entered, he saw Dan, but too late. 'What's he...? Look out!'

Tam and Billy turned and froze. They were looking down the four barrels of two sawn-off shotguns. And Dan Mackay, no longer old and bent, was standing tall and grim.

'No one moves a muscle, unless I say so,' he said calmly. 'Your hands on the table, Mr Moncrieff. Jake, hands on your head. And Mr King, very slowly, put your piece on the table and then your hands on your head too.

'Three of these barrels could blow your heads off, and I'd still have one left, just in case.'

They each obeyed. Jake was shaking. 'That's Dan Mackay…' he stuttered.

'That's right, Jake, but I'll tell the story. You keep your mouth shut. Yes, I'm Dan Mackay, and I'm a God-fearing man. But tonight I've come in judgement not in grace.'

The colour drained from Big Tam's face. But he managed to speak. 'For Christ's sake, what's the problem?'

'Yes, it's for Christ's sake, Mr Moncrieff. And I'll tell you what the problem is. A friend of mine has some family here in Edinburgh. Seemingly one of them got mixed up in the drugs world—but not with you. He was involved with the competition, as you might say. But it wasn't enough that you took him out. You killed his wife and three children.'

'But that wasn't any of us,' protested Big Tam, 'it was a toe-rag called Mark Fulton…'

'Shut it!' snapped Dan. 'I do the talking and you do the listening.

'And then there's the little racket you run in The Paradise. Some Paradise! Where you ruin the lives of girls and women with threats of violence—and not just threats. You're a coward, Big Tam. Isn't that what they call you—Big Tam? Only you don't look so big now, do you? You're shaking in your expensive shoes.'

Big Tam was stung, but he managed to swallow his pride and said, 'Now let's be reasonable…'

Dan cut him off, 'I thought I told you to shut it!' and he put the barrels of one of the sawn-offs right between Tam's eyes. 'I'm not finished yet. In fact I'm only starting.'

Tam Moncrieff turned pale and beads of sweat stood out on his brow.

'My daughter had a son,' Dan continued. 'He was her

only son. He was a good boy. A bit wild at times, but he was young. He was at University here in Edinburgh. He loved the hills. We used to walk there and climb there together. Now he'll walk there no more. He loved his music. He could make his guitar sing. Now it will sing no more. He loved his girl. And I believe she loved him. He had hope and a future.

'But one day his path crossed with three evil men, and he threatened to expose them. But they couldn't have that. So they took away his future. They injected him with heroin, made out he was a junky and left him to die. They dumped his body in a dark lonely place as if he was garbage.

'Yes, Big Tam, Rory Williams was my grandson, and you're the three cowards who put him in the ground.

'Now, I've killed a lot of men, men who were fighting for causes they believed were noble causes. And I've killed a lot of noble beasts. And not one of them did I kill lightly.

'But I could squeeze these triggers now and not give it a second thought.'

All three thought their time had come, and all they could think of was to play for time. But Dan gave them no time.

'Now, close those cases, Mr Moncrieff, and set them up side by side on the table.'

Tam obeyed, setting each case directly in front of Dan's guns, his hands shaking and sweat beginning to trickle down his face. Dan grasped the case handles with the ring and pinkie fingers of each hand and lifted them, still pointing the guns in Tam and Billy's faces with his trigger fingers still on the triggers. He walked backwards towards the door to the front shop, pushing it open with his back, and paused in the doorway.

'First one through this door gets it.' He let the door swing shut behind him.

He passed quietly through the front shop, putting the guns back in his coat and gripping both cases in one hand.

He laughed and shouted, 'Just wait till word gets out about Dan Mackay—the man who made a fool of Big Tam Moncrieff!'

He opened the door quietly and let himself out.

CHAPTER EIGHTEEN

Dan ran to the van, opened the driver's door, threw the cases and his coat and hat onto the passenger seat and fired up the Cosworth engine. It growled and roared into life and Dan swung out onto the road.

Tam, Billy and Jake tumbled out the door just in time to see Dan giving them a little wave as he passed. But before Tam and Billy could raise their handguns, the van rocketed down the road towards South Clerk Street where it turned left heading out of town.

Tam was in a towering rage. 'Get in the car! We're going to catch this Dan Mackay. He's not getting out of here alive! He's a dead man!'

He ran to his BMW, the others following him. They dived in. Tam swung the car round, had to do a four point turn in the confined space and then roared after Dan, tyres squealing. Billy was in the passenger seat and Jake in the back. They screeched round into South Clerk Street and saw the tail lights of Dan's van only two sets of traffic lights ahead.

'I knew we'd catch that heap of junk in no time,' said Billy.

'Eh, that may look like a heap of junk,' interjected Jake, 'But, believe me, it's not.'

'What do you mean?' snapped Tam.

'I don't know exactly, but the story goes it's fast.'

'How's that?' asked Billy. 'It's a Transit. What can they do? And anyway how do you know?'

214

'Look, I never said this before, but my father has a place in the Highlands, in Wester Ross, and Dan Mackay lives not two miles from there.'

'What!' Tam exploded, 'Why didn't you say any of this before? If I'd known...'

'I had no reason to say anything. I had no idea you were meeting Mackay. If you'd let me in on it...'

'But you could have said before that—way back at the beginning of the year—that you knew that runt and his family!'

'I didn't think it was relevant', responded Jake sulkily.

'I don't pay you to decide what's relevant. And any-way—not relevant that his grandfather had a fast van and can handle guns! You idiot!'

Tam's attention was now focused on the chase as he raced through three sets of traffic lights, two of them red, and quickly overhauled the van. He went to overtake, but the van pulled away as if the BMW was standing still.

'What the hell?' Tam gaped incredulously at the van rapidly diminishing in the distance. He kicked the accelerator to change down the automatic transmission and raced after the Transit along the straight stretch of Minto Street and Craigmillar Park, and then up Liberton Brae. The occupants of the few vehicles on the road, seeing the van going through red lights pursued by a white car, thought they were witnessing a police chase, mistaking Tam's white BMW for an unmarked police car.

Dan was approaching the City Bypass, the A720, the dual carriageway that circles the south side of Edinburgh. He checked the BMW in his door mirror, went under the Bypass and round the roundabout very fast and turned on to the slip road heading west.

'Right. Let's show them what this old van can do!'

Dan held the gear shift lightly in this hand. He changed smoothly from second into third gear. The rev counter

215

raced up towards the red. Dan checked the mirror again and smiled.

As Tam followed Dan up the slip road on to the Bypass, they saw the van accelerating away from them.

'Bloody hell!' Billy was dumbfounded. 'Look at that crate go!'

'I told you,' said Jake, 'It's rumoured it can outrun anything the police have.'

Tam sneered, 'The polis haven't got this baby though.'

Tam accelerated hard and the car jerked and bulleted after Dan. As they hit the Bypass the speedo said 100, rising to 130. But it was clear that the van was still pulling away from them.

'Put the hammer down, Tam,' shouted Billy, 'We're losing him.'

'I have the bloody hammer down!'

'I tried to tell you,' said Jake, a little too smugly.

'What the hell do you know, College boy?' shot back Tam. 'If you're so clever, tell us what we're supposed to do now!'

'Well, why don't you just call the police? They could stop him.'

'The polis! Are ya aff yer heid?'

'Just think. He's got a million pounds of smack and two firearms. He'll go down for a very long time.'

'Aye, and take us down with him!' Tam was scornful. 'This would be a traffic job, and Lawson and Reid have no influence there. Na, no polis. We'll settle this ourselves. No one gets to know about this. And I mean no one. Not even anyone else on the team. If this gets out, we'll be a laughing stock. And nobody… nobody makes a fool of Tam Moncrieff.

'Look, he's no' gaining on us anymore. That wreck is no' going to keep this up for long.'

Round the Bypass and heading west onto the M8, the

van kept tantalisingly ahead of them. As it turned off onto the M90, they thought they were catching it. But Dan accelerated round the tight slip-road, and as he shot down the motorway towards the speed camera under the flyover, he saw a big artic truck in the inside lane and took his chance. He pulled alongside of it just as it was passing the camera so that it shielded him, and then he accelerated hard away.

'The camera under the bridge, Tam!' Billy shouted, but it was too late.

Tam braked hard, but the camera flashed. Even Billy winced at the string of oaths and curses that erupted from Big Tam's mouth. He didn't want there to be any record of his movements, quite apart from the points on his licence.

'Where's he heading?' asked Billy, 'Stirling?' But a sign for the Forth Bridge flashed past and Dan's brake lights showed.

'No,' said Jake, 'He's heading home.'

Dan took the turn on to the slip road for the A8000. They were catching up with him as he braked, but then he accelerated fast round the tight cloverleaf. The BMW's tyres squealed as Tam tried unsuccessfully to keep up with the van.

In the faint midsummer twilight and starlight, the Forth Bridges were lying like sleeping dragons across the Firth of Forth. The peace was shattered by the high-pitched whine of approaching vehicles. First the Transit van and then the BMW roared over the Bridge and on to the M90 motorway.

Dan slid the gear shift into sixth and stretched, easing his back. He loosened his collar and pulled off his tie. The speedo showed 155.

'If he goes any faster than this, we'll lose him,' said Tam, his frustration at boiling point. 'This is as fast as this thing goes. I can't keep this up all the way to Inverness or wherever Mackay is heading, or we'll run out of fuel. But just as well I had her filled up today. What's under the bonnet of that thing?'

'Well, it's rumoured,' said Jake, 'that it's some sort of racing car engine.'

'What would some sort of wealthy landowner like him want with a racing car engine in an old van?' asked Billy.

Jake laughed, 'Mackay's no wealthy landowner. 'He's a crofter and a poacher.'

'So,' said Tam through gritted teeth, 'the whole thing he spun me was a load of crap!'

Billy was staring ahead intently at the tail lights of the Transit. 'He's no' gaining now. I bet he's going to blow a gasket any minute.'

But the Cosworth engine didn't blow a gasket. In fact it was well within its capabilities as it cruised up the M90 to Perth and then onto the A9 in the early hours of the morning doing a steady 130mph. Even allowing for hills and bends that weren't designed for such high speeds and the junctions and roundabouts round Perth, Dan was easily averaging over 100mph. Any time Tam tried to catch up, Dan accelerated away again.

So the BMW made no headway against the van, even at the Broxden and Inveralmond roundabouts around Perth. But equally the van didn't pull away from the BMW. It was a kind of stalemate. The only worrying times for Tam and the others were when they approached traffic cameras. As Dan slowed, Tam had to follow suit. He didn't want any more points on his licence, and he certainly didn't want his presence recorded on the A9. Strangely Dan didn't seem to take advantage. Each time they caught him up after a while.

'The bastard's playing with us!' Tam was exasperated.

There were not many people on the road in the early hours of the morning, and those who were, thought they were witnessing a police chase. There was the occasional campervan or caravan and the odd truck, all of which Dan easily overtook even on the single carriageway sections, but he usually did so just before bends, so Tam had a worrying wait until he could see it clear to overtake.

On a stretch of single carriageway of the A9 just north of the dual carriageway in the pass of Drumochter, a Nissan saloon was cruising north. The couple inside were arguing. The man was driving.

'Slow down!' said the woman. 'There are unmarked police cars on this road.'

'Relax! I'm only doing 70.'

'More like 80. And the speed limit is 60 on a single carriageway.'

'Isn't it 70? Anyway, there's no police cars around at this time of night.'

He suddenly saw the blazing lights of the Transit in his rear-view mirror. Before he could even brake, the Transit flashed past.

'It's the police! I told you!' shrieked the woman.

'Well if it is, they're not interested in us. Anyway that didn't look like any police vehicle.'

In a white flash, the BMW screamed past.

'That's the police!' he exclaimed.

'No unmarked police cars, hmm? You're lucky they were chasing the van. Now slow down!'

Meanwhile, Tam had cooled down and was thinking more rationally.

'I've been thinking, Billy. Sharon set up this deal with you.'

'I thought it was for real, Tam, and I'm sure Sharon did too.'

'But how can this Dan Mackay be that shite's grandfather, and her not know!'

The mention of Sharon suddenly jogged Jake's memory.

'Uh, I forgot with all the excitement, but I tried to tell you at Montague Street, Sharon wasn't at the Paradise tonight, and neither was Claire.'

'What! That proves it. The bitches were in it together.' Tam was getting irate again. 'And you forgot! What were you doing at the Paradise anyway?'

'Eh, Claire had asked me to bring her some stuff there.'

'Couldn't you have phoned? Then we would have known something was wrong!'

'Uh, there was a note saying Billy had phoned, telling me to be at Montague Street at one. I thought I'd get there quick enough. I didn't think.'

'Didn't think!' mocked Billy. 'Thought you students were paid to think! Anyway I never phoned the Paradise or left any note!'

'Shut it, the both of you!' snapped Tam. 'You were set up. Think about it. The only way Mackay could know that the three of us were involved, was if someone in the Paradise that night saw what happened. That can only mean Sharon or Claire, or both of them.'

Suddenly the light dawned on Tam. 'Of course, the camera room! The two-way mirror! The bitches!' The irony in one of his own devious ploys being turned against him was lost on Tam. It only doubled his anger and his desire for revenge.

'And all this time they never let on. But it makes no difference now. But when I finish with this Dan Mackay, I'll see to that pair of slags. We'll give them a little farewell party before we ship them out to the Russkis. They'll wish they'd never grassed on Tam Moncrieff.'

As they approached Inverness, they crested the hill and the whole vista opened up. There was a pale glimmer in the north-east sky heralding the coming of the new day. The slate blue mountains of the north and west were slumbering in the eerie northern twilight. But the Transit and the BMW streaked down the hill, through the Longman roundabout in Inverness and across the Kessock Bridge to the Black Isle.

Dan's brake lights glowed as he approached the Tore roundabout. The sign said ULLAPOOL A835.

'Like I said, he's heading home,' said Jake. 'If you're going to stop him, it will have to be on this stretch. It's 50 miles of twisty roads, but he knows it like the back of his hand.'

'What do you know about this Dan Mackay?' asked Billy as Dan accelerated away from the roundabout.

'He's a small-time crofter and poacher. He's had several run-ins with my father over shooting deer. Never been caught though. He's reputed to be a crack shot. Seemingly he was in the army at some point.'

'Bloody hell!' rasped Billy. 'We're up against a hitman! He could pick us off anywhere in this country!'

'All I'm saying is: don't underestimate him. He's trying to get you on his own ground. I think that's his idea. Oh, and he's a religious nutter as well, but not your namby-pamby type. Believes in blood and judgement and hell and all that stuff.'

'A hitman and a religious maniac! That's just great!' Billy snorted. Under the humour, he was getting worried. 'Are you sure this is such a good idea, Tam?'

'Not got the bottle for it, Billy?' Tam smiled disparagingly. 'King Billy going to be dethroned by this teuchter? Na, if this gets out, we're out of business. We finish it today one way or the other.'

Past Conon Bridge the road becomes much narrower and twisty and passes through the small villages of Contin and Garve, but after that there are several long straights. Here Dan could easily have lost Tam, because the automatic BMW hadn't the same flexibility in accelerating as the van, but he restrained himself.

As they approached Loch Glascarnoch, the panorama opened out, and twenty miles away in a gap in the hills the peaks of An Teallach above the mists were catching the first rosy light of the approaching dawn.

Billy was awestruck. 'What's that?'

'That's An Teallach. It means The Forge,' explained Jake. 'Those who know reckon it one of the very best mountains in the Highlands. Sheer thousand foot cliffs, narrow ridges—pretty frightening. That's where we're heading. Mackay's place is not far from there.'

The Transit and BMW were soon approaching Braemore Junction where the A832 branches off for Aultbea and Gairloch. Some distance ahead they saw the Transit's brake lights as Dan slowed to turn off. They rapidly caught up with him. Tam braked late and the tyres squealed as the BMW skidded round following Dan.

'Don't lose him here!' advised Jake. 'It's a very twisty road and it's the road he knows best. It's called the Destitution Road.'

'He'll know destitution all right by the time I'm finished with him!' snarled Tam between gritted teeth.

'Why's it called that? Destitution Road?' asked Billy, interested.

'Oh, something to do with impoverished crofters in the Potato Famine in the nineteenth century. Oatmeal was doled out to them in return for building the road. They're always going on about things like that up here—a chip on their shoulder about something or other.'

The car slewed from side to side as Tam tried to keep up with Dan. One moment they were nearly right behind him, as he braked for tight corners, the next moment they found he was disappearing round a distant bend.

*

All was quiet in Dan's croft house. Even Fleet was sleeping. But he was restless. He whined in his sleep. Claire had fallen into a deep sleep but troubled by wild dreams where the threatening faces of Tam Moncrieff and Jake loomed out of dark surreal windows and doorways. Then Rory had appeared, reaching out his hands to her, imploring her to come to him. She threw her arm round him and felt his long hair. She felt a wet kiss on her face. But it felt wrong. There was something nightmarish about it.

She gave a little moan and she suddenly woke up with a start, staring wildly at a wolf-like face inches from hers.

'Oh goodness, Fleet, what a fright you gave me! I was dreaming...'

Fleet wagged his tail and went to the door, looking expectantly back at Claire. When she didn't move, he went back and pawed her.

'OK! OK! I'm coming!'

She stumbled out of bed and followed Fleet as he went down the stairs to the front door.

'Oh, you're wanting out. OK, just a minute.'

Claire unbolted and opened the door and Fleet shot out. Claire took a step outside, shivering in the grey light of the approaching day. There was the breath of a cold wind from the north. She watched as Fleet ran across the field down towards the burn and east over the old township of Cill Donnain towards An Crasg.

'Fleet! You crazy dog! I hope I haven't done something stupid...'

*

Dan looked in the door mirror at the BMW sliding all over the road and smiled.

'OK, let's lose them.'

He slid the gear shift down from third to second as he approached a tight bend and accelerated hard.

Tam came screaming round the bend only to see Dan disappearing round a distant corner.

'We're losing him!' Billy wasn't sure whether he was

worried or glad at the prospect.

'What has he got in that thing?' Tam growled.

They came round a series of bends onto a long straight stretch and the van was nowhere to be seen.

'Well, whatever else, he can drive!' said Billy.

'Drive! I'll drive my fist down his throat when I catch him!'

'But first we've got to catch him,' observed Jake rather needlessly.

'Shut it, smart boy!' Tam was rapidly losing his cool again. 'I'll catch him. I'll catch him all right, and then we'll see who's the fool! He must have turned off somewhere!'

But there were no turn-offs. In spite of two hours in the car to think things over, Tam's burning anger and frustration had not lessened one little bit, and he was not thinking clearly. This was partly due to the adrenalin coursing through his veins as he tried to keep up with the Transit van. He had never driven at such speeds for such a prolonged period of time and on such roads. But it was also due to his failure to realise he was being drawn into a landscape that was utterly alien to him.

And always as they drove west the ridge of An Teallach with its stupendous cliffs and pinnacles was growing ever larger in their vision.

*

Muhammad was finishing getting dressed quietly, trying not to disturb Jasmine. She stirred.

'What time is it?' she asked sleepily.

'It's just gone half past three. I'm just off to Edinburgh, remember?' He kissed her.

'Oh yes, bye-bye, take care.'

'The roads will be very quiet at this time. Bye.'

Outside the air was still and chilly with mist lying in patches over the land. Muhammad climbed into his old white Fiat van and drove off. He was going down to Edinburgh to visit some of his cousin's family who had been so tragically bereaved, and he planned to pick up some groceries at the wholesalers on the way back.

CHAPTER NINETEEN

At Corrie Hallie the Transit van screeched to a halt in a lay-by on the right. Dan cut the engine and jumped out. All around there was a profound silence in the still, misty morning air. He opened the back door of the van and put on his camouflage jacket. He carefully removed the hundred £100 notes from his case and stuffed them inside his jacket. He slid one of the sawn-offs into a hidden compartment in the floor under the passenger seat. Then he tipped the bags of heroin into his large rucksack.

He grabbed an old sack from the back of the van along with several stacks of the cut newspaper "notes", stuck a lighted match in them and threw them down behind the van. He threw the empty briefcases across the road scattering some of the other cut papers at the start of the path on the south side of the path leading up the hill. He shouldered the rucksack, took the remaining gun in his right hand and his long stick in his left.

In the stillness he could hear the high-powered whine of the BMW approaching. He closed the van doors, and sprinted up the path. If anyone who had seen his bent figure limping around Edinburgh saw him now, they'd have been utterly astonished.

The BMW screamed down the brae at Corrie Hallie, round the bend and there was Dan's van parked at the side of the road with grey smoke billowing from its rear. Tam slammed on the brakes hard, and they stopped about 50 yards from the van.

'Ha! He's finally blown a gasket!' Tam gloated.

'Back up, Tam,' shouted Billy. 'It could be some sort of ambush!'

'I'm no' going back one inch for the son of a bitch. It looks like his van's finally crocked. Look at that smoke.' He paused. 'Jake, now's your chance to prove yourself. Billy, give him the piece in the glove compartment.'

'I'm not going out there!'

'Perhaps we should pay a visit to your old man then— you said he lives near—introduce him to your friends...'

'OK! OK! Give me the gun, but cover me.'

Jake took the handgun and opened the door. He rolled out of the car and into the densely overgrown ditch on the left hand side of the road. He crawled along until he came to the path leading up the hill. He made a crouching dash across it, noticing as he did so the open cases and scattered papers, and also that the smoke was coming from some sort of bag. He dived into the ditch on the other side until he was level with the van. After watching for a couple of minutes and seeing nothing move, he jumped up, ran across the road round the back of the van to the driver's side. He couldn't see any face in the door mirror, so he rushed forward and pointed the gun at the driver's window. There was no one there and nothing except Dan's coat and hat lying on the passenger seat. He beckoned to the others.

The BMW roared up. Tam parked right behind the van. He and Billy leapt out, automatic pistols in hand. Jake kicked the smoking bag aside, scattering the still smouldering note-sized bits of newspaper, and opened the back doors of the Transit. There was nothing of any interest there.

Billy looked at the smoking bits of newspaper, and then at the empty cases across the road with other bits of newspaper flapping around in the little eddies of air. 'Hey! Look at this!' He picked up Dan's empty case. 'He never had a million. Just bits of newspaper! He's packed the smack and cash in something else and he's off up that path.'

Tam turned to Jake. 'Where does that go? Is that where he lives?'

'No, his house is miles away yet on the other side of the river. That's the path to An Teallach,' said Jake, turning the colour of the surrounding mist, 'But I wouldn't go up there after Dan Mackay!'

'Why the hell not?'

'Uh, like I said, An Teallach is one dangerous mountain... And Mackay's on his own ground.' He hesitated. 'And there's a dangerous bog up there. If you go in there you don't come out.'

'No' half as dangerous as me!' shouted Tam putting his gun in Jake's face. 'Let's go! You lead the way.' He waved the gun up the path.

But still Jake hesitated. 'But Mackay's just going to bury the stuff. It could be anywhere.'

'The only thing that's going to be buried here is Dan Mackay. We'll put him in that bog you were on about. Now move it!'

Jake reluctantly headed up the sloping path, Billy and Tam close behind, as they heard the sound of a vehicle approaching from the west.

*

Muhammad was heading east along the A832 past Dundonnain, the road that loops through spectacular West Highland scenery from its junction with the A835 at Garve near the east coast, round by the west coast at Gairloch and Poolewe and back to the A835 at Braemore. Suddenly he had to brake hard, as a dog shot across the road in front of him and ran off over rough ground on his right.

'That is Dan's dog—Fleet. Well, that is very strange. What is he doing here on his own? There is something wrong.'

A few miles further on, he was approaching Corrie Hallie just as the trio left the road. As he passed, he clocked Dan's van with the doors open, the strange car and the three on the path. He drove on.

'Something is not right,' he said under his breath.

He slowed and looked for a place to turn. He turned in the entrance to a track and headed back. He parked in front of the Transit and got out and investigated Dan's van. He picked up Dan's coat, looked up the path and stood undecided for a good minute. He shivered as he looked at the mist that seemed to be coming down, and he put on Dan's old hat and the coat which was rather too long for him. Then he headed off up the path.

*

Jake was pulling away from Tam and Billy. He was younger and a bit fitter and, now an idea for getting out was forming in his mind. He could disappear in the woods and then double back and head to Dundonnain Lodge. He shouted over his shoulder, 'OK, I know this country. I'll go ahead and spy out the land. Just follow the path. I'll meet you further up.'

'OK, but don't do anything stupid!' gasped Tam, beginning to feel the effect of his weight. 'We're right behind you.'

They saw him disappear into the Gleann Chaorachain wood. None of them realised that by separating they had done the first foolish thing.

Jake was running warily up the path, pointing his gun from side to side and looking for a good escape route. So he never saw the snare wire that was taut across the path between two trees and partly hidden by bracken. He went down hard, cracking his head on the rocky path. The gun flew from his hand. Before he recovered, Dan was on him. He pinned him to the ground with the sawn-off to his head. He whispered in his ear, 'Make a sound and you're dead.'

Dan bound and gagged Jake with duct tape, removed the snare wire and threw the hand gun into the bracken. He put Jake over his shoulder, as if he was a young stag and carried him off the path slightly downhill towards the burn. He trod carefully so as not to disturb the undergrowth and dumped Jake none too gently in a dense patch of bracken.

No sooner was this done than he heard the sound of Tam and Billy approaching and he lay low in the bracken. He watched them pass, and could hear Tam's heavy breathing.

'I'll deal with you later,' Dan whispered in Jake's ear. Jake's eyes opened wide in fear and he shook his head. With that Dan was off, weaving through the trees off the path and across the burn at the bottom of a short incline.

A few minutes after Dan had gone, Muhammad approached cautiously, looking around. He spotted some crushed bracken and looked over to the side of the path. He took a few steps in that direction, noticed the gun and picked it up. 'Now, what is this doing here?' Then he saw Jake.

'Jake! What is going on? Where's Dan?'

Jake looked wide-eyed with terror, and made some muffled sounds. Muhammad knelt over him and ripped off the gag, none too gently.

A little further up the path, Tam stopped, looking round. 'Where the hell is Jake?'

'It's no' Jake I'm worried about—it's that Dan Mackay, he could be anywhere here,' said Billy looking up the path.

Suddenly they heard a shout back behind them down the path, 'Tam! Help!'

The yell seemed abruptly cut off. They raced back down the path. Tam saw Dan kneeling over the bound figure of Jake with a gun in his hand. Tam fired and saw Dan topple over on top of Jake who was screaming. The gun fell from Dan's hand.

Tam grabbed the fallen body and yanked him off Jake who was covered in blood. Dan's hat fell off and Tam saw Muhammad's face.

'Who the hell is that?'

'Muhammad!' screamed Jake. 'Muhammad! You've shot Muhammad!'

Tam was stunned. 'I thought it was Dan Mackay. He's wearing his coat and hat. I don't understand! Who the hell is Muhammad? Is he one of the Edinburgh gang?'

'Edinburgh gang!' spluttered Jake. 'No! Muhammad's a local shopkeeper!'

Muhammad had been hit in the chest and was clearly dying. He was gasping for breath, but was trying to say something. Billy bent over him and asked, 'Why were you wearing Dan's coat and hat?'

'Tell Dan…' Muhammad whispered.

Billy put his ear near Muhammad's mouth.

'Tell Dan… I understand… redemption… Tell Dan...'

Muhammad's head fell back. He was dead.

'What did he say?' demanded Tam.

'I don't know,' Billy replied quietly. 'Couldn't make it out.'

'Right, this is a bloody mess. Cut that fool loose.' Tam pointed to Jake with his gun.

Billy produced a flick knife and proceeded to cut the tape binding Jake. Meanwhile Tam picked up Jake's hand-gun and swapped it with his own, being careful not to remove his expensive leather driving gloves.

'Not so clever now, college boy. You'd better clean up this mess. Get rid of that.' Tam indicated Muhammad's body.

'What? How am I supposed to do that?' Jake was nearly hysterical.

'Your problem. Put him in that bog you were going on about. Here take this.' Tam handed him the murder weapon. 'Right, let's get this Dan Mackay. We're losing time here.' He and Billy headed back up the path.

Tam called over his shoulder to Jake, 'Better do it. You're covered in his blood, and your prints are all over that gun in your hand.'

Jake stared at the gun in his hand and realised it was Tam's gun.

'Bastard!' said Jake under his breath, as he sat running his hands through his hair. Then he got up, wrapped Dan's coat around Muhammad and, stooping down, lifted his body over his shoulder.

Tam and Billy were hurrying along the climbing path up Glen Chaorachain and the mist was rising in front of them. Some way up they came to a fork in the path, and they were just about to take the main path to the left when Billy caught Tam's arm and hissed through clenched teeth, 'Look way up there, just where the mist is clearing. There's someone there. It's Mackay.' It was too far for a shot and they set off up the right-hand path in pursuit.

As they half ran, half walked they scanned the path and the hillside above them. Suddenly Billy caught a glimpse of Dan again on the edge of the mist up the mighty slope of Sail Liath on their left. He pointed. Tam raised his handgun and got off three hurried shots. Dan disappeared into the mist. 'I got the bastard!" exclaimed Tam, clenching his left fist.

'Well, maybe,' said Billy, sounding unconvinced, 'But we'd better make sure, and take it canny. You might have just winged him and he's maybe hiding behind some rock.' Tam and Billy turned off the path up the hill after Dan. A few hundred yards up the hill, a dark shape loomed out of the mist and Tam raised his gun to shoot, but Billy pulled his arm down and said, 'It's an animal! Look at the horns!

I think it's some sort of goat!'

Half an hour later after some steady climbing they reached the white quartz-strewn summit of Sail Liath, Billy in front. There had been no sign of Dan. But now the mist was receding rapidly in front of them, retreating into the abyss in the corrie of Toll an Lochain, and the sunrise behind them revealed the awesome red sandstone rocks of Stob Cadha Gobhlach, the Corrag Bhuidhe Pinnacles and Sgurr Fiona.

Tam was blown, and could hardly get his breath. Billy was looking intently at the path leading down and up again to Cadha Gobhlach and on to the pinnacles.

'There he is!' They caught a glimpse of Dan near the summit of Stob Cadha Gobhlach.

Tam waved Billy on. 'Don't lose him! I'll follow you when I get my breath back.'

Billy ran down the slope with a new lease of life.

*

Jake staggered off up the path, Muhammad's body across his shoulder. He was terrified he'd be overtaken by some early morning hill climbers, but there was no one around. The forecast of mist had probably deterred them. After a while he took the right hand path and soon veered off it downhill to the right into the heather and long grass. He'd been carrying Muhammad's body for nearly a mile, and he staggered and fell several times, but eventually he reached a group of small lochs, some no bigger than ponds, known in the Highlands as dubh lochans. He trod warily and finally stopped at the edge of a black morass. He held Muhammad's body in his arms, swung back and then threw it with all his strength out into the peat bog. He almost overbalanced, slipping on the soft ground, but he managed to regain his balance and he watched in horrified fascination as the body sank beneath the oozing black surface.

At that moment a blood-curdling howl broke out behind him. He jerked round and saw what appeared to be the monstrous silhouette of a wolf against the skyline not 30 yards away. He staggered, slipped on the soft ground, lost his balance and toppled backwards into the bog with a scream of terror. No human eyes saw the last struggles of Jonathan Kenneth Hetherington, and no human ears heard his cries as he sunk slowly into the cloying liquid peat sucking him down to his death. But Fleet watched until the last bubbles ceased to rise, then he turned and set off at a steady loping pace up towards An Teallach.

High on Stob Cadha Gobhlach, Dan heard the howl followed by the scream echoing up through the ravines in the still, clear air. He turned his head this way and that as if to detect the source. He turned away and hid behind a rock on the edge of the ravine. The mist was still swirling in the ravine, boiling up from Toll an Lochain.

Tam and Billy both heard the howl and scream. Billy was on the ridge between Sail Liath and Stob Cadha Gobhlach. He headed off again. Tam, still on Sail Liath, set off after him.

As Billy approached Cadha Gobhlach, gun in hand, he was looking from side to side as he ran. Suddenly, up out of the mist there reared a ghostly figure. It was Dan Mackay. One blow from his hazel stick sent Billy's gun flying, and the second took his legs from under him sending him tumbling backwards down the rocks with a scream. He ended up on a precarious ledge. He could hear stones clattering down the steep gully behind him.

'For God's sake, help me!' he screamed. 'I can't move. It's my leg. I think it's broke.'

'You should thank God you're alive!' said Dan grimly looking down at him. 'For what you did to Rory, you deserved to die.'

In that lonely place, lying in agony on that precarious ledge, with a grim-faced Dan glaring down at him, the last veils of deception were torn away from Billy King like the shredding mist. 'I know that, Dan… I'm sorry about your grandson. I was there, and I knew it wasn't right. I tried to stop it, but I didn't. But don't leave me here, Dan! It hurts like hell.'

'All right,' Dan's burning anger was receding before his long instinct of compassion for someone in agony, even his worst enemy. 'I'll get help for you as soon as I can. But first I have to deal with Tam Moncrieff.'

Billy was gasping in pain and terror as he clung to the sharp rocks. 'Thanks Dan… but you need to watch out. Big Tam is one vicious bastard…'

'Billy, what was the first shot back there?'

'It was Tam… we heard a shout from Jake and there you were bending over him with a gun… Tam fired, but it wasn't you. He was wearing your coat and hat. Some Pakistani.

'What! Who was it?'

'Don't know. Never seen him before. But he knew you. Jake said he was Muhammad…'

'Muhammad! No! Not Muhammad,' groaned Dan, 'Muhammad, what did you think you were doing? Is he dead?'

'Afraid so.' Then he called, 'Dan?'

'What?'

'He wanted to tell you something.'

'What?'

'He said he understood… redemption, I think it was. I don't know if it means something?'

'Aye, Billy. It means something.'

Dan turned to go.

'Dan!' Billy's voice echoed up from the ravine.

'What?'

'You're going to kill Tam.' It was more of a question than a statement.

'I don't know that, Billy, but if he comes off this mountain on his own two feet, he'll be a changed man.' As he turned to go, he asked, 'What about Jake, Billy? Where's Jake?'

'Tam told him to get rid of the body. Jake was talking about some bog or something…'

Dan looked up to the Corrag Bhuidhe buttress ahead. His face was grim. 'Maybe I won't have to bother about him then. Tell Tam I'll see him on the top. See you, Billy. Don't go anywhere!'

'Ha! Ha! Very funny!' Billy grimaced in pain.

Dan turned, shouldered his backpack and set off up towards the Corrag Bhuidhe buttress. Minutes later Tam came gasping up, gun in hand. Billy saw him on the ridge, and called out, 'Tam!'

Tam looked around, confused, trying to determine where the voice was coming from. Eventually he located Billy below him.

'What the hell happened to you?'

'Dan Mackay happened to me, that's what.'

'Get up here, you fool.'

'Tam, I can't move. It's my leg. I think it's broken.'

'Great! Do you want me to put you out of your misery?'

'For God's sake, Tam!'

'Only joking, Billy boy! I'm going to get the bastard who did this to you, Billy. Where did he go?'

'He went straight up.'

Tam turned to look at the buttress ahead. 'What? Up there? How am I supposed to get up there?'

'Don't know. But he said he'd see you on the top.'

'Oh aye? Right, I'm going to finish this. It'll only take one hit.'

'Tam! Maybe you should leave it, eh? He's already taken out Jake and me.'

'But I'm no' Jake or you.' Tam turned to head off up the ridge, but he stopped. "Where is that damn fool, anyway—Jake? He should be up here by now.'

'Dan didn't seem to think he would come.'

'Aye, a streak of yellow a yard wide running down Jake's back!' Tam said moving off. His voice came echoing down faint and ghostly, 'See you later, Billy boy!'

As Tam reached the great slightly overhanging buttress, he stood perplexed. He looked up and realised he couldn't climb up there. Suddenly he heard eerie laughter echoing in the rocks. He looked up and down and all around, but could see no one.

'Lost your way, Tam?' said the unearthly voice that seemed to be coming down from above, 'Or just not got the bottle, eh?'

Tam pressed himself against the rock and pointed his gun in various directions, but couldn't see anyone. 'You'll rue the day you ever tried to sting Tam Moncrieff!'

Tam heard more laughter, receding into the distance. 'Mackay!... Mackay!' he shouted. There was no answer. After waiting a little, he started searching around for some way up. To the right was impossible and the cliff was sheer. But to the left he found a path heading round the side. He took it. He skirted to the left of the Corrag Bhuidhe buttress and then slanted up towards the pinnacles.

As he neared the top of the ridge, he constantly scanned the slopes. He reached the top between two pinnacles and just as he did so, the mist retreated down the cliffs, the sun came shining through blinding him, and he realised he was standing on the edge of a fearful abyss. He swayed unsteadily on his feet. As he took a step back, he didn't see Dan emerging from the pinnacle behind him to his left, only a few feet away. A sawn-off shotgun was in Dan's left hand. His right hand held the rucksack. It was open, revealing the heroin glistening in the sun.

Tam sensed something and whirled round, but as he had to use his arms to balance, he was unable to aim his gun. Instead he found himself staring down the barrels of the sawn-off.

'So, we meet again, Mr Moncrieff,' said Dan 'You may wonder why I've brought you up here. Of course, I wanted you on my territory, not yours. But there's more to it than that.

'Rory and me used to come here. It was one of his favourite places. I thought it fitting to bring his killer here.'

'Look, Mackay, be reasonable,' said Tam, his face a mask of suppressed anger, but playing for time. 'It's a pity about the boy, but nothing is going to bring him back.'

Dan made no response, his face unmoving.

'You've got something there that belongs to me, but I'm a reasonable man,' Tam tried to sound business-like. 'You give me back my property and that's the last you'll hear from me.'

'And ruin countless more young lives? No, I can't let you do that. Anyway, a million pounds of heroin won't be any good for the journey you're going to take.'

'OK, OK. You can take me back down and phone the police...'

'That's not the journey I was thinking of. You'd never get the justice you deserve down there. Too many policemen and lawyers you've corrupted. But you know there's a higher court, Tam, one where you have no power or influence, where no threats or bribes or blackmail will work.

'You'll have to stand alone there, Tam, alone with your crimes—the ruin of young girls, the wrecking of young men's lives, the devastation of communities, burning a whole family to death, the shooting of my good friend Muhammad and the murder of my daughter's only son.

'But there's time to change, Tam. I brought you here to give you that chance.'

Tam was getting agitated. 'I don't believe any of that mumbo-jumbo, pie-in-the-sky-when-you-die stuff. There's no one going to judge Tam Moncrieff. And anyway, you're not going to kill me. If you shoot me, you'll spend the rest of your life in prison. And I've got a lot of friends there. By the time they've finished with you, you'll wish I'd shot you here.'

'Your move then, Tam. But let me warn you, by the time you move your little finger, I'll have blown you off the cliff. It's a long way down.' Dan glanced at the rocky edge.

Tam gingerly looked into the abyss.

'But even if you did get me first,' said Dan, 'this is going with me.' He held up the rucksack. 'Down there. You'll find it difficult to collect your million pounds there.

'So it's decision time. Is your million pounds worth more than your life? Is your reputation worth more than your soul? Time to ask for forgiveness, Tam.'

'Screw you!'

Tam's gun hand moved, but froze again as Dan pointed the sawn-off and squeezed one trigger. It clicked, but didn't fire. Tam flinched, then suddenly coming to life he went to raise his gun again, but again he stopped as Dan said calmly, 'Must be in the other barrel,'

He squeezed the other trigger. Again it just clicked.

Realisation dawned on Tam's face. 'You bastard! It was empty all the time!' He stepped back from the edge and raised his gun. 'But all your schemes have come to nothing now, you fool. Hand over my property right now—and the money.'

But at that moment Fleet came bounding up the rocks and leapt straight at Tam, snarling. Tam whirled and shot him, but Fleet's momentum carried him right into Tam who staggered back to the edge of the cliff.

Tam turned the gun back towards Dan to squeeze the trigger, but at the same moment Dan heaved the rucksack at him. Tam's shots went echoing wide and the gun was knocked out of his hand as the rucksack hit him on his right side. Tam managed to clutch the rucksack and let out a shout of triumph as he swayed precariously on the edge. 'Ya beauty!'

'Don't be fool, man. Give me your hand!' shouted Dan. For what seemed like an eternity, Tam teetered on the edge, waving one arm wildly trying to regain his balance, but he wouldn't release his grip on his precious drugs, and with a scream of terror he overbalanced and plunged into the abyss, his body smashing into the cliff face on the way down. And the rising east wind blew the powdered heroin up over the cliff's edge like pure drifting snow.

But Dan paid no heed. He knelt beside the fallen Fleet and took his head in his lap.

'Aw, Fleet! What were you doing here, boy? Poor Fleet! You've always been a great dog, and now you've saved my life.'

Fleet looked into Dan's face, until gradually his breathing stopped and his eyes stared blindly, still looking into his master's eyes. Dan hugged Fleet, his faithful dog, and with eyes brimming with tears he looked up into the sky. With his blurred vision he saw a dark shape against the blue. It was Iolair soaring high in the pathways of the heavens.

Iolair took in the whole scene, then he swept down along the cliffs where the heroin was still blowing across the cliff where each rock shone like a knife, and he focused for a moment on the crumpled body of Tam Moncrieff at the bottom of the cliff a thousand feet below. He rose on the thermals and glided over An Loch Beag and Dundonnain, and eventually over Dan's croft house at Cill Donnain.

*

Fiona's phone rang. She turned over in bed and looked at her phone. It said 7:15am. And it showed the number phoning was her Dad's mobile.

'Dad! Where are you?...

'What? On An Teallach?!...

'Are you all right? What's happened?...

'Yes… yes, I've got that. I'll tell them.

'Take care, Dad. We'll meet you there. Bye.'

Claire, who had slept fitfully after letting Fleet out, heard Fiona speaking and got up. The creak of the bedroom door woke Sharon and in a minute they were all in Fiona's bedroom.

'What's happened?' Claire stared at Fiona.

'It was Dad. He said you're free.'

Claire looked at Sharon and they hugged each other and started crying.

'Did he say anything else?'

'Just that the cost was high. What did he mean?'

'I don't know. When will he be back?'

'He's on An Teallach—the mountain—there.' She opened the curtains and pointed out the window across the Loch. 'We'll go to meet him.'

Claire stared at the mighty bulk of the mountain glowing in the morning sun, a wholly alien environment to her, and she shivered, wondering what had taken place there.

*

As Dan was descending with the dead Fleet across his shoulders towards the spot where Billy lay injured, he heard the unmistakeable thudding noise of a helicopter approaching. Suddenly the mountain rescue chopper rose into view over the ridge. Dan had phoned Jim Matheson who said he would arrange everything. And now, not much more than half an hour later, the RAF Sea King from Lossiemouth was here at the exact coordinates Dan had given.

Dan pointed the pilot to where Billy lay. He watched as they lowered a paramedic and a policeman down. One of them asked Dan if he wanted to go in the helicopter, but they couldn't take the dog. Dan said no, he was OK. He then spoke briefly to Billy as they strapped him into a stretcher and told him he would try to put in a good word for him, and then he set off down the mountain, as the helicopter rose behind him and headed for Inverness.

*

In addition to Dan's Transit, Tam's BMW and Muhammad's van, there were now several vehicles at Corrie Hallie: Fiona's car, a mountain rescue Land Rover and two police cars. Superintendent Jim Matheson was there, taking command. He had had the rest of the layby cordoned off and told some early morning would-be climbers that An Teallach was closed. Along with some other policemen and the Mountain Rescue team, he was looking at a map spread on the bonnet of one of the police cars. Fiona, Claire and Sharon were standing together, looking up to the mountain.

Claire glanced up the path. 'Look!' she could hardly get the word out for the feeling of compression in her chest, 'There's Dan!'

They all turned and looked. Dan was coming down the path, bent but steady, still carrying Fleet over his shoulders. They ran towards him. Claire and Fiona nearly knocked him off his feet as they threw their arms round him.

'What's happened, Dan?' asked Jim.

Dan said nothing until he'd opened the back door of his van and laid Fleet gently down inside. 'Fleet's dead. Shot. The very last evil deed of Tam Moncrieff.'

Sharon pointed to the blood on Dan. 'Are you hurt, Dan?'

'No. It's Fleet's blood. He saved my life.

'Jake and Muhammad are in the Dubh Lochan bog, Billy King is on his way to Raigmore with a broken leg, and Tam Moncrieff lies at the bottom of the Corrag Bhuidhe cliffs.'

'I see there's a story to be told, my friend,' says Jim.

'And you'll hear it, Jim. And then you will have to decide what you have to do.'

*

In Edinburgh, a dark blue Audi drove into the car park at St Leonard's Police Headquarters. DI Lawson and DS Reid got out and entered the building, where they were informed that they were wanted in one of the interview rooms. There they were confronted by a Detective Chief Superintendent and DCI from the Serious Crime Squad, who informed them they were under arrest on suspicion of involvement in organised crime and murder.

In the Crown Office and Procurator Fiscal Service, two police officers knocked on Carruthers' door. He called, 'Come!' They entered and introduced themselves as members of the Serious Crime Squad. They informed him he was under arrest on suspicion of perverting the course of justice. The colour drained from Carruthers' pink face.

In Tam Moncrieff's mansion in the Grange, Gayle Moncrieff was agitated. As usual, she was elegantly dressed in a white blouse and beige pencil skirt and high heels. She went to a front window and checked the drive. Then she picked up the phone and dialled.

'Gina? Hello, it's Gayle Moncrieff. Can I speak to my husband, please?...

'Oh... He hasn't come in yet? Did he say anything to you about what he was doing last night?...

'No, not to worry. It's not the first time he hasn't come home, and I don't suppose it'll be the last.' She tried a chuckle, but it didn't quite sound convincing. 'But I've been trying his mobile—it's dead...

'You'll let me know if he calls?...

'Thank you, Gina. Goodbye.'

She went to the kitchen, poured herself a large glass of red wine and, picking up the glass and the bottle, returned to the lounge and sat on the white leather sofa, staring out the large picture window looking over the manicured lawn to the ancient trees, some of them actually older than the house. She had just poured herself another glass when the intercom from the front gates buzzed.

'Yes?... Oh... I suppose it's my husband you want to see. He's not here... Oh I see. You'd better come in then.' She pressed a button and went to the front of the house and looked out. She saw a police car coming up the drive and then two police officers, one male, one female, getting out and coming to the door. She straightened her hair, answered the door, wineglass in hand and invited them in.

She stared at them in disbelief as they told their news. They asked her if there was someone who could be with her and if she wanted them to stay until they got here. Looking dazed, she shook her head. She escorted them to the door. As they drove off, the wine glass slipped from her fingers and smashed on the stone doorstep, the blood red wine splattering her elegant beige stilettos and nylons.

*

In a corner of the garden in front of Dan's croft house, Dan and Neil Cameron had dug a deep hole about five foot long and two wide. Fiona, Claire and Sharon were standing round. Fleet's body lay on an old tartan travel rug.

Dan wrapped Fleet's body in the rug and gently lowered him into the grave. He and Neil then filled in the grave.

'Will you say a word, Neil?' asked Dan.

'Well, I've never conducted a funeral for an animal,' Neil smiled. 'But if any animal deserved it, it was Fleet.'

He brushed the earth off his hands, closed his eyes and tilted his head heavenward. The women put their arms round each other and bowed their heads.

'Lord, you are the creator of man and beast. The life of animals is mysterious to us, but known to you.

'We thank you for Fleet—so fast, so powerful, so brave. We thank you that he gave his life for Dan. Fearful things have happened. We pray that the sacrifices made will not be in vain.

'I to the hills will lift mine eyes,
  from whence doth come mine aid.
My safety cometh from the Lord,
  who heav'n and earth hath made.'

Dan gazed up to An Teallach with open eyes.

*

A week later, after picking up his luggage and stick in Edinburgh, Dan walked into Harry Brown's pawn shop in Kirkcaldy and laid a wad of £100 notes on Harry's desk. Harry looked rather disappointed. He'd hoped that whatever Dan had been up to would fail, and he'd be able to sell the valuable necklace.

He carefully counted the notes, fumbling a few times.

'Eh, there's only ten grand here.'

'Yes, that's right. You gave me ten grand for the necklace and I gave you the necklace. Now I'm returning the ten grand and you're returning the necklace.'

'Eh, that's not how it works. I need my commission— 10%. I've got to make a living."

'I wouldn't worry about making a living, Harry. If I were you, I'd worry about just living, .'

Harry got the message and reluctantly went to his hidden wall safe and took out the dark red box and the brown envelope containing the provenance. Dan checked the contents of both and stuffed them in his pocket.

'What have you been up to?' asked Harry.

'Judgement and redemption, Harry, judgement and redemption.' He walked out of the shop and headed north on the long road home.

AFTERWORD

This story began life as various pictures and scenes in my imagination which all coalesced into a song. I let a couple of friends hear the song—broadcaster and journalist Tom Morton, and Calum Macdonald of Runrig. Both were enthusiastic. Tom said 'It's a film that song', and Calum even began to sketch out ideas for a film! I began to think there might be something in it and so I started to read up how to write a film script.

Eventually I managed to write the screenplay and hawked it around various contacts in the film world, all to no effect. But then one day I thought, 'Why not write the book?' And so what you have in your hands was produced in exactly the reverse direction of most creative projects, that is, first the book, then the film and finally the music.

In addition to Calum and Tom, others must be thanked. Karen Murray and Jimmy Yuill read the film script and offered much sound advice. Several people read various drafts of the book and gave helpful comment and encouragement: Calum Macdonald, historian and author Owen Dudley Edwards, William Lytle of Edinburgh Books, retired Detective Inspector John MacRae, my daughter Katharine Duffy, my daughter-in-law Anne MacDonald and Evelyn my wife.

Needless to say, any mistakes, inaccuracies or infelicities are entirely my own.

Alex J MacDonald

ACKNOWLEDGEMENTS

Scripture quotations are taken from the HOLY BIBLE, NEW INTERNATIONAL VERSION®. Copyright © 1973, 1978, 1984 by International Bible Society. Used by permission of Hodder & Stoughton, a member of the Hodder Headline Group. All rights reserved.

Sing Psalms version of Psalm 23, Copyright © Psalmody Committee, Free Church of Scotland, 2003, used by permission.

Quotation from *Going Home: The Runrig Story* by Tom Morton, © Tom Morton and Runrig 1991, Mainstream Publishing, Edinburgh, p.217, used by permission.

GLOSSARY AND PRONUNCIATION

(In Gaelic, 'ch' is pronounced as in 'loch', not as the 'ck' in 'lock' or the 'ch' in 'church')

A bhalaich – boy (pronounced *uh vallich*)
A ghraidh – my darling (pronounced *uh ghry*)
Allt Mor Chill Donnain – the Big Burn of Kildonan (pronounced *alt more chill-donnan*)
An Crasg – a crossing over a ridge (pronounced *an crask*)
An Loch Beag – The Little Loch, Little Loch Broom (Pronounced *an loch bek*)
An Teallach – The Forge (pronounced *an tyaloch – y* as a consonant)
Barry – Edinburgh slang for fantastic, great (pronounced *barray*)
Bealach – a pass or watershed (pronounced *byalloch – y* as a consonant)
Beinn nam Ban – the Mountain of the Woman (pronounced *beyn nam ban*)
Bidein a'Ghlas Thuill – Peak of the Grey Hollow (pronounced *beetyan a ghlas hil*)
Buccleuch – (pronounced Bu-*clew*) from an area in the Scottish Borders, originally Buck Cleuch—the ravine where a deer was killed
Cadha Ghobhlach – Forked Pass (pronounced *ca-uh gollach*)
Cill Donnain – Church of Donnain (pronounced *kill-donnan*)
Coir a' Ghiubhsachain – Corrie of the Fir Trees (pronounced *Cor uh yoosachan*)
Corrag Bhuidhe – Yellow finger (pronounced *korak vooya*)
Dubh Lochan – Little Black Loch (pronounced *doo lochan*)
Dundonnain – Donnain's fort (pronounced *Dunn-donnan*)

Garbh Coire Beag – the Little Rough Corrie (pronounced *gariv cor-uh bek*)

Garbh Coire Mor – the Big Rough Corrie (pronounced *gariv cor-uh more*)

Glas Mheall Liath – the Grey-green Hill (pronounced *glas myowl lee-uh*)

Gleann Chaorachain – the Glen of Plentiful Rowan Berries (pronounced Gla-oon Choorachain)

Iolair – eagle (pronounced *yoolar*)

Oidhche mhath – Goodnight (pronounced *oychuh vah*)

Radge – Edinburgh slang for crazy or in a rage

Ruadh – red (pronounced *roo-agh*)

Sail Liath – Grey Heel (pronounced *sal lee-uh*)

Sail Mhor – Big Heel (pronounced *sal more)*

Sgurr Fiona – White Peak (pronounced *skoor feeana*)

Shan – Edinburgh slang for terrible, bad

Teuchter – Scots word (disparaging) for a Highlander (pronounced *chewchter*)

Toll an Lochain – Hollow of the Loch (pronounced as it looks)

Yowe – Scots word for ewe (pronunciation: rhymes with 'now')